Tom Toomey was born with severe cerebral palsy, making him non-verbal and prone to uncontrolled body movements.

Despite his disabilities, he is very intelligent and has a charming personality. He is very proud of his many accomplishments, including attending the University of California at Berkley and obtaining a degree in World History, as well as realizing his dream of becoming a published author. After seven years of hard work writing it, *Dark Secret in London* is his first novel.

I would like to dedicate this book to my mom because she encouraged me to write. I miss her and love her very much. To my dad because he encouraged me to write as well. I also dedicate this book to my teacher, Mrs. Bowman, because she found a way for me to be able to write.

Tom Toomey

DARK SECRET IN LONDON

AUSTIN MACAULEY PUBLISHERS™
LONDON * CAMBRIDGE * NEW YORK * SHARJAH

Ordering Information:
Quantity sales: special discounts are available on quantity purchases by corporations, associations, and others. For details, contact the publisher at the address below.

Publisher's Cataloging-in-Publication data
Toomey, Tom
Dark Secret in London

ISBN 9781643784878 (Paperback)
ISBN 9781643784885 (Hardback)
ISBN 9781645367932 (ePub e-book)

Library of Congress Control Number: 2019910944

www.austinmacauley.com/us

First Published (2020)
Austin Macauley Publishers LLC
40 Wall Street, 28th Floor
New York, NY 10005
USA

mail-usa@austinmacauley.com
+1 (646) 5125767

I would like to thank my caregivers, Leslie Ochoa and Autumn Pollard, for helping me write this book. I also thank God for my intelligence.

Chapter One

When I was thirteen, my nanny helped me dress in my tuxedo and my father told me to be on my best behavior because I would be meeting important people that evening. When I looked in the mirror at myself, I thought, *Flawless*. But looking back now, on the inside I was anything but perfect.

I walked downstairs and opened the door to our ballroom, where the fingers of a pleasingly small orchestra were dancing on their instruments, playing Chopin Berceuse in D-Flat. As I ventured in, I noticed the fragrance of a bouquet of flowers floating on the air as white clouds float on a summer's breeze. It was a smell I recalled from the first time I attended this ball at five years old. I saw many people there conversing with one another; the men wore tuxedos like mine. I saw my best friend's grandfather, Mr. Jesting Heddwyn, wearing a tailored tuxedo. The wives were all wearing very elegant dresses. I could tell they were prestigious people, and I couldn't help but look all around at the refinement. It was 1973. My attention snapped back to my immediate surroundings when a man took my hand to shake it. "Hello, my name is Fitzgerald," he said. "Your father and I work in the British Parliament."

I greeted him politely, but I left to look for my name card on the dinner tables, where I sat down in my assigned seat to watch this scene. I anxiously recalled my manners and looked down at the table settings: four forks, a napkin, a bread plate on the left, two knives, one spoon, and my glass to the right. Slowly, people began to wander, looking for their own name cards, and sat down at their assigned places in anticipation. The *maître d'* and his assistants came out to serve us; they came with appetizers and served us from the right. I looked at my mother to see if she had plucked her napkin and unfurled it…she had. I reached for the fork with two prongs to begin eating, but suddenly, I felt strange. My body was shaking—uncontrollably and violently shaking. I felt as if I were in a bubble, knowing everything and everyone that was around me, but being unable to reach them. I fell unconscious for the first time.

When I came to senses, I heard the beeps of the machine that was monitoring my heart. I heard my mother say, "How are you feeling?" and felt her check my forehead. After scanning my father's face, I felt he might be either concerned or furious—or both.

"I feel like I ran a few thousand miles...my body is weak," I said. "I'm sorry, Dad, I ruined your social."

Before he could respond, the doctor walked in. "How are you, Alban?"

Mother said, "My son is exhausted."

"I want to run couple of tests in the morning. Alban has to stay until tomorrow." The doctor was calm and wrote something in the file resting in his hand.

"I was reading about seizures in a medical journal," I said. "There are different kinds. Some people shake violently like I did. An electric current naturally runs in people's bodies that controls their heart beat, breathing, and movements, but if the electric current short-circuits, it floods the cells and the brain unloads the electric current. The result can cause seizures, just as the drain in a shower would overflow if it could not handle all the water. The type of seizure depends on how severe that short-circuit is, and some can be long and ferocious. Are the tests you will do in the morning the EEG and blood tests?"

The doctor clicked his pen and said, "Yes, your test is the EEG. You are an intelligent young boy. Why are you reading medical journals?"

"I like reading medical periodicals and all the books of the intelligentsia to increase my analytical thought."

The doctor cracked a smile. "I need to see other patients now."

My father said, "I'll join you in the hallway," and both parents followed the doctor out.

My mother is the emotional, caring, tender one in my family, but she is a rag doll compared to my dad. All my father sees is black and white, morally correct or morally wrong, and he's always demanded that his family perform with precision. He has always expected the house to be managed perfectly. He can be severe, but his high standards were put to good use in writing British law in the House of Parliament. My parents devoted themselves to education: I had learned three languages before I was five years old, and I had an exceptional home instructor. Due to my parents' dedication, I was set to graduate from high school in just a few months.

Through the open door, I could hear them talking in the hallway. My mother asked the doctor, "How come my son is having a seizure? Will his life ever be normal?"

"Your son will never be a normal boy—whether or not he has seizures—due to his intelligence," the doctor said. "In case studies done on boys and girls in early puberty, the type of seizure that occurs from overloading the brain with electrical current and hormones will be a non-recurring type. However, a few do keep on having seizures, and if their medicine and diet are well managed, they can have a normal life. I have to go. See you sometime tomorrow afternoon."

Chapter Two

Within three days of being discharged from the hospital, I'd had two more seizures.

On one of the occasions, I was having lunch with my father. We went to lunch every single Saturday with others who worked in parliament. As they didn't have quality time with their kids on weekdays, the luncheon was created for the parents to spend time with their children. At my first luncheon after I'd left the hospital, I was talking to my friends when I felt a strange sensation. Suddenly, my body was shaking uncontrollably. My friends were laughing at me. Their parents came over to see what was happening and tried to help me. When my body had stopped convulsing, Robert handed me a glass of water. I looked at my father, who was looking at me and everything around me, and I interpreted his expression as exasperation. It hurt to know how much our relationship had deteriorated, as my father had to take control of everything; nevertheless, he couldn't control the problems that were looming in my body.

A requirement of home-schooled British children are the graduation exams. My teacher handed me the final, and I was working on it when I overheard my parents arguing about me. My father said, "The seizures our boy has—this family isn't able to do enough for him. I do not have time for my son's problem and you don't have time either. Look at our house! It's in shambles! My boy falls and shakes and threatens our old vases and the character of our house. Our maids thought there was an evil spirit inside his body the time they saw him shaking! I know that it's not true, but they're going out and discussing his problem with maids who work for people we know. People are talking about us."

My mother said, "I realize that, but you talk about our flesh and blood as if he was the seizures. He cannot control them. You make it a command, as if stopping them should be as easy as tossing out an old newspaper. This is a control issue with you."

If I could have seen my father at that moment, his eyes would have been rolling up to the sky as he paced backward a few steps, then stopped. He said, "I want to help my boy out. I talked to the administrator of Eastman Hospital."

He paused and stared my mother right in the eyes. "He told me his cottage hospital is an excellent place to be if a person has out-of-control seizures, just like our son. After he graduates, we will enroll him in that hospital. "

Mother said, "A few days from now, Alban will be the youngest ever to graduate. Your father worshipped him... He thought our son was intelligent enough to do great things throughout the world. Now you want to put him in some mental institution. I know you did not like your father, but don't treat Alban the same way you treated your father. Your idea of celebrating is committing my son to the mental institution with patients who are insane! All of England would talk about that for a long time, since you work for our queen. They believe you are thinking to the highest standard. But you are not, in view of the fact that you want to commit my son to the mental institution for seizures that he cannot control!"

I knew my father's stance when he got madder: his chin stuck out and his fists tightened at his sides. "I know you cannot read my mind," he said, "but I do my damnedest to help our boy out. I recognize that he will be in shock and furious with me, but after a while, our son will adjust to his environment."

I heard Mother crying as if her heart were breaking. I heard his footsteps move across the room, and he opened and closed the bedroom door. I said to Della, my instructor, "Okay...I guess the final was unchallenging to me." She placed her hand on my shoulder, and when I looked at her, her face showed the same devastation I felt. I handed over my exam to her.

"How was the exam? You are the most intelligent young boy I am teaching. Your father didn't mean what he said about the hospital."

But I knew that he did mean it, and knew my mom could not prevent him from doing what he said.

My father had an insurmountable desire to be in charge of his family, unless it meant throwing away someone or something. But in America around the 1800s, men used the idea of *manifest destiny* to allow the death of the native people and march them to barren places where they were forced to live. The Indians never returned to their previous homes. They discarded them as a different kind of people, and my father's attitude toward me was becoming like that of the Americans toward the Indians.

Della said, "All men have the issue of being controlling, but strong determination like mine and intelligence like yours keeps them in line. I will help you someway, somehow." Her hand grasped my shoulder softly. I know she meant it.

"I am exhausted, can I go now?"

"Yes. I will see you on your graduation day."

I walked off, thinking of my plan for later tonight.

I read my history books at great length, but in their manuscripts, the historians never recorded who had a disability. We don't know what they were doing in their time, but I believe the peasants were afraid of everything different about them. The king used their pagan religion against them to make them fearful and keep them loyal. Christianity at that time was a new religion, and the king told the peasants that he would fight off the pagan gods for them. It made the peasants angry that their king chose Christianity over their paganism. The king told them that their pagan gods will be haunting them in ways they could not imagine. Their pagan gods could take their very souls and turn them toward the darkness. This paralyzed them with fear of anyone who acted differently.

The king required his people to let the priest see their babies and allow him to place his benediction on them so the pagan gods would not take their souls away. It was believed that the pagan gods could easily take possession of their young souls. From then on, beginning at three years old, the children were required to learn the tenets of the Catholic Church. The priests told the king about the children that had the mental or physical signs of harboring spirits. The king commanded that those children be killed because the pagan gods had taken the children's souls from them and had replaced them with their demonic gods.

A thousand years later, the Christian Church was flourishing, and its churches continued to bless babies to protect them from evil. Most countries were still requiring their children go to school. But after all that time, what was happening to those born disabled? After many years, that king died. The Pope commanded the new monarch of England to stop taking the life of innocent children that had physical or mental problems since they had realized that no gods took those children's souls; those problems occur naturally. The king told the Pope, "I will do that for you." From that time on, when peasants had a disabled child on the rare occasion, they felt disgraced by others. This is why the families of disabled children could not have them work to help them out as the other children did. And the peasant families who had a disabled person would hide them at a distance from others.

From the 900s to the 1500s, England's population increased greatly, and the number of children born disabled increased as well. Most peasants cared for their disabled children, but a few families had no concern for their special needs children—they lived on the streets in England and begged for food. The king was not happy about that, so he mandated that the disabled be placed into a building at other end of the town, in an area where the poor and impoverished lived. That building was the first of its kind. The buildings of today that represent this function are classified as mental institutions.

I opened the door to my architecture room where we built models of England's and Europe's great architectural buildings. I remember when Robert and I put up the models of the Tower of Pisa, the Eiffel tower, and the Vatican Square, they filled the table ... Houses of Parliament, Big Ben, London Bridge, and the Tower of London, too. As I looked at them, I was thinking about running away. The first idea I entertained was to go to San Francisco in California, but there were some problems with that—one being that my passport said I was 13 years old.

Airport authorities would want a letter from my parents... I could write that letter and sign my father's name on it. Another substantial problem if I went to San Francisco would be how to get money for a means of support, as I was too young. A second plan I had mapped out was to go to the burgs deep in northern Britain. England built them in the Middle Ages, as the king at that time had his nobles living there. However, I realized that I did not want to live there for seven years, until I am 20 years old. That's too long to be all alone, like being Tarzan in England. Another option I had was to stay where I was, go to court and fight my father, but I doubted that I would get a fair deal out of the judicial system.

As I touched my model of London Bridge, I reflected on its history. The actual London Bridge is simple in structure but has overcome the tests of time. I do not know who built it, but I know that the bridge was first built in the 9th century and was destroyed by England's invaders. It was restructured several times. The countries wanted supremacy of England, and time after time their armies withdrew in London, so perhaps the bridge was named in remembrance of that. I walked to the doorway and turned around to look at my models of European architecture. I spent thousands of hours in here building, but I must have spent at least that much time learning about European architecture and design throughout the centuries. I captured the image of the layout of the models in the room to my memory, I closed the door behind me, and I walked away. I began wondering if I could live in the Middle Ages if I am even afraid to go to San Francisco. Nonetheless, if I were living back then, I would have to fight for my king. They didn't feel afraid, but went proudly to die for the King of England. I don't know why they did, but I know they did. At any rate, I needed to go whether I was frightened or not. I had made up my mind—I am going to San Francisco tonight.

Chapter Three

I went quietly to my bedroom and wrote a phony letter, putting my father's precise signature at the bottom. I pulled out my dresser drawer, took out my map of the burgs, and I rolled it open on my desk so that the light was shining on it. I looked at the longitude and latitude of London, as I wanted to know the exact location of the burgs in case the airport authorities didn't accept my phony letter and I had to live off the land.

I looked in that drawer and saw my grandfather's gold Rolex watch. I recalled the day he gave it to me. It was one of the last days of his life; he was in his bedroom, and I was there with him. We played chess together and we talked about life. He told me he thought he wouldn't be living too much longer, but that he had a good life and that he had discovered amazing things in the Middle East about the history of their culture. He took off his Rolex watch then and he gave it to me, saying, "Look on the back." The back of the watch was engraved: *"When you look at this watch, remember me. Every move you make, I make with you."* He said, "I know I am not your father, but I saw my young self in you. I know you cannot wear this watch now, but you will know when it is the right time to wear it."

I took my grandfather's Rolex and kissed it…it flooded my brain with memories of my grandfather and our intelligent conversations about the world's cultures. I ripped off a piece of my wool blanket and rolled up my watch in it tightly. I had a loose board in my floor, so I picked up the bundle with my watch and I put it under the floorboard between the joists. Then I piled together my money, my compass, a flashlight, an old British Army canteen, and my pills for my seizures, and stuffed them all into my backpack.

I had thirty days' worth of pills. I was thinking to myself, "If I go to San Francisco, I will need to go to the library and look up alternative medicines for seizures. If I have to go to the burgs, could I put together comparable pills off the land, just as the medicine man did for the Indians? I started to roll up the map, but I heard someone walking in the hall. I quickly turned off the light and was surprised to notice that it was already dark outside. Grabbing my backpack, I zipped it as quietly as I could, slid it onto my thin shoulders, and moved to the window. It opened silently. I climbed over the sill one leg at a time, steadied myself on the massive branch that had grown near the outside wall, then turned…and I suddenly felt the heavy weight of leaving my familiar room. Closing the window was like a silent farewell.

The oak branch I was on was wet, but I crouched down onto it and crawled carefully toward the trunk of the tree. And then, like in a dream, I was climbing down. I jumped down to the ground and gave thanks for that hundred-year-old oak. I ran to the tall fence around my house, made of blarney stones, both rugged and wet, and carefully placed my footholds up one side and down the other. I was drenched. The clouds had burst open on me, and I kept on running, soaking wet. "Now I am home free," I said out loud as I ran.

Two hours later, walking on the road to the airport, the sky continued emptying up its life force onto me. I liked to see rain coming down onto the trees, but I was too drenched and chilly to enjoy it now. I heard a siren and saw red highlights on the raindrops coming down, and then I felt the splash of car tires soaking me. The police officer parked in front of me and jumped out of the vehicle in one movement. He strode through the rain to me, and seemingly turned on his flashlight just to blind me with it. "What is your name…and why you are walking on this road in the middle of the night?"

"I am Sir Alban III, and I am going to the airport. I have to catch a 4 a.m. flight."

"I see…but why are you walking? Why didn't you drive your car?"

"I do not have my car because it broke down three miles back," I said, doing my best imitation of someone who actually had a car.

"I see. Hand over your driver license!"

"I left it back in the car." I hoped that this kind of maneuvering, which sometimes worked with parents, could also work with the police.

"How old are you?"

"I am 16 and half…even though I do not look it."

"No, you do not look that old. I think you're trying to run away from your parents. You wait here while I talk to my dispatcher." The police officer walked to his car, where I heard him mumbling with someone into his radio. In the meantime, I thought, it would be no good to go to the airport because the police will be looking for me there.

There is a point in time when a young person's actions can alter their life forever, and that point in time for me was now. Still, better that I change it myself rather than having my father change it for me. I looked at the officer, who was still talking, and took a deep wet breath. I noted my position on the north-south road, and thinking of the map, I realized one of the burgs was about 40 miles northeast from where I stood. My thinking stopped there—and as I started to run, I heard police officer slam the car door—but I was in the woods already and weaving around the trees. I could still hear the police officer, and I hoped that he had a good heart because the ground was thick with mud, and I almost couldn't run.

Ahead of me, I saw the 200-year-old Hadrian's Wall, which had been built by the Romans. They built the wall over fifteen feet tall and 40 miles long as protection against invaders who wanted to conquer England…but over time, the ages took hold of Hadrian's Wall and brought it down to two feet tall and just a few miles long. I jumped over it. I reached into my raincoat pocket for my flashlight and compass, and I quickly checked to see if I was going in the right direction for one of the burgs. I heard several police officers calling my name with a slight echo, running to the northeast.

I needed to scale England's rolling hills. I was running toward one of these hills, green and muddy. I thought to myself, *What happened when the people in the Middle Ages had to climb this hill? What were they thinking when they started up this hillside, fearful and running away from the king? And were they wondering what was out there, outside the kingdom walls, just like me?* I was afraid and wondering, too, as I ran away my family and a safe place to live. I searched my spirit for the answers. I knew if I stayed at my house, my father would have me committed to the mental institution for life. Out there, I knew what they were thinking when they were running away from the king—they felt the same as I did, that my fate was better taken into my own hands.

I looked around with my flashlight to find a walking stick so I could find out how deep the mud was on the slope of the hill. I had to know if I could safely climb it. And at last, I found the ideal walking stick for me: it was as tall as a yardstick, and it got narrower at the end, which would work for driving it deep into the mud. With my walking stick in my right hand and my flashlight in my left, I started to climb this hill. I drove the walking stick down in the mud ahead of me. When I stepped up to the stick, my foot sank into mud that was ankle deep. I slid my walking stick out of the mud, put it further away, and drove it down in the mud again. I swung my other foot forward toward the walking stick, and this time the mud was only half as deep. Finally, one step at a time, I reached the top of that hill.

As I turned to the east, I saw at the horizon that the sun was appearing from behind the clouds, and all of a sudden, I felt peaceful. In the morning light, a soft rain appeared, and there was a beautiful rainbow. It was taking my breath away. But although I had been traveling all night, I could still hear police officers shouting out my name closer than I would have liked. Suddenly I was running again, down the hill this time, as fast as I could. I used my compass to see what direction I was going, and I turned to face northeast. I was running to one of the burgs against all odds.

An hour and a half later, I was running through tall wet grass in a countryside that I had never seen before. I was famished, so although it was still raining, I made it a priority to search for nuts and berries. I knew what kind of berries people could eat and which ones were poisonous, but I wondered how many people throughout London's glorious history had traveled this route and died from eating poisonous berries.

I had read about William Wallace, a Scotsman who spent his life fighting England. If Wallace had simply walked this land, I imagined he would have thought England's countryside was marvelous. But the king of England was bloodthirsty against Wallace and his country's people. William Wallace looked around the land and saw Scottish peasants' blood staining the English soil. He successfully rallied together an army to fight against the English. But the king eventually captured him and maliciously commanded that he be executed in the king's courtyard, where Wallace was beheaded in front of everyone. That way, the peasants could see what would happen to whoever went against the king's power. The king ordered that his head be placed on the London Bridge to scare the peasants and keep them under his control. Wallace's message to all was that one must control their emotions, for whoever can keep their emotions under control will win their battles. I need to take control of my own emotions now since I have to win my battles, just as William Wallace did throughout his lifetime.

I had been looking carefully on the downhill slope and found some edible berries in a low bush to dull my hunger pangs. While I was stopped, I saw that rainwater was flowing down over the leaves on the hillside and creating small waterfalls. I reached for my pills in my backpack, got out the ones I needed for now, and I popped them into my mouth. Quickly, before they dissolved, I crouched down, cupped my hands, and held them so that the rivulet filled them like a cup. Once the pills were down, I quenched my thirst. Then I took out my canteen and refilled it. The calling of the police officers had stopped, and the air was still, which felt odd. I checked my compass again and headed northeast.

I walked five long miles after my small breakfast of berries. By early afternoon I was feeling very tired, and I wanted to take a nap, but I didn't have an alarm clock to wake me up. I had been thinking about this problem for hours as I walked through the wet landscape. For my plan, I needed to find several large leaves, so I walked under the trees, and I broke off seven leaves that were larger than my hand. They were young and supple, and just right.

Now, I needed a source of water, which was easy: it was all around. The best waterfall was fifteen feet away from the spot where I wanted to sleep, but

I saw that the ground was sloping where the water was falling, and that was good. By this time, I was so tired I wasn't sure I would finish my project, but I had to make sure I wouldn't sleep too long. I dug a hole right next to where I wanted to lie down, and then I lined the hole with the leaves. I arranged them nicely and cleanly, stacking them so that I was sure the water couldn't percolate through to the mud below. This is where I would sleep.

My next move was to dig out a channel from the hole to the base of the waterfall, which would divert the water. I added four dams along its length as I continued to dig toward the waterfall. This would allow the water through at a slower rate. They looked adequate, but there was no chance for a trial run. When I finally dug out the last bit of the channel, and the water started to flow toward the leaf-lined hole, it was time for me to go lie down. I put my hand in the hole. With two more leaves placed carefully over my eyes, I fell asleep.

Suddenly, my hand was wet. My heart was racing as I woke up out of a deep sleep. The forest was silent—there was no one around—but then I realized what had happened. I had had a bad dream, and the cold water inching its way up my hand had roused me. My idea worked.

I stood up, now fueled with a little rest and adrenalin, and I kissed the leaves that I'd had over my eyes. They did the job well. I threw them up in the sky for the wind to carry them away. They needed to return their nutrients to the soil. I looked at my compass and walked again toward the northeast. Ten miles to the burg.

The terrain had become more rugged, suggesting that I was near the southern border of Scotland. I turned on my flashlight in the dusk to scan my surroundings, knowing that my final destination should only be a mile away. It got dark as I headed toward the burg, and I heard nocturnal animals beginning to scamper around searching for food. As my pin of light swayed back and forth, it suddenly caught the face of a wolf, with amber eyes shining back at me. I stopped short—I heard two or more, and in fact, they were on both sides and behind me, still a bit far off. *Uh-oh*, I thought, hoping hard that they were just curious about me. I turned off the flashlight and stood dead motionless, and they began to growl. A quick survey of my surroundings revealed a tree on my left side, ten feet away. I estimated the wolves' distance from me, and from the tree; I took a couple deep breaths and I prayed.

I walked very slowly toward the tree, daring myself to take each quiet step, but knowing that I had no other choice. I heard the pack of wolves in motion around me, and though I had turned the flashlight off, I knew they were coming closer. Inch by inch I approached the tree until it was about five feet away. I knew that the wolves could attack me at any second, and that the time was right to run for the tree. Feeling the adrenalin energize me, I took an enormous stride, and I jumped, reaching for the first limb of the tree. I grabbed it, pulled myself up, and climbed onto the limb of the tree—not a moment too soon, either—a wolf's nose touched my back leg as I swung up. The pack of wolves was shaking the tree and trying to climb it, but their claws only stripped the bark. Wolves are canines, so their nails aren't the type that can climb up a tree. Still, my heart was pounding as I climbed up to next limb to be safer. I stabilized myself and felt my pockets…my flashlight was missing. I decided to look for it in the morning. All I could do was make myself more comfortable…as comfortable as a person can become while spending the night in a tree. I closed my eyes and heard the wolves shaving the bark.

Chapter Four

I woke up as I felt the foggy morning air hitting my eyelids. I opened my eyes and saw the wet air dancing over the British countryside, so beautiful, and in total contrast to my fear the night before. I looked down—no more wolves—and carefully climbed down from the tree. The wolves had clawed up the tree trunk so much that there was a lot of bark on the ground. I found my flashlight…it looked like the wolves had tried to chew it up. Thankfully, it was still working when I turned it on. I went back to the tree, touched it, and thanked it for my life.

I put my battered flashlight in my backpack, looked at my compass, and turned to the northeast. It was less than a mile to the burg. I put my backpack on, inhaled deeply from the excitement, and began walking into what had suddenly become driving rain again. You might think that I would be disheartened, but I'm always strangely energized by walking in the rain. Maybe it's because I'm British.

Finally, far in the distance, I saw a gate for the burg, and behind that, rooftops of buildings. I ran through the open green field toward the gate, which grew larger in my sight as I ran to it. Close to it now, I saw that the gate was elephantine and antiquated. It sat ajar, and it was not long ago that someone or something pushed the gate open since its path on the ground was smooth. There was a ridge of mud from the corner of the gate that was recent… *That's peculiar*, I thought to myself.

I walked to my left along the outer edge of the ancient fence. Back when the burg was inhabited, it was ten feet tall. In the Middle Ages, the king had constructed the ten burgs; they were metaphors of his domination over his people. The king wanted to ensure that he could control the different regions, especially the tax collection, which was the job of the nobleman stationed in each burg. The nobles were totalitarian rulers empowered by the king to watch over the burgs; they oversaw landowners and dictated the cultivation of their land, which ensured more food and more tax monies for the king. But there was a secondary reason for the burgs: the nobleman that lived in this particular burg had jurisdiction over the south of Scotland, and his job was to seek out any evidence of a military campaign against the king of England, uprisings just like William Wallace was famous for.

This was the only burg that had stood the test of time; after centuries, the other nine burgs had fallen into ruin. This fence was still standing, but it was decaying and had holes throughout, allowing me to get easy footholds for climbing. I climbed up the fence from the outside of the wall, and paused at the top. Surveying the burg, I saw something strange about seventy-five feet away. I saw that the high grasses had been blown down by the wind, creating a large, flattened square.

In hindsight, I should not have gone over the fence, but I went anyway. The first thing I noticed was that all the buildings had disintegrated, and then I saw between them some edible berries had grown. My hunger took me to the bushes, and I ate as many berries as I could find. I took out my pills and swallowed two of them with a swig from my canteen.

A search around the complex revealed that the buildings were in an 'L' shape. The lookout tower was half gone. I went inside a room that was filled with dust and dirt. It had spider webs on the walls, and the floor had been reclaimed by the earth so that it couldn't be seen. I walked through it, and I felt that at one time it was a banquet room, or something like it, because it was so enormous. I went through a long galley to a room that had been the kitchen. It was dusty and dirty. I could see some animal droppings on the ground, and inside the two brick fireplaces, which might have been an oven and stove, were two nests that small animals had made.

I wandered back to the banquet room and stood in front of the gigantic fireplace. I imagined that its large, granite stones must have filled up the whole wall once. I saw the nobleman's living quarters just behind the fireplace, and as I walked there, my imagination took hold of me. The past was alive again and I was thrown back in time. The nobleman's power cascaded out of his room and out into the community. His stone fireplace had become sculpture, the stones formed into ornate art. I walked upstairs and his bedroom was paneled in knotty pine, with yellow, purple, and blue fabrics making his bed. I looked downstairs and saw the same colors on the chairs and table, and a bearskin rug on the floor between two chairs in front of the fireplace. I went downstairs and moved over to his desk. I saw a letter from the King of England, Henry VII. I was thinking to myself…should I open it and read it? Why not? It was my imagination! I carefully opened that letter and read it. Henry VII said in his letter:

"My noble, who is in authority over the north part of my province, the High Council and your Lord command that your proprietors increase their taxes. Thus, my soldiers will have better equipment to protect them from our Scottish neighbors. But, if they do not do this willingly, my noble should remind them, your Lord possesses power over the pagan gods, and he will unleash them on their crops, leaving their land unproductive."

Wow. I had read a 400-year-old letter from Henry VII, the King of England. I put the letter back on his desk very gently. On the noble's desk, I saw a feather pen and a thimble full of ink, and he liked to write hard. Every word he wrote made an impression in the wood of the desk.

A rumbling in the banquet room drew me back there. When I walked in, I felt the heat of the fireplace and saw a blazing fire glowing against the granite stones. My attention then turned, as men were walking into the room wearing richly styled clothes from about the 1550s. They sat down at the ten-foot table to discuss events with their noble about the king's increasing leverage on their taxes. Although the men filling up the room were apprehensive, one person spoke up against the king, saying, "The king is going to harm our crops. Huh…that's like throwing my money into the wind and then hoping it rains buckets full of cash. Also, this weather is changing—this is the worst year of crops I've had in the last year or two. Five bushels of wheat over one-and-a-half acres was what I used to get, but because of the colder weather, I am now getting only two or three bushels."

Another man said, "That is true, but the king allows us to be landowners of his land; in turn, he wants a large amount of our gains. Also, all the men in here have a wife and a few children. We do not want the king to destroy our families."

This meeting went on for hours. I walked to the heavy double doors and pulled on them… pulled and pulled… pulled again… Finally, the doors moved and opened. I walked outside for some fresh air. That man was right: it was much colder out here. I saw the lookout tower with a guard from the king's army serving as a lookout across Scotland for any peasants who were antagonistic against the King of England. I saw peasants working at their repetitive jobs, cleaning the horse barn, feeding the horses, and carrying pails of water from the well to the army's living quarters.

Suddenly I heard, "Freeze and put your hands up in the air! Drop to the ground!"

Cold, hard reality shook me out of my vision and took hold of me. I fell down on my knees and then down onto my stomach. Someone took my arms, placed them on my back, and clasped handcuffs on me.

He said, "What is your name, boy!"

His voice was powerful. I wasn't thinking, and I said, "My name is Sir Alban III."

He pulled me up by the handcuffs and spoke into his police radio. "I captured the boy. Send out the helicopter."

He pushed me, and I started to walk. I asked him where he was taking me. The police officer said, "My orders are to hand you over to the Eastman hospital, and I will do that."

"Who made that request?" I said, knowing already who delivered these orders: my father. The police officer told me the same thing.

I was forced to walk out the gate, and I was headed for the square patch of grass I saw earlier today. It had to be the landing pad for the helicopter. "Who told you where to find me?"

"Your father did."

My father must have known I was going to be here because I left my map out on my bed. He read my markings and knew it was where to find me. Damn it! My father was right about one thing: always put your odds and sods in their proper place. If I had listened, he wouldn't have found my map.

I heard the chopper and felt it thump the air as it came to take me. My heart was beating faster and faster as I struggled to get away from the officer like a dying person struggling for one last breath. I almost got away from him, but he kicked my knee and knocked me onto the ground and sat on my body. My legs were kicking and the mud was flying. I was fighting to the end for my freedom and my life. The helicopter was landing and people were running to me. I saw someone insert a needle into my arm to inject something, and right away, I felt tingly all over.

I don't know what time it was or what might have woken me. I simply found myself lying down with my arms and legs strapped to a hard gurney. I was in a pink, padded room and I felt sick to my stomach. They had an I.V. in me, I knew only because I could hear it dripping. I knew how they made *non compos mentis* people out of commonsensical people like me. Put them on boards, strap them down, and make them listen to drip, drip, drip, drip sounds all day long.

I was thinking I would try to ignore the dripping sound, but it filled my brain like the firing of a gun and the rip of flesh. The door opened and a nurse walked in.

"Hello," I said.

The nurse looked at my file and said, "Albin."

"No. I am not Albin. My name is Sir Alban III. Can you take these straps off of me? I need to stand up."

"Don't you be making trouble with me! You want to be a good boy, then be quiet!"

"I asked you a question. Normal people who are in the same shape as I am right now would ask you the same kind of question."

"Who is normal in here? Surely not you. If the boffins had your medical condition, they wouldn't run away and hide in the forest, so they are obviously smarter than you are. You decided to run off into the forest with a medical condition, and it's very dangerous for you out there. So, your dad put you in this padded room." She was giving me a mean look, like I got what I deserved.

"But that is not true. My dad had planned to place me in here after my graduation. I heard him say that, and I made my mind up to run away. Furthermore, regarding my seizures, I take control of them; I took my pills as my doctor prescribed for me. Hey, what did you just put in my I.V.?"

"I'll give you medicine that will make you sleep forever."

As she injected the medicine in my I.V., my dreams and aspirations for improving our civilization dissolved. I was screaming my lungs out and praying to God. I don't remember everything going black.

Chapter Five

From that blackness, I felt a hand slapping my face gently. "It's time to wake up," the man said. When I didn't respond, he quickly unfastened my legs and arms from the straps and helped me sit up. He tried to rouse me again, but I barely opened my eyes. He said, "I'm a doctor. Focus on what I say. What is your name?"

I searched my fuzzy mind for a moment, but it finally came back to me. "My name is Sir Alban III," I said. I felt stiff from head to toe. I asked him, "How long have I been unconscious?"

"Nearly a week. By your cognitive skills, I can tell that you won't have ill effects from your ordeal, but can you tell me your name again?"

"I am Sir Alban III," I said forcefully.

"Okay, calm down. I believe you."

"I do not think you really believe me."

"Well, are you able to stand up and walk? Wait a second—I will take off the I.V." He removed the needle from my arm, checked the bag, and muttered, "That is peculiar…"

"What is?"

"Your I.V. bag is full of sugar water. Someone refilled it last night."

As I scanned the room for the first time upright, I saw that I had a catheter bag trailing off the gurney. It was empty. That told me that either my kidneys weren't functioning while I was unconscious, or someone had been emptying the bag. I hoped it was the latter. "Where is that nurse who wants to snuff out my life force?"

"Wilma is the nurse who gave you the shot; the board of directors fired her before this could go any further."

"Do you know if any of the doctors or administrators in this hospital are tied to British Parliament? Sir Alban Christopher?"

"Yes, I heard of him, but I never talked to him personally. Why?"

"Because that is my father."

"Really! Your file states that your name is Albin Sebastian."

"Can I see my file?"

The doctor left it open and held it open in front of me. I couldn't believe my eyes. "That's not my name in this file," I said. "Do you do think all this information is true?"

"The doctors would believe the file over the patients. Your case has been rather abnormal, so I think it could be possible. In your case, the name could have been changed."

"You are not going to believe anything I tell you, are you, just because I sit here in the mental hospital. I will prove that I am Sir Alban III, and it will only take a few minutes of your time. Where are my pants...my wallet...my identification is in there."

"We have a storage room where we keep new patients' things. I imagine they were put there."

"Please get my I.D. for me. Just give me a chance to show you."

"Yes. I'll be right back."

I tried scanning the room and making a mental note of everything I saw, but my dread threatened to overcome me. This time my emotions could not be overcome with intellect.

The doctor returned quickly. "What's wrong? You look terrified."

As if he didn't realize that since my identity was stolen, I was in a strange place, and I didn't know how I would get out! But, I said, "I was thinking about my circumstances in here. I have a big problem. Whoever did this to me, whoever they are, they want to kill me. And what is going to happen when they find out that I am not tied down with straps to this bed, that I'm conscious now? That is what you see on my face. So, do you have my I.D.?"

"I searched for it, but it wasn't there. I looked at the sign-in sheet, and whoever took your identification did not sign the sheet. But I have a pair of pants that were in a bag. The name on the bag is Albin Sebastian. Are they yours?"

I wouldn't know until I unfolded them. "Hand them to me," I said. I took the pants from him, and I looked for holes in the knees. There they were. "Yes. These are mine."

The day I put those holes in the knees—I recall it as if it were yesterday. My friend and I made a bet about who could climb to the top of a tree the fastest. I lost that day because the bark from the tree slashed my knees. My friend said, "I want to be in a cloud because the air will hug me and be my friend."

I said, "What am I, chopped liver!"

And he said, "No, you are my best friend. I mean that down there on the ground my mother doesn't want me, and she gave me away to her parents. But

the car, and he landed on his back and head. He was knocked unconscious. The hospital said that from that moment, he would not recover because of the irrevocable damage to his brain. The standard policy of the hospital is that if a patient is in a coma for two weeks with no sign of improving, the patient must be transferred to another hospital. That's why Robert Zachary is here."

Reeling, I lost my composure and started murmuring. Not to Robert or to the doctor or anyone else, only because I couldn't believe that things could go so wrong. "I ran away from my dad too quickly...I never thought about anything else but myself. If I am intelligent, and some people think I am, why did I think only of myself in the heat of the moment? I failed to put back the map of the burgs... My father found it on top of my bed, so he knew where I went, and two police officers captured me... So, now I am here... I also failed to consider that what was most important to me was Robert. I believe I am at fault for what happened to him. He had only me to count on... What is going to happen to my only best friend and me?"

Aaron asked, "How long did you think about running away before you did it?"

"About two hours."

"In the very short time since I met you, I can guess that you made a back-up plan in your mind in case your first plan of action didn't work. What are the burgs, anyway?"

"Do you like history?"

"Not really."

"That is why you don't know about the burgs. Henry VII built them. He wanted know who was coming in his country and whether they challenged England or not. That's it in a nut shell." Aaron didn't respond. "You were nearly a doctor, so how long do you think Robert could last in a vegetative state like he is in now?"

"Well, the coma involves a delicate process of reconstructing brain cells that have been damaged in some way. I do not know how long this procedure takes, but I do know that if you talk with him, he will awaken earlier."

"Then I have to stay here and talk with Rob. It is my obligation to him."

"Doing that is going be a problem for you."

"I realize that, but our two intelligent brains will work on it together and figure it out one way or another."

"Do you have a proposal for your little problem?"

I thought about it hard. "I have two ideas. Do you know where they keep all the patients' files and records?"

"Sure, but that door is locked up, tight as the skin on a drum."

"I know how to loosen the skin of a drum," I said with a wink.

"You want to go there now?"

I squeezed Rob's hand and said, "I am coming right back to you. We are going to talk about the good times we had."

I reached for my crutches and stood up. I had more strength in my legs than I did before, and as I put down one crutch, I saw the box of rubber gloves. I took two pairs. Then I reluctantly walked to the door and left Robert's room.

Aaron led me to a hidden stairway, and we climbed slowly to the fifth floor. This floor had all of its lights turned off and was pitch black. "Do you know where a flashlight is?"

"I don't know," he whispered.

"Did you see my backpack in the storage room? My flashlight was in there."

"Easier to turn the light switch on..."

"No. You cannot turn on the lights because we do not want someone to see us break into the office."

"You're right. I'll run back and get it."

I stayed in the palpable darkness and got lost in my thoughts. I couldn't get Robert out of my mind. Suddenly, I felt someone touch my shoulder—immediately I jumped and pulled back to throw a punch.

"It's me!" He turned on my flashlight and illuminated his face.

I tapped him with my hand and said, "You scared me half to death! Now where is that office?"

"Hey, what's wrong with your voice?"

"Nothing, why?"

"I heard it crack."

"Where is the office?"

"Follow me."

My flashlight's beam demolished the darkness, just as if humans consumed all the oil around the world.

We walked through the stuffy air down a long hallway that had many offices on either side. As I looked around, I noticed a name on one of the doors: Fabron Rahman. I know this man—my father mentioned that name before.

"Who is Fabron Rahman?"

"He's the chief of the doctors at this hospital. I saw him one time when he was furious at a doctor, and I heard he fired him. Here it is. This is the records office."

I took out a pair of rubber gloves and handed other pair to Aaron. We hurried to put them on, but tried not to make a sound. I checked the doorknob. "It is locked, but I know how to remedy this problem quickly," I said. "Do you have paper clip or old pen?"

Aaron stuck his gloved hands into his pockets. "Just my keys, paycheck and pocketknife…here, I have a pen."

I took his pen and pocketknife. I unscrewed the pen and took out the tube of ink. It was a quarter full of ink. "Take this tube. Hold the end and place it horizontally." I began to carefully cut the tubing at about a sixty-degree angle with the knife. I copied the knife's serrated edge onto to the plastic ink tube, and I felt it was not perfect, but in this dim light, close enough to a key's teeth. I knelt down at the doorknob and carefully placed those teeth into the lock. I cautiously turned the tube, and miraculously, I heard a click, so I turned the knob and opened the door. "There it is! Now put tape on that ink tube and hide it in a trashcan."

"Okay, but you didn't tell me anything about why we are here."

"I am sorry. My brain is working overtime, I guess. Do you know how to type up a death certificate?"

"Yes, who died?"

"Me."

Chapter Six

The concern on his face told me that he didn't know my capabilities and the deep understanding that I had of my situation. "You know how to get the death certificate?"

"Yes, I do," I whispered. "The head physician will check the dead person, check for heartbeats for twenty seconds and for *rigor mortis* that will set in after about one hour… which is good for me. One of the doctors will want to keep me unconscious if he finds out I'm awake. Do you know what he will do to me?"

"Yes…he wants to kill you…but can you stop your heart for twenty seconds and your breath for five minutes? Can you do that?"

"I can do it because I learned transcendental meditation. While I do that, it helps me control my heart rate and my respiratory system. My heart rate will be about one beat per sixteen seconds. I am not Houdini. However, I need a little help from you, so the doctor does not notice my heart beating four seconds earlier. I also need twenty minutes in order to focus my mind and body to relax to Cosmic Consciousness in transcendental meditation."

"Okay, what do you need me to do exactly?"

"There are four things you must do in order for me to help my friend. Do you know anyone working in the funeral parlors?"

"Well yes, but why?"

"I need you to call that person to transport a body after four o'clock to that funeral home, and immediately put it in the crematorium and cremate something."

"I like your plan, but the funeral parlors do not have crematoriums. The bodies that are to be cremated have to go to a separate location. When your father admitted you to this hospital, he was given a form to fill out in case of death, and that's what he would have had to sign to get your body cremated promptly."

"Thank you for sharing your knowledge. I feel ignorant for not knowing that," I said.

"Don't feel stupid…in the short time I have known you, I can tell that you're intelligent. You're just too young to be thinking about death."

"Okay… now show me where that file cabinet is."

"Here it is," Aaron said. It was one of a few file cabinets up against the far wall.

I pulled the top drawer a bit, and found that it was not locked… it was easy. I pulled the second drawer out, and I searched for my name. *Sir Alban III* was not there, but right away I knew why. I quietly slapped myself on the face—my father and the head doctor used different names for me. I searched for the other name and found it.

As I read my file, I couldn't believe my eyes. I was right—my father put me here. "Look at this."

"What?"

I turned the file so he could see it. "I am here because my father admitted, 'My son, *Albin Sebastian*, is profoundly mentally retarded, and that while the children next door were playing baseball, one of them hit the ball into our back yard, where it hit him in the head and put him into a coma.' He told them, 'My family cannot care for him this time.'"

"I can't believe that your father would say that. He's in the British Parliament… He is one of the people who make the laws so that our lives are better. How can this be?"

"I do not think that all of them in parliament are like my dad. I hope not, anyway. But probably many are. It is human nature to want authority over people, just like in the Middle Ages when the kings ruled over the peasants. Years change, but human nature will not change. Those people who like control over others like it because it makes them feel like a god."

"That's true. A lot of the doctors feel that way, too."

"Look… Here is the cremation form that my father filled out, and he checked the box to cremate my body immediately… but he included that he wanted to see my body first."

"Well, do you have another plan?"

"Why?"

"Your father is methodical. He wants to see your body, watch them seal the coffin, and maybe he even wants to see the coffin put in the crematorium."

"Yes, I understand that, but do you know where to find a blank form like this?"

"I was working in admitting at some time or another. Let me see if it's still in this desk." He took the flashlight and left me in the deep darkness for a moment. "Here it is."

"Good. Can I have the flashlight, too? Let me see." I took it and checked the box, just as my father had, and I also signed his name on it, just the same way. I took out the old one and put my version into the folder.

"I hope you know what you're doing!"

I smiled at him. "Can you burn this form in a toilet?"

"How can I burn a paper in a toilet?"

"The first thing you have to do is drain water from the back of the toilet tank until it is empty. Then flush the toilet until there is no water left in the toilet bowl. Then, let water fill the toilet tank again. Ignite the paper, drop it in the dry toilet bowl, and close the lid. Wait thirty seconds, then flush the toilet." Aaron was silent. "Do you know why you have to do all that?"

"I have no idea."

"The smoke... It cannot get in the air or it will set off their alarm system."

"Hey, your voice did that thing again. It cracked,"

"Go burn it! Okay?" I let him take the flashlight, and I waited for him in the dark office so I could think for a while. Then, in the distance, I heard the faint sound of a toilet flush.

Before long, he was back in the office. "Really, it worked like you said!"

"How much smoke was left in the bowl?"

"A little bit... I opened a window just a crack because I didn't think the smoke would all go down in the sewer pipes."

"The flushing causes a natural vacuum. Therefore, you can be sure the smoke went to down the drainpipe."

Aaron smiled at me, and mused, "Whoever cleans the old bricks in our sewer is happy with you. He or she is happy to clean smoke off the bricks...otherwise they would be cleaning something else."

"What time is it?"

"3:17 a.m."

"Okay we need to hurry up. At about 4 a.m., you need to inform the doctor of my death. The people are in a deep sleep at that time. And you have to be a little antsy because you want to make the doctor be a little confused. Who is the doctor in charge tonight?"

"I think...uh...Richard Coition is the head doctor tonight. Yes."

"I need a few things before 4 a.m."

"There you go you again!" he whispered. "What things do you want this time?"

"Can you type up a birth certificate?"

"Yes, but you know it's not recorded."

"Duh. I am not stupid... you know that...Anyway, can you?"

"Sorry. That sentence came out of my mouth wrong. I know you're not a stupid person. I meant that the birth certificate isn't real. If you want to get a passport, there are other ways to do that."

"I know that. But ever since the first kings began levying taxes, they recorded the people's names that lived and worked on the king's land. They wanted to know how many peasants there were. The kings wanted to know how much money in taxes they were getting from their land. In modern times, governments still record our birth certificates from the hospitals; they are using them to keep track of us. But people also need the government's record of our births because after we are gone, it's proof that we were here. I know it is only a piece of paper, but I know it is going be in my pocket."

"I understand perfectly. I'll go ahead and type it up for you, but I need a little information from you: what do you want the name of the doctor to be on the certificate, and also, what is your new name and how old do you want to be?"

"My mother talked about her obstetrician. She thought he was great: Dr. Quintin J. Celestine. I am going to forge his name on my certificate, and I want to change my name to Alex T. Ottoman. Can you type up two pages in Latin?"

"Yes. I learned that in 4th grade."

"How did you master it at such a young age? I learned that in my first year in college."

"I don't know, but I can understand it, and I can write it, too. Anything else you want to know?"

"I want to know if Cambridge students volunteer in this place."

"Yes, but the Cambridge dean won't let just any student volunteer in this mental hospital. He'll allow it only if the student majors in psychology and development of the mind."

"I see." My fingertips tapped at my chin. "Can I make a call?"

"Sure, but it's already 3:30."

"I know about the time." I picked up the phone and dialed. Della answered.

"Hello who is this?" she said in a sleepy voice.

"Sir Alban III Christopher, the best student you had."

"It can't be. His father told me that he ran away deep into the forest and that a pack of wolves tore up his body and ate it. There is nothing left of his body."

"The first thing you thought of was a story my father told you."

"Yes, and it doesn't make sense. My rationalization is that he's an intelligent young man. He knows that wolves cannot climb up trees. And there are many trees in the forest, so I suppose he climbed up a tree."

"I did."

"Who is this?"

"Me! Alban III Christopher. I will prove it to you. Remember when my mother and I first interviewed you?"

"Yes..."

"The first thing I asked you was, 'Why are you wearing a Rolex watch?' Your answer was, 'Good teachers are worth their weight in gold. My watch reminds me of that when I look at it. And if you want me to teach you, you have to take my test first. I will see if you are a candidate for my teaching skill.'"

"God, really! I'm talking to you now?"

"Yes, it is me."

"What happened to you?"

"It is a long story. I have to go right now, but I would like to meet with you later this morning."

"Of course! What time? Where?"

"I will meet you about two hours from now at your lobby."

"I will see you then," she said. "Bye."

I hung up the phone and wiped it with my shirttail.

"Here they are," Aaron said.

"Why did you sign my certificates for me?"

"Because you were busy. I saw you talking on the phone. I see time is 3:39."

"Okay...we need to hurry up a bit. Do not forget to get my file out for the person who takes me to the crematorium, and remember to make the doctor more confused. I can prevent my heart beating for only sixteen seconds." I grabbed my flashlight and we ran back through the dark hall and rushed down the stairway toward my room. I stopped to touch Robert Zachary's door as a teardrop fell down my cheek, and for a fleeting moment I remembered all the good times we had. Then I ran back to my bed, and Aaron Isaac hooked me back up to the I.V. "You remember that you need to get the doctor twenty minutes from now?"

"Okay, and I want to pick you up from the rear of the crematorium after you 'die.'"

I nodded to him. Aaron walked out of my room and took my flashlight and pants with him. I thought it was good of him to take them out: a doctor could see those things in here and think it was strange. I lay back on the hard gurney, focused on my breathing, and with each breath I took, I slowed down my heart rate. My concentration heightened, and I felt the air flowing through my bronchial tubes, my lungs filling up with air, and the red cells forming a junction with the oxygen in my lungs. I started to gently slow down my heart rate; I was falling deep into transcendental meditation.

In the meantime, Aaron walked in the direction of the office of the doctor on duty. He overheard the doctor talking on the phone with the chief doctor of the institution. Aaron rushed back to the secretary's desk to the multi-line phone, pushed on the lit button, and picked up the receiver.

Chapter Seven

He listened in on Fabron Rahman telling Richard Coition, "My client requires a male child. I am not going to disappoint him! I want you to give that child in room 498 an injection of the cocktail. His heart will stop, you write out his death certificate, and you will put him in the hearse. My client will intercept his package. My client must have a young boy, but whatever he wants to do to him, I do not know and I do not care."

"Nevertheless, it is wrong," Dr. Coiton replied. "I will not ever do it again to these adolescent boys!"

"You will! Because I am the chief doctor of this place. If I want to, I can fire and hire to my whims. I know people in the administrations in the hospitals of England and Europe—you will never work again as a doctor if you don't obey. I look at it differently than you do, Richard. We are serving our country greatly because my client represents the affluent and the powerful. His servants do anything he desires. If he wants a boy, his servants have to capture an innocent boy at a park or on the streets somewhere…maybe your boy. We have the boys he wants, the ones that this society discards. Some because they aren't right in their head, or because they need little help with their lives. Our culture has decided to put them in medical institutions like ours."

"You are right… we do not see eye to eye, Rahman. The citizens put their loved ones in the hospitals because the doctors all took the Hippocratic oath. Its utterance by us will keep our innocent patients from harm and injustice. Who will prevent me from saying anything to the Bobbies?"

"What ages are your children? I recall Nancy and Dan are two and 11 years old. Do you want them to have more birthdays, Richard? Do you? I am sorry for saying that to you, but my client would do that if something happened to me."

"Well, the boy's parents…what are you saying to them?"

"His dad and me, we are friends, and we golf together. I Informed him of the terrible catastrophe concerning his son. His dad put him in here under a different name—he doesn't want people to know his boy is in the mental institution. So he told them he ran away, deep into the forest, and that a pack of animals ate him. His name is Sir Alban III."

"That name rings a bell... His dad is Sir Alban II. He is working for the British Parliament."

"Yes, he is.... Did you hear that? Someone is breathing into the phone!"

Aaron hung up the phone quickly. He looked at his watch: half a minute until four o'clock. His heart was beating so swiftly and his blood was flowing in his body as if a train were out of control. The salt-water filled up his sweat glands, and adrenaline pumped into his blood instantaneously. He ran to Richard's office, just like a medical student who for the first time witnessed a death of a patient. He flung open the office door.

Aaron loudly and nervously pronounced that the boy in room 498 was dead! The doctor dropped his phone and stood up, put on his white coat and followed Aaron. They ran to my body as fast they could. The doctor searched all his pockets for a stethoscope as they ran. "I left mine on my desk—can I use yours?"

Perfect, he thought. Aaron handed it over to him.

Suddenly, the doctor opened my door, and there was a lot of activity. He shouted, "You check his airway and pulse on the carotid artery! I'll check his heart!"

Aaron fretfully told him that my airway was clear and that he did not feel a pulse.

"I don't hear it either. Okay, we need to start cardio pulmonary resuscitation! You give one breath to him, and I will give four chest compressions. Start now!"

Three minutes later, Aaron said he could not do CPR anymore, that he could not breathe any air into my lungs. Dr. Coiton said, "I cannot do compressions on him either." Both of their faces were beet red. The doctor said, "What time is it?"

"4:03 and twenty-seven seconds."

"I will go to write the death certificate for him, and I need to make a call. Get him ready for the undertaker."

The doctor left my room, and Aaron whispered in my ear, "Are you okay?"

I motioned to him that I'm okay, and he whispered to me again: "We have another problem...I'll tell you about it a little later." He pushed my gurney outside the room and down the hall to the cold storage.

Halfway there, a person stopped us and said, "I am presuming that body is Albin Sebastian."

"Yes, but who are you, and what are you doing here in front of cold storage?"

41

"I am the hearse driver. I need to take this body to its final resting place."

"That is peculiar…you waited down here for Albin Sebastian to die? I think that is odd!"

"Wait, damn it, one moment…My boss called me up and said that Eastman Hospital has a person who died; will you pick him up? His name is Albin Sebastian."

"Really? Who is your boss and who called him?"

"My boss's name is Bob Haritian. I do not know who called him, and I do not care! I DO care about how long is taking me to pick up this dead body, and my boss does, too. Well, what are you going to do? Will you give him over to me, or do I call up Mr. Haritian?"

Aaron's hands were clutching and quivering out of fear. I could feel my gurney shaking. I knew that Aaron was thinking to himself that he didn't want to give me up to him. But if he didn't hand me over to him, Fabron Rahman would know that Aaron listened in on his call with Dr. Coition. I knew he must be apprehensive of being fired by Mr. Rahman…or worse.

But I was hoping he knew I wanted him to let the hearse driver take me. I need him in the hospital to watch over Robert Zachary. I hoped so much that he would realize that. For a moment, I worried he would lose composure.

Aaron said, "Sorry, I had a bad night…I'll help you put this body in the body bag."

"Okay then." They pushed me into a cold storage room and opened up the body bag inside the pine casket. Together, they lifted me into the coffin. Aaron zipped the bag nearly all the way, and under his breath, said, "Remember—I've got your back covered."

The driver put the lid on my coffin, he took it to the hearse, and put it inside. He asked Aaron, "Whose beautiful black Indian bike is that?"

"It's mine," he said.

"Where did you get a fine bike like that?"

"In America, when I was living there. I had it shipped to me here."

"Well, I have to go now."

Aaron quickly asked, "What route are you taking to the crematorium?"

"It's odd that you ask. My boss informed me to take a different route tonight."

"Which is?"

"The Gallows Green Road and turn off on Lindsell. I have to run." The driver folded his large frame into the driver's seat, and soon the hearse with me inside it was rolling beyond the hospital grounds.

Aaron ran for his bike and threw his white coat down. He put on his leather coat, started the bike, and rode away after me. Aaron rode through dark wet air, and it enveloped him as if a beam of light shone on darkness. The hearse was driving on a zigzag road for nearly half an hour, with Aaron not far behind me. I started to breathe deeply again and felt oxygen circulating and flowing in my veins. It was resurrecting the cells throughout my body, like a river that's rushing and carrying nutrition in its riverbed.

I unzipped the body bag and moved around. It felt good. I slipped the top of the coffin off and I sneaked out of it. I inhaled deeply and felt pain in my chest. I crawled along the bed of the hearse and looked for something to use to notify Aaron that I was all right. I also needed to find some weights to put into the casket so when they lifted it out of the hearse, it would be heavy enough to have a body inside. I searched every square inch of the bed of the hearse, but I did not find anything. Just in case there were something under the coffin, I moved it. I found a loose rug and I pushed it out the way, and in my amazement, there was an old trapdoor there. I tried opening that door but I still couldn't lift much. I tried lifting it with all my might…and the trapdoor finally opened. I spit out some blood. I reached down inside and felt something soft. I pulled out a blanket… *Is this useful to me?* I thought. *Yes, I think so.* I put it aside. Then, I reached farther inside and to the left, and I felt something big with a handle. I grasped it and managed to pull it where I could see it. It was a toolbox. I tried to pull up on it, but I couldn't lift it because I was so much in pain. I spit out more blood. I opened the box up…there were a lot of tools in there. I picked up every tool in the box and, one by one, I lined them up forming two columns inside the body bag. I zipped the body bag back up, putting the cover on the same way the driver did.

The hearse was bouncing around and it was hard to keep my balance. I reached around on the right side inside the trapdoor. It felt like something was there, but it was slipping away from me. I reached around harder, and then the tips of my fingers grabbed hold of it—a round flashlight. I hoped that it would work. I switched it on and it shone into my eyes. Quickly I turned off the light. I put it on the blanket, closed the trapdoor, and laid the rug over the door the same way as it was before. I tried to lift half the coffin and pull it over the rug, but it was too hard to do. I lost my balance as the hearse went around the curves going faster and faster. I had a sharp pain in my chest each time I tried, but finally I pulled the casket over the rug.

I spit out so much blood I couldn't believe it. I felt weak, but I knew what I would have to do to get through this. I had to keep a cool head. I got the flashlight and hoped that Aaron knew Morse code. It was used in America in the late 1800s for telegraphs, which was the main communication between people in U.S. cities. My timing had to be accurate. I couldn't know how far Aaron was behind me, and the road was curvy, so I would have to send the

Morse code while the hearse was on a straight way before it zig-zagged. I counted two turns so far, so next there would be one straight section for about nineteen seconds until the next couple of turns.

Now was the time. I paused for six seconds, then I started signaling the light on and off, hoping he'd understand. I told him: I a m ok I wait for hearse to stop.

I could only hope that he got the message. The driver abruptly stopped, and the coffin slid and pinned my body against the wall of the hearse. I felt sharp pain in my chest and I coughed up blood. I heard the car doors shut with force... *Oh no*. With all my strength, I pushed the casket back to where it was, I covered myself up with the blanket. I heard two people walking over to the driver's side, and then I heard a big thud. A second after that, one more thump, and then footsteps coming toward the back of the hearse. I held my breath. A man said, "Here it is...the package our boss is lusting after."

"Yes, it's here," said a second voice. "This is easy. You remember two weeks ago, our boss asked that we get the boy? That S.O.B. that rode away from us on his bike?"

"I remember. The boy got what was coming to him. A car hit him and he bashed his head on the road."

"Yes, but I saw his body fly over that car like Evel Knievel did many times, and lived... Okay, enough chatter. You get the left side and I'll get the right side." They lifted the coffin and carried it to their car. I heard two car doors slam and their vehicle took off.

The boy they talked about was my friend Robert Zachary. Immediately, I got out of the hearse, and Aaron pulled up on his bike right in front of me. "Are you all right?"

"I am okay. Check on the driver." Aaron handed me my pants and I swiftly pulled them on, trying hard not to move much. I leaned on the side of the hearse as I walked along the driver's side. "How is he?" I could barely speak.

"He is still alive, but unconscious from the blow to his head."

"Turn on his emergency lights and put his head on the horn. Someone will come and let somebody know he is here."

While Aaron did all that, I slowly and painfully got myself astride his motorcycle, and then he ran over to the sound of his motorcycle and got on it, too. We rode fast to catch up to the bovver men.

"What kind is their car?" I asked weakly.

"I don't know. I think a van... What's going on? Your breathing sounds like gurgling."

"I think my rib is broken." It was difficult to speak louder than the sound of the engine. "From when the doctor did CPR on me. I spit up a lot of blood and I am weak."

"What are we doing trying to follow the gangsters? I need to drive you to the hospital if your rib punctured your lung!"

"You cannot do that."

"Why can't I do that!? Oh, I know why, right? You are dead!"

"You can care for me after I find out where they are going... I saw the sign for Lindsell... You have to turn there."

Aaron turned the bike with precision as rain began to hit us. As Aaron went faster, the water splashed onto our legs. I saw the car—it was a quarter mile dead ahead. Aaron accelerated. Wet wind whipped our faces as if we were riding into a dust storm in the desert. I was drowning in my own blood. I forced myself to continue. We were nearly in London, and we were behind them, just one car's length away. I was close enough now to see their license plate and memorize it.

They soon slowed and turned into a parking lot. We rode around the block before we dared to park within sight of them. We saw them open the coffin. We heard their fury with my replacements inside the body bag, and we watched them destroy the car with tools I gave them, cursing and shouting. I barely heard them.

I was distracted by the sight of a long limousine that turned into the parking lot, slowed, and picked them up. As it drove off, I spit out pool of blood.

Aaron asked me, "Are you okay?"

I took a long time to answer him. "I want to follow the limo."

He started his bike again and we sped up toward the taillights before they were out of sight. We were in London, and the city lights were reflecting on the streets and shining in my eyes. The limousine was stopping at the Landmark Hotel. We parked near there and watched them go inside the luxurious lobby.

I needed to pursue them, but I could not stand up, and breathing was so difficult. Aaron turned around to me and said, "You want to die right here, or are you going to tell me where Della is?"

I knew that my wounds had made the decision I could not make, so I told him she lived just a few blocks away—The Berkeley Hotel. But whatever else I did in this lifetime, I promised my friend Robert that I would find the person lusting for innocent boys like him—the person who, tonight, was in the Landmark Hotel. And I know that when I find him, his body will be gripped in pain from the tortures I will commit against it, and he will wish his body had already expired. When it finally does, his spirit is going float in a sea of ungodliness, and then, only then, will he feel like the young boys he craves. After that, those innocent souls are going to rest peacefully.

My physical pain melded with this deep anger and grief, and I barely noticed Aaron speeding me to Della's place, but the sight of the opulent hotel brought my attention back to the present. He parked near the hotel entrance and helped me get off the bike, and then my body fainted into his arms. Aaron carried my lifeless body into the lobby. My long, wet hair drip…drip…dripped onto the shiny marble floor as my brain drift…drift…drifted into darkness.

Chapter Eight

In an instant, my life force catapulted back in history. I was suddenly marching in England's army amongst a thousand men, just eight rows behind the men holding the flag of the Royal Coat of Arms of England. I tried to see what kind of emblem was on the flag. It was hard to see it, but I could make out that it was the French three fleurs-de-lis on a blue field, quartered with the Royal Arms of England. That emblem was used from the years 1399–1603, but knowing that didn't help me out one bit. I saw the king riding on a white stallion in the middle of the first row. He was wearing the royal crown on his head and a long royal blue cloak that flowed from his body onto the back of the white horse, and sunlight flowed through the king's crown jewels. As the stallion walked through the mud, pieces of mire flew up and hit the end of his cloak; so lovely, and so powerful. I asked one man who marched beside me, "Do you know who the king is that rides the horse in front of us?"

He smiled and belly-laughed and screamed to the troops, "Thus, you see a young boy right here amongst us who doesn't know our king, our royal lord accompanying us to battle with the French!" All of the troops raised their swords up and yelled loudly together, "NOBLE KING HENRY THE FIFTH!"

Early the next morning, I saw the men huddled in a group, so I went and joined them. Henry V started to talk to his troops, telling them, "Do you see how the beautiful sun rises and lights up the French territory like it's done for millennia before this day, as God made it! God did put you here to fight for magnificent England! This day defines a moment in the glorious history of England. From this day forward, old people will tell their children about this day, and they will tell their children and their children! Do you remember yesterday, how a young boy did not know my name? But from this day forward, when people speak of England, they will think back on this day! This will be the day that defines English history!" The archers lined up behind the right side of me, and put up the archery flag as he spoke. "All of my men fighting on this day will be immortalized in England's history! Do you hear that rumbling sound? The Frenchmen are coming! It is our predestination—it is calling us—it is time for war! Get ready!"

I heard someone on my right say, "Kid, go to the archer rows."

"Why?"

"Kid, you dress like the archers, and you don't have a sword or shield. That's why."

"I guess so."

I walked off, and I heard the king calling out, "Get ready, entry-men, line up to the left side of me and put up the entry-men's flag! Horn player, play on my command!"

I found an old sword and shield laying between the bushes. The sword was not rusty. Before me were the tools of war; my heart was beating rapidly, and I felt proud to fight for my king. Henry V communicated very well with his troops, but my inner voice told me, "Don't go!" I heard the horn sound off—this war was starting now.

The king commanded that the archery flag be dropped, and then the archers shot hundreds of arrows in the air. A few seconds later, I heard the arrows piercing men's flesh. The brutalism on the field of war! The men were bellowing out the sounds of the wounded and dying. It was piercing my soul, as if I could hear lost spirits crying out from the fires in the underbelly of hell! The archers again shot hundreds of arrows in the air, and they pelted the enemy like rain falling from the sky. These archers shot rains of arrows for several minutes. Then, the king commanded the entry-men's flag to be dropped, and the men charged onto the field of war.

I heard a sound that I've never heard before, one of torture and torment from the depths of hell. My mother had read the Bible to me, and a passage I liked talked about teeth gnashing together in the lake of fire. I had wondered what sound the teeth made, but now I know! I imagine that teeth gnashing in the lake of fire sounds just like our metal swords and shields coming into contact with the enemy's.

I looked at the sword and shield that I found... I thought to myself, *Could I go into this battle?* I felt proud to die for England, but I did not know if I had enough backbone to do that. When I touched both sword and shield, their powerful energy surged through all of me, and the energy transformed my instinct to pure animal aggression. I looked at tools of survival, and I grabbed the violent sword and shield. I felt powerful as I ran to this field of bloodshed!

I was engaging in battle with England's enemy, and I fought for both my life and England's survival. I had their blood and guts spattered everywhere on me. My sword was covered with blood, too. This morning, the field was golden brown at sunrise, and it was illustrious to me, but now the field was enveloped with bodies—half dead, and the and other half mutilated. Those still alive cried out, "Kill me!" I heard them loudly, but I had to focus on fighting as strongly as I could for my life! I was in the middle of the battlefield, and human flesh was surrounding me. The air was stagnant as it filled my lungs.

As I engaged in battle with a Frenchman, I heard my name spoken softly. I kept on fighting, and I heard my name again and again, a bit stronger now. The Frenchman turned to fight with another British enemy behind him, and I had a moment to choose my next move. I walked on blood and human remains towards a voice calling out my name. I searched for that voice as I carefully avoided more of the adversaries. I walked through the cesspool of war. I took my steps closer to that voice, and it was getting stronger, but it sounded ghostly.

I tripped over a body, and the voice said, "Be careful what you wish for, it might come true. Look around here… You see too much torture. Those bodies that were once human, all they want now is to expire for a little peace! You wished for torture and torment, and now that person is dying. In your lifetime, you saved many innocent people. You may kill evil men, but you cannot revel in the killing of them! You have the gift, so use it wisely. Watch out!"

Suddenly, my awareness focused in on the war again. I turned and saw the Frenchman walking up to me. Of course he wanted to kill me, so I stood up abruptly and grabbed my sword. I blocked his sword with my shield with all my strength! His sword reverberated through to my arm, and it told me that he was a strong challenger for my life. I thrust my sword at his chest and he blocked it with his shield with authority! The powerful force of my sword hit his shield and stunned my grip. As I let go, it flew and landed about ten feet away. Suddenly, he was thrusting his sword forcibly at me, and I barely blocked it. His force threw me backward, and I landed on my side. I rolled over and over nearer to my sword and reached for it. I managed to grab it and stand back up immediately. But, while I did all that, he was simply waiting, and he thrust his cold, sharp sword into my warm body

I gasped for air as I lifted my head, and Della said, "Are you all right, Alex?"

"I am fine, I guess." I took a moment to adjust to my new surroundings. It seemed as though I were up on her dining room table. "You remembered my new name. That's good. Did Aaron fill you in? How is Robert?"

"Robert is fine, but he is unconscious, the same way you saw him before," Della said. "You, on the other hand, you are fortunate that your friend is a good doctor, young man! Aaron came in my front door carrying you. He put you down on the table, and he had to perform surgery on you on that table. He used the tube out of a pen and my good knife. Don't worry, I sterilized them. He tapped your chest with his finger, and he heard the hollow sound everywhere except for one place on your chest. That's where he cut a little incision. I used my nice towels to mop up your blood from the table and the hardwood floors while he cleaned out the blood in the wound."

She barely stopped to breathe as she continued, "Your rib punctured your chest wall and went into the pleural cavity. That's why you've been coughing up blood. Your chest cavity had also filled up with air, and that's why it was so hard for you to breathe. So, he inserted the tube in there to help suck the air out of your chest. He told me that you would breathe much better. And he said that he couldn't do anything about the small hole in your chest, but he did say that it would heal over time. He said the body can heal itself."

I said, "How long have I been out, and where is Aaron?"

"I am right here." He rose up next to me, from the floor.

"Why were you on the floor?" I asked, feeling a little silly because I was still on the table.

"I was sleeping, and I stayed here because I wanted to help Della watch over you after you woke up. You needed to see some friendly faces. We are going to remind you to keep your movement to a minimum, and I am sleeping here for four nights."

"Something is blocking my deep breathing."

Della said, "My good linen is twisted around you. Aaron wrapped your abdomen up with it. Your rib needed extra support."

Aaron said, "It's also so you don't reinjure your chest."

"How long until I can move around like I did before?"

"In a few weeks you will be good as new," Aaron said.

"Della... You cannot call me Alban anymore. To protect my life, you must call me Alex from now on. Did Aaron tell you what happened?"

"Not much. We were a bit busy with your chest. I trust you will tell me all about it, though...Alex."

"You are a very good professor. You taught me the history of the Middle Ages and about life in general. I was dreaming about William Shakespeare's play about King Henry V, the famous speech he had with his troops. I don't remember if I quoted him word for word or not."

"Thank you. I like being a good professor, and you are very a great student."

Aaron said, "I am going to lie down and go back to sleep. And Alex, you need to lie back and go to sleep, too."

Chapter Nine

Three weeks later, my injury was healing just fine, but my ribs were a little sore. I looked out of Della's family room window and saw that fog was rolling into London. The wet dew touched the London Bridge. The Thames flowed and kissed its embankments.

"Hey, what are you are thinking about? Enjoying my view from up here?" Della teased. "It is glorious, I know."

"Many times I've seen fog rolling into London, but after going through such difficult times for the past few months, I look at things differently now."

"I know what's wrong with you. Aaron said that for the past few weeks your voice has been changing."

"Yeah. Another problem I have on my plate."

"No, don't think of it like that," she said. "Since the beginning of time, girls around eleven or twelve years old and boys between about twelve and fourteen have physical changes. Girls come into womanhood and boys move toward becoming young men, as your body is doing now." Della sauntered over to the window and looked out with me. "Generation follows generation. Life just a cycle moving through history, and quickly it will be gone. A hundred years from now, some person will read about you in a history book. What they perceive about your life is up to you. I know they will be acquainted with your intelligence and strategy."

"Thank you. I hope they will. But now I look out there at the great big world and think about the extraordinary people in it. But some people want to devastate innocent lives for their own gratification. I understand that our culture wants them in jails, but there are too many of them for that."

"I know you want to get that guy who destroyed Robert's life, Alban, and almost your life, too—but you can't be angry. If you're angry, you're making a big mistake. A few weeks ago, you just about died, and that guy will tell his goons to kill you. He won't think twice about it. You must be the Machiavellian."

"I know. I need to be more cunning this time. But I could not believe that the head of doctors there, Richard Coition, did CPR on me. I realize why, too. Fabron Rahman told him that his client would kill the children."

"That is true," she mused. "But you were faulty in one way. Do you know what it was?"

"You think I gave up my control while I acted dead. But I manipulated the doctor, and he thought I was really dead. I told you a little earlier about my mistake."

"Your plan was exceptional. I could never have thought of it, and the doctor would never have thought of it, either. You need to understand something. People's actions are like a cup of water. You can manipulate the water easily inside of a cup, but if you spill it at the top of a slope, it's difficult to control. Do you understand?"

"Yes. I didn't hold the cup tightly enough. So, Della...how is your cardiomyopathy these past couple of weeks?"

"Good, I guess. I went to my doctor, and she told me that my tests were actually good, but with heart disease it's difficult to tell. It can be good today, not so good tomorrow. You know that already."

"I don't believe your heart is bad," I offered.

"Out of your mouth and into God's ear."

The doorbell startled us both. "I'll get it," I said.

"Your food is here! Who's hungry?" Aaron said, as he walked in carrying several bags.

Della asked, "Hey, how is Robert doing?"

"He is okay."

"Can I see Robert tonight?" I asked.

"Sure. I'm leaving here to go to work. You want to come along? Oh, and did I tell you, Alex? Fabron Rahman is missing."

"No! You didn't tell me when he left!"

"Two days after you faked your death. And tomorrow his family will be moving all his stuff out of his office."

"That is strange. I'm wondering...if we go to his office after I see Robert, we can look for his private papers. Maybe some information about this attacker of innocent children is there."

"Dinner is served—come and get it."

We sat down in her dining room with the air filled with the glorious smell of a cottage cheese pie, hot gooey biscuits, and couple pieces of key lime pie.

"I overheard your plan for tonight, boys. Do you think Mr. Rahman has evidence of a connection to this person lying around in his office? Or any connection at all?"

"Perhaps not. But I think other people are involved who are in the British Parliament. It's possible that his office has information that will lead me to a contact of his," I said with forkful of pie hovering near my mouth. "We have to try."

We were all deep in thought, even though the wonderful treats seemed to be our main focus. "I just remembered," Aaron said, mid-chew. "About three years back, all the newspapers wrote an article about Scotland Yard not finding a child molester who killed six children. Newspapers stopped writing articles about Scotland Yard altogether about three years ago, right around that time. Anyways, I see why you think your father could be involved with this ring. Be careful with your emotions. It will affect your judgment."

"I don't think my father is associated with him. I do think the man knows someone in parliament, though, since Fabron Rahman has given this guy the *compos mentis* children before. Now listen to this. The doctors write their death certificates, they send the papers to the registrar's office in their district, and some employee there makes a copy of the death certificates. Those copies are sent to the General Registry office at the British Parliament, where they keep an archive. The funeral director would have written down the time of cremation or where they were buried, and those copies are also kept. It's in their files."

"You're right…the board of directors of England's hospitals all work in the parliament," Della added. "They oversee the death rate in the hospitals and what kind of medication the doctors had prescribed their patients."

"I want to see Eastman's file with the death certificates tonight. I want to see how many doctors wrote them out in there. You know where they are, right Aaron?"

"I worked in admitting. You know that. I think you're trying to distract me from that last piece of key lime pie," he said with a smirk.

"I saw that file somewhere in the office next to Rahman's office. I'll find it."

"Do it carefully, and I want to help you out if ever I can!"

"Thank you, but due to your heart condition, I think that's not a good idea."

"Well, I never thought you'd think I sit around here like a vagabond waiting for my heart to stop beating! Look at me. I am still a vivacious woman. My wisdom and knowledge have served me well. You need my astuteness, as it could get serious out there! I'm sorry for being so defensive, but it's true."

"I'm the one who should be sorry, not you. Please accept my apology."

"Yes, of course."

"Do you want to do a favor for me? Tomorrow, can you go to two places? The registrar's office in the district for Eastman hospital, for one, and ask them for a copy of the death certificates for boys that died at Eastman. Also, go to the police station and ask for a police report on Robert Zachary. Then, write down the information, and see if the police captured the child molester three years ago. I believe that the child molester and his hired hands tried to abduct Robert Zachary. The same child molester killed children three years ago and he is still around, but he went underground. I mean he hunts for innocent children in the mental institution. Society did not miss the children because they were already forgotten citizens, and he knew that."

"In all my life I've never heard a thing like that before. If that is true, he's intelligent enough to not be caught by the police. They would never think of this! I don't want to believe it, either, but I'm listening to you and Aaron, and I know what happened to Robert…wait one minute! If all of it is true, where are the lifeless young bodies?"

"You recall reading the history of Viking cultures? Do you remember how when a Viking died, they put his body in the sea? I think those bodies are in the Thames, unfortunately."

Della looked flabbergasted. "I know the assistant commissioner. I know what needs to be said in order for him to give me the right information."

I looked at Aaron. He took a look at his watch and said, "Ready to go, Alex?"

"Yes. Do not wait up for me, Della. I will take his bike."

I walked out the door, and I heard her say, "Wait." She handed me money for a taxi, and we drove off.

Dark and windy rain came from the northwest. We drove through it as though nothing was there. It felt like a glorious night in England.

Chapter Ten

Aaron dropped me off about a quarter mile away from the back side of Eastman Hospital so the employees wouldn't see me, and he went ahead of me to unlock the back door. I walked through the driving rain to the hospital, thinking to myself that in the Middle Ages, the European leaders wanted take a control of England, and few ever did. I reasoned that there were two factors: one was geographical—the Celtic sea, the English Channel and North Sea; the other was England's weather. England's kings used the elements to their advantage.

I finally made it to the door. I opened it, slipped beyond it, and it was dead silent and pitch-black inside. I felt all over inside, looking for another door. I could feel my heartbeat thumping in my ears as I located the doorknob and quietly opened the door. There were faraway sounds and dim light inside. I took off my wet shoes and tied them together, then hung them up around my neck. I snuck in silently and noted the stairs about fifty feet ahead of me. I walked towards those stairs.

I climbed up out of the basement, unsure of what I would find, but all I saw at the landing were the lamps, dimly lit along the long hallway. I checked my mental map of the layout of this floor, then headed for Robert's room. It wasn't hard to find. No one seemed to be around. I looked into to his room, and I thought to myself, *Inside that motionless body is my friend.* Life is so delicate. That there are people who want to take life away from the innocent among us, is atrocious to me.

I walked up to Robert and I held his hand. I asked him, "Do you remember when I poured cold water on you when you were sleeping? You were so furious with me! You ran after me all around our neighborhood. And when you caught me, I saw your sweat and the rain on your eyebrows, and the expression on your face told me you were about to laugh. We walked to our homes, laughing all way there. You remember that? Of course you do. One time you challenged two boys to a tennis double match. One week later, they were teasing you in terrible ways. We didn't know how to play tennis! I got my father's tennis racket and you got yours from your grandfather, and we practiced a lot that week. You complained…yes you did. I told you that your willpower would win the game and would help you for the rest of your life, if you let it.

"We practiced serving the ball all week. It's hard to toss the ball and hit it near its apex at a diagonal so it falls inside the correct opponent's service box. And we practiced rallying. Our arm muscles were aching, remember? Finally, that day came, and we knew our tennis game was inadequate to challenge them. We went to play them anyway. There we were at the tennis court, and you told them to be there at one o'clock. We waited and waited until three. I remember you told me that whether the bullies come or not, they will always keep teasing you about something. Of course, they will still poke fun at our tennis skills. After all, you nicknamed me 'hit it sidewinder' and I nicknamed you 'missed it again.' We knew deep down that the bullies wouldn't show up. And then you said, "They keep on teasing me for the way I act, but I only have truly one friend, and that's you. You like me way I am."

"We played tennis that day with each other, and we had more fun that day. Do you know what I thought while we walked home? No? Well, I'll tell you then. I thought about what makes bullies in school mistreat the kids who are different. Like you, for instance. I think that all people are jealous of other people. Most people tell racial jokes with friends, and their children overhear them. They teach children that it's human nature to poke fun at people who are different. The parents unknowingly ingrain into their children the values of prejudice, violence, discrimination of other ethnic groups, and different appearances of people. It is resulting in school children forming their own groups and becoming antagonistic against other groups. There lies a key problem in society today. Children will grow up being more prejudiced and discriminating toward different ethnicities. It leads to violence of all kinds…even sexual violence.

So, that person who wanted you for his sexual desires…He is a type of personality that would have been a bully at his school, maybe."

As I finished talking, the door opened, and Aaron shut it quietly behind him. He said, "Are we talking about bullies? Guess what. I was bully at my school."

"But why? You don't seem like a bully to me."

"Well, my father is good doctor, but he liked to move a lot during my childhood. I didn't have many friends, and when I did, I moved and I lost them. My mother told my dad, 'Do you want your only son to be alone?' He said, 'No, but…' And she said, 'But what? Only four years left until our son graduates from high school. After that he is going to get in a good college, and you and I can move around any time you like.' So, surprisingly, we lived in one place throughout my high school years. It was a small town in upper New

York. It was quite nice there. It had a big, peculiar high school…well, I'll keep this long story short.

"I hung out with the wrong crowd, and they bullied others, and so I did, too. We especially poked fun at a girl who was disabled and had to use a wheelchair. She drooled, and her body trembled with her every movement. My so-called friends were merciless as they mocked her about her body, and she cried after we were done. That went on for most of the school year. But one day, halfway through the semester, she transferred into my geometry class. That day we had a test. The next day our teacher told us that he was going to grade on a curve this time, and that someone got a hundred percent. The students were booing at whoever got the perfect score.

"The next Monday, I went to that class early and saw that disabled girl waiting for the door to open. I hesitated a moment to talk with her, but it was hard for me to talk at all because I saw the drool and it nauseated me. I said, 'Hello, glorious morning in New York, isn't it?' Her voice was just above a whisper, but she said, 'Great day to be alive!' I said, 'I heard that! Earlier I heard that only one person got a perfect grade on the test. I'm wondering if you know the name of the person who ruined our test curve?' She said, 'I know who; I ruined the exam curve.' I asked her how she accomplished that when she had transferred in the same day we took the test. She said, 'I transferred out of the same class, just with another teacher. I learned all of the same material and I got an A+. I am not dumb. Some people look at my body and they think I'm retarded. You and your friends have teased me ruthlessly, as if I don't have a mind or feelings.'

"I was put on the spot. I said, 'Well, I am wrong. I'm so sorry about that.' I was hoping the conversation was over, since the time was getting close for others to show up, but she kept going. 'Sorry is just a word in our language. It doesn't mean much. By the way, are you Mr. Bernelle's son?' I said yes. 'Your father is my doctor,' she said. 'He's a good doctor, but you, on the other hand, why do you hang out with bullies?' I only told her that I didn't know. I was still hoping no one would see us talking, but it wasn't unpleasant anymore.

"She continued, 'My life is grueling enough. Your friends are sarcastic about my body. I look at myself in the mirror and I think to myself, what they're saying about me is really true! They see only the outside of me, even though the inside is what really matters. You and your friends never thought about that, did you? Well?' I said, 'I guess not.' She continued, and I remember this part so clearly, too, 'Whoever is doing the teasing is having fun. I know that. But if they could wear my shoes a little while, they'd know their teasing hurts deep down in my heart.'

"On that day, I stopped anyone who was teasing Suzan. She and I were friends over that summer, and she taught me to look through another person's eyes. When I do that, I take a different point of view, and I have a greater understanding of people's needs. She was also the reason I became a physician."

"What happened to her?" I asked, mesmerized by his story.

"She was normal one year prior to her symptoms. She had dreadful headaches, and her mother took her to the doctor, but nothing came of it. For months, she was still having horrific migraines, and she started losing her balance a lot. Her mother took her to the doctor again, but he said he didn't know what was going on. He agreed to make an appointment with the neurologist. Before she was able to see the specialist, she started to lose her fine motor skills. She had to use a wheelchair, and she started drooling. Finally, Suzan went to the neurologist. He ran all kinds of tests. Two days later, the doctor told Suzan and her mother that she had a tumor deep in her brain that was growing rapidly. Her mother asked the neurologist if the tumor could be removed, but he told her that in order to take out the entire tumor, he would have to move half her brain with it. That would mean Suzan's body would be in a vegetable state. The doctor asked her what she wanted to do, and it was her quality of life that was her biggest question.

"She said that all of her life she wanted to help children from deprived families…that she understood how they felt to not have anything in their stomachs. She said that she and her mom sometimes didn't have anything to eat in their apartment, either. She hoped to teach the children to see their future as a lot better than their present. But God had a different idea than to make her an angel for unfortunate children. On the morning of July 14, 1956, I was holding her hand at her bedside. God took Suzan home. I hope he made her a beautiful angel like her own spirit that was inside her."

"Wow. Suzan was a good person. I know she is looking over Robert right now."

"Yes, I believe she looks over all the children in the mental institutions, too."

"God gave us the knowledge of right and wrong. The people who desire young children for sexual gratification—that is immoral. God has certain people in civilized societies sit in judgment on others who sin. I will find the wrongdoer and put him through torture just like he served to Robert and all of the children he abused."

Aaron looked at his wristwatch. "It's time to go to Mr. Rahman's office while the staff works on their charting."

"Okay!" I was holding Robert's hand, and I told him, "I know you do not like goodbyes. See you later, then." I squeezed his hand gently and put his hand down on the white sheet, and I slipped my shoes back on. They were dry. I grabbed two pairs of rubber gloves, and we left his room.

We walked through the dim hall again, and then upstairs…déjà vu all over again. Aaron asked me if I wanted to use the hidden stairway or the normal stairway. I asked, "If I go on the regular stairway, will the staff see me?"

"The staff is a skeleton crew tonight. The staff won't notice you in here if you're very quiet." So we went up the normal stairway, and he opened the door to the first story. I walked through the door, and the sterilized hospital air breezed past my face. I looked into the extremely large hallway—all white, and about one hundred feet long and thirty feet wide, and somewhat alarming. I looked down the hall with its many doors on each side, and looked at the two red lines going along the center of the floor, about five feet from each other, disappearing into the distance. Aaron opened the door to the second story stairwell, and we climbed up there. I opened the door, looked around, and then opened the door to the third story staircase. I saw the same things and smelled the same disinfectant on every floor.

We were on our way to the fourth story now. It was dark, so I took out Della's flashlight from my pocket and turned it on dim. Aaron said, "This way." We snuck down the hall as quietly as we could. The night doctor was in his office, six doors ahead of us. Aaron was pointing at the door of Fabron Rahman's office, and I nodded. Aaron reached down into his pocket very calmly, silently took out a cluster of keys, and searched for the right one. He held them between his hands so that they wouldn't jingle. The right key was pinched between his thumb and finger, and the rest of the keys were bundled inside his hand tightly so that they wouldn't make any noise. Aaron put in the key in the lock and turned it until it released the mechanism, then pushed the door so gently that it couldn't make a sound. We went in, and I aimed my light toward Rahman's big desk. His cabinets were next to his large sofa. I suddenly felt an odd sensation of cold, wet air hitting me that sent a shiver down my spine. I motioned for him look for all of the death certificates in the cabinets as I handed him my flashlight.

I walked over to Rahman's desk and touched its top. The heavy lacquer felt smooth as glass. I sat down in his black desk chair with my back towards the large picturesque window. I was lucky, since as the clouds moved, the moonlight illuminated the room a little too much. I looked across his desk and thought to myself what a powerful man he was. If I were Mr. Rahman, where would I put things that I didn't want anybody else to know about?

On top of the desk was a big blotter-style calendar lying flat on its mat, and I looked at April. He had many meetings listed here. The last meeting he noted was on Tuesday, April 23rd. He had a meeting, but with no mention with who or where. To the left of the calendar, there was a pen holder with just one pen. I reached for it, and I could tell that he used that pen a lot. In the moonlight, I saw the Russian flag on the pen. I put it back in the holder. I saw his Rolodex on the other side of the mat and started flipping through it. It looked like about fifty names. I looked at Aaron, and he was still in the cabinet searching. I looked more closely at the cards in the dim light. In there were the thirty-five names of doctors in Europe and ten names of attorneys in England. But Jesting Heddwyn's name was in there, too! He worked on the board of crimes in England in the British Parliament, but he didn't work on the board of Physicians. How does he know Heddwyn? Social gatherings, or business dealings? I looked at Aaron again and hoped he would find the death certificates soon.

The desk had four drawers. I pulled out one drawer—it was empty. I pulled out other one, and it was empty, too. I thought he was an eccentric person to need anything as clean as my father did. But I pulled out a third drawer, and there were two of his ledger books. Pulling them out carefully, I opened one of them and found it contained his comments about his employees. I was curious about Mr. Rahman's observations of Aaron, but I closed that book. I picked up the other ledger book, and it contained the miles he traveled each week. I looked at April 23rd, his last entry in the book: 41 miles.

Aaron nudged my shoulder and whispered, "Here it is… Two years of copies of death certificates."

I took them from his hand and searched them for children under thirteen who died in Eastman. I found fifteen children who had died in the last two years. Of those, thirteen died in Eastman: four last year and nine this year in this place, all of boys! I whispered to him, "You see it…what do you think?"

"I do not know right now, but that is serious data. How can you take those documents and figure out who is the head of this grotesque operation?"

"I will figure it out somehow. Can you search this ledger book?"

"Okay, for what? We need to hurry."

"Let me see. The first child died on May 8. Search a week before that."

"On May 1st it says sixty-eight miles, and the second day says thirty-four. The third and fourth were on the weekend, and he didn't write his miles. The fifth day it says forty-one miles."

"Hey wait, what?"

"Forty-one miles! Shhh!"

"The very last entry was also forty-one miles. Look for others between the dates that are the same. June 17, July 24, and September 18… On June 17, the second child died in here, and on July 24, the fourth child died in here. It's just a few dates. I hoped to find more of the key to this…the name of the murderer. Keep looking for forty-one miles in the week before those dates."

"I did. There was a forty-one miles on June 15, too. And he traveled forty-one miles five days before that."

"Can you check the death certificates against those trips in June and July? I want to check if they were all after he made the first expedition."

"You are right. It's all right here. He traveled forty-one miles one week before fourteen innocent children died in here."

"I am curious about his dreadful habit…why he wrote down miles each time he went out from his job."

"What are you thinking? Why did he go forty-one miles the week before each child's death in this hospital?"

"I need a little while to grind it around in my mind. I know someone knew about this operation in Westminster because the British Parliament goes over it with a fine-tooth comb, as they do for all the deaths at all the hospitals. But I do not know who it is."

Aaron looked at his watch. "We have to go now!" He put back the file of death certificates, I put back the ledger books, and when I did, I saw a white envelope in the bottom corner. The envelope was addressed to Mrs. Rahman. I couldn't move. Aaron hissed, "What is wrong with you!"

"This letter." By then, I had it in my hand. "Should I read it?" Frustrated, Aaron took the envelope from me and opened it. He unfolded the paper and started reading very quickly, very softly:

Dear Love of my life,

If you find this letter, then you know that I am dead. I loved you from the first time I met you. I hope you know that. I remember when our sons were born and I was rejoicing. I wanted to protect them always. And I did that, but I know you heard the rumors about me. The boys did not know any of it, and I tried so hard to keep all England's children safe. But in order to make that happen, I made an arrangement with the devil to stand aside from England's innocent children in this hospital. Unfortunately, England's citizens abandoned some innocent children into my care, those who couldn't care for themselves. I erroneously took their innocent lives… Oliver, Alfie, Joshua, Jack, Charlie, James, Harry and Thomas… during my deal with the devil.

I know that as you read my letter, you will blame yourself for my death, but I hold myself responsible for my own death, and my actions have sealed my fate. Although I deeply regret that I will not see my children go through each step they are taking to adulthood, but I know deep down in my heart that you will educate them properly. Finally, I am going to miss you and I growing older together. I want you to make a new life with someone who loves you and your family.

I love you.

Chapter Eleven

The sound of the doorknob rattling snapped us to attention. There was no time to analyze the letter. A woman in the hallway said, "The door is locked. I'll get the key from the head physician in the next room..." and then her footsteps faded away. Quietly, I folded the letter, put it in envelope, put it back in that corner and closed the drawer.

I felt Aaron's nerves buzzing. My mind was working at sonic speed. I looked around his office and noticed a chair next to the tall file cabinet, and then looked up at the two-foot-square ceiling panels. I whispered, "Follow me."

I leaped onto that chair and then hopped onto the cabinets. The flashlight was still up there, so I picked it up and put it in my pocket. I pushed one square of the paneling up and over into the ceiling and checked out the upper side of the ceiling configuration. There was a steel horizontal beam just beyond my reach that I'd have to jump for. Quietly, I jumped up and grabbed the beam, not letting my body touch the metal grid! Success... I pulled my body up to the beam, threw my torso over it, climbed to a crouch, and stood up.

I faintly heard her say, "Thanks for the key." Aaron looked terrified. I motioned for him to move quickly and do what I did. I heard the nurse's footsteps getting closer as Aaron was pulling his body up to the girder. He looked down suddenly, and I followed his gaze: his shoestring was stuck in the grid! I cautiously hooked my feet on the beam and reached for his shoestring, heard a key in the lock, untangled his shoestring, and instantly, Aaron pulled up his foot. I pushed the panel back in place as she opened the office door.

Aaron got both his feet under him, and we froze. It took a few moments to feel our heartbeats slow down and feel the adrenaline slack off. Down underneath us in the office, she said, "Hi Jack..." And then, I heard the door shut, and it was strange that he didn't answer. But now instead of hearing my heart thumping, I could hear them: they were kissing each other passionately. My emotions and hormones raced through me like a wildfire burning a harmless meadow. After that, the meadow would never be the same again...

just like my body. I became a young man in that moment, as the generations transcended before me.

Aaron nudged me, and my brain, body and spirit awakened to a cold, hard realization. I needed to figure out how to climb down and not be noticed. I looked over our surroundings and saw that the central beam we stood on extended east and west in both directions, with a brace beneath it every eight feet. The nearest perpendicular crossbeam was near the center of a row of steel crossbeams oriented north and south above the doors along the hallway. I saw huge bundles of electric lines everywhere for the lights and outlets on the fourth floor, and I felt a glimmer of hope. At the far end in front of me, using my flashlight, I saw a room. Just below the floor of the room, I saw a massive pulley... the room could be the machine room for the elevator. If it was, I would be able to get down to the basement undetected.

I motioned to Aaron to follow me and pointed to the power lines so he would see them. I put my flashlight in my mouth and held my arms to the side for balance with every footstep. I set my sight on the next bracing and set my foot carefully over it. My body was at the midpoint, shifted out to the side with my hands holding each side of the vertical support beam. My weight shifted to the other foot, and I cautiously brought my trailing foot to other side of the bracing. I needed to walk sideways so that I could shine the light on the beam for Aaron, and I turned back to watch him as he stepped onto the beam that was only the width of his shoe. Aaron shuffled over to the vertical bracing and copied my movements. We were both solid and ready to move on.

Stealthily, we moved along on the thin steel beams and stepped over the electric power lines. Slowly and diligently, we made it there. I was right about the machine room, thankfully. Underneath it, a gigantic pulley and massive cables hooked to the top of the elevator down in the bottom of the hoist way.

Aaron asked me, "What are we doing?"

I said, "Do you see the service ladders in the shaft?"

"Yes! I got it. How do you think of these things?"

"Well, I know a little about the architecture of buildings because I have made several models of European buildings."

"It helps to be as intelligent as you are." Aaron looked at his watch and said, "I need to go my nurse's rounds." I nodded my understanding to him silently.

I walked to the edge of the elevator shaft, put my flashlight back in my mouth, and carefully placed my feet on one of the rungs. I climbed down the ladder, and about a quarter of the way down Aaron began to follow me. I thought to myself, "*I hope nobody wants to use this elevator right now, or we are S.O.L...*" But if the elevator started, I already knew what I needed to do.

My feet touched top of the elevator, and Aaron was close behind me. I felt like being in a tin box, and every sound reverberated back to us and up the shaft.

I quietly opened the panel in the top of the elevator, and Aaron carefully hopped down. I placed the panel halfway over the panel next to it and climbed partially down. I was standing on Aaron's shoulders to be able to lift up the panel and place it over the opening, and then I jumped down. I landed on my feet, hoping that the panel would cover the entire opening...looking up, I was happy to see that it did. Aaron said, "Good job. Can I call up the taxi for you?"

"Yes, please. What are you doing this afternoon?"

"Nothing...just sleeping. Why?"

"Do you want to have a cup of coffee?"

"I thought Englishmen like you liked drinking English tea?"

"You thought wrong. I am not a normal English guy!"

"That is the honest-to-god truth! Where is good coffee in London, anyway?"

"The Costa Coffee. You know where that is?"

"I think so ... Wigmore Street?"

"Yes. I'll meet you in front of the coffeehouse about two o'clock. Are you ready to go?"

Aaron smiled, and I pushed the button. When the elevator doors opened again, we ran out and went our separate ways.

I ran to Robert's door and put my hand up to the window. I closed my eyes for a few moments, then suddenly, I felt like my old friend's spirit met mine, and I was content. I opened my eyes and said, "Thanks, Robert." Then, I ran quietly back the same way I came in.

It was cold outside, and damp air whipped at my skin like a chisel. I kept moving and finally reached the road to meet with the cab. Ten minutes later, it drove up, and I threw my sopping, dripping, wringing wet body inside. I was colder than I'd ever been. The taxi driver asked me, "Where are you going, wet gent?"

"The Berkeley Hotel."

"Ah, you are a *rich* gent, too."

He pulled up to the hotel entryway, and I paid the fare. Inside the lobby, my clothes were dripping on the shiny marble floor again. Their custodian surely hated me because I kept messing up their beautiful floor.

I walked up to Della's door and pushed her doorbell. She said, "Who is it?"

"Me. Alex."

"Okay, take your shoes off, and leave them on the little step by the door and come in," she said. I walked in, and the magnificent fragrance of fresh bagels, cream cheese, and hot honey buns was swirling around me. All of a sudden, I felt ravenous. "Go ahead, eat!" So I helped myself.

"So, what did you find out last night?"

"Well, we didn't find much. But I did discover a few things. Fabron Rahman knew Jesting Heddwyn … which is a little odd because they don't work with one another. I happen to know that Jesting did not like his grandchild Robert Zachary. What if the child molester told Mr. Rahman he desired live boys, not half-dead ones? If Rahman knew that Jesting Heddwyn didn't like his grandchild…"

"That is speculation."

"Okay, then the only fact I know is that Fabron Rahman knew Mr. Heddwyn. I know that because his name was in Rahman's Rolodex."

"That is fine, but what if they were golf associates?"

"Even so, they would have conversed with each other. Talk with Heddwyn for just one hour, and anyone could tell he didn't like his grandchild. It's a shame, but it is true."

"It is not likely that Mr. Heddwyn had knowledge of Rahman's dealings with this murderer. I don't believe that he did."

"Our culture today is untrustworthy, and this is just an example. Mr. Heddwyn told Rahman his private thoughts, and Rahman in return gave a predator his knowledge about Robert in hopes of getting that person off his back. It's an old saying… Loose lips sink battleships. But this time, I lost my friend."

"It was a famous saying in World War II."

"I need to get that person, whoever it is, that wrecked Robert's life. You know that."

"I do. We need to be as cagey as William Shakespeare's treatment with his own manuscripts. But it's a real person we are looking for, not characters out of his plays. If that person hears we are searching for him, he will to try to kill us for real."

"I know that. I said earlier that loose lips sink battleships. I meant that. Do you want to know when Fabron Rahman started injecting young boys? Last May. The chemical composition of the shots causes the heart to stop temporarily—I guess for two minutes—enough time to put them in a body bag and a pine casket. That child predator's gang hijacked the hearse. They abducted innocent children from the hearse, gave the children to their leader, and…"

"Why are you giving me a synopsis of what happened to some boys in Mr. Rahman's mental institution? I know what happened in there already. I want to know about specifics of your findings last night."

"I am sorry," I sighed. "My brain is a little tired. Here are the specifics from last night. Last May, Mr. Rahman took the first boys from his mental institution, and ten months later, nine innocent young boys lost their lives. The odd thing about it is that five days previous to the date in May, Rahman drove forty-one miles—hey, one second. Do you know what the taxi rate is?"

"All of the taxi cabs have the same rate. Two pounds per mile. Why?"

I smiled. "Perfect. I gave eighty-eight pounds to the cab driver... 88 divided by 2 tells me your apartment is forty-four miles away from Eastman hospital. And how far is it to the Landmark Hotel?"

"It is about three miles away from here," Della said with her trademark crooked smile. "Your math also tells me that you didn't tip the driver."

"Right. I guess I am not very polite when I am worried about catching a murderer. So, the Landmark Hotel—is it closer or farther from the Eastman hospital?"

"I don't know. It would depend on the route the taxi took to get here. There's a long way and a short way. What street did the cab take?"

"Lindsell."

"That's the short way, though the Landmark Hotel is still closer to Eastman than that."

"I know where Rahman went five days before they abducted the boys. It was the Landmark Hotel. At least, I think so, but I do not know who he was meeting there."

"Wait a minute. You're not the only one who's having a revelation... Do you remember when I told you about the newspapers, and how they abruptly stopped writing articles about Scotland Yard and a child molester? That was last May!"

"Yes... I guess so."

"I understand your body is a little tired. That's okay. I'll talk plain English: The child molester killed children last May, and the press was printing articles about it. What if that person got hold of Mr. Rahman and told him, 'I'll kill your children unless you give me boys from your mental institution. Our society won't mind me getting that kind of boy anyway.' If that happened, then no one would know more children were missing, and the press would have stopped writing their dreadful articles about him. I have my friend who works as a maidservant in the Landmark Hotel, cleaning the higher-level suites where the affluent people stay. I will talk with her and see if she can tell me who stayed there on those dates."

"I feel like an ignoramus sometimes, and this is one of those moments. Reason is that I think I have the big picture, but I really only have the pieces. You have something there. That person is intelligent enough to push all the right buttons and get anything he desires. I am wondering if they worked in government somewhere, just because of their abuse of power over the people. They could meet at the Landmark Hotel, and the child predator could stay there!"

"I want to inject some motherly advice into this conversation. When was the last time you went to bed?"

"Let me see. It was yesterday at midnight."

"My dear, your mind needs to rest. It causes you to feel like a cretin. I know you don't have a sub-par brain, as I taught a lot of students back in my tutoring days, and I never knew anyone more intellectual than you. But I'm worried about you!"

"Why?"

"Young people are thinking about their futures, but you don't think about your own future. You think about Robert's destiny and the person who changed it for the worse!"

"Well, I thought you would be proud of me. Reason is that I have not been influenced by my father. He thought about his own future all the time. His own son, he threw into the mental sanatorium because he does not want to deal with seizures. It might interfere with his social status and his ascent up the hierarchy of British Parliament."

"By the way, you haven't had a seizure, have you?"

"Oddly, I have not had one since my father had me in the park for the luncheon. That doctor might be right. He said that some young people in puberty have only a few seizures, as their brains are overloading with electric current and hormones. Just like mine, hopefully."

"When was the last time you took any medication for your seizures?"

"The last time I took the pills my doctor prescribed, I was running away from my father. It was a few months ago."

"It sounds like that might be the case, then."

"Nevertheless, you did not answer me. Do you think I wanted to conduct myself as my father does?"

"You're growing into a young man. All people around your age want to loosen the ties with their parents, but you, young man…your situation is quite different."

"Do you miss your husband? Your voice tells me that."

"Yes, I do. All the time."

"I remember the first time I met him. We met him in an extravagant restaurant, and I was a little apprehensive toward him. We sat down at the table, and he told an off-color joke. I did not know whether to laugh or ignore it. He smiled at me and said, 'Go ahead and laugh!' So, I did. I laughed my head off, and we had pleasant conversation that night.

"I know my husband really liked you, and from that night, he and I started talking about having children. He said, 'If I could clone Sir Alban III, I would!' Unfortunately, we did not have children. A few days later, my husband was driving to a meeting and he was in a car accident. It killed him instantly, and my life was forever changed... Please forgive me, my phone is ringing."

I waited for her to answer her phone and sat patiently, observing that I was still sitting barefoot in my wet clothes. I had barely noticed.

Chapter Twelve

Della came back and said, "My yellow cab is waiting for me at the front entrance. I have to go now, Alex. We will finish this conversation later about your future."

"Where are you going?"

"You don't remember? You told me at dinner last night that I should go to the police station and that registry office. What you're going to do, I hope, is get a bit of shut-eye today."

"I forgot! I have the list of names of the boys who died in Eastman hospital this year. Oliver F. Mabsant, Charlie H. Radbourne, Samuel A. Easton, Joshua G. D'arcy, James William S. Wahchinksapa, Daniel I. Zackary, Jack L. Saith, Harry B. Rogelio and Thomas W. Edmond. There is one other thing you can do for me. Can you go see if my mother is doing okay or not, and wish her a happy birthday?"

"Yes, I guess so."

"While you are there, ask about Jesting Heddwyn."

She smiled and walked out the door.

I woke up a few hours later, and my brain felt alive again. I took a long shower and looked at myself in the mirror, feeling like my body has now changed, just as generations behind me and before me. Della was right. I have the power to change future generations for the better. I hope they look back and perceive me to be on the good side of history. I saw Della's cup of bobby pins on the counter, and I remembered that my mother had the same cup of bobby pins by the mirror. I took one of the bobby pins from Della's cup and kissed it as if it were my mother.

I could faintly smell the bagels and cream cheese, and my stomach told me that I was hungry again. I went into the other room and took a bite of this morning's leftovers. The bagels still tasted fresh and the cream cheese was still good. I checked the time, and it was exactly one o'clock! I have to go to meet with Aaron! I closed Della's front door, locked it, and walked away while I ate.

I strolled down the sidewalk thinking, *"Great day in England...rainy and blustery."* Three sides of the country are bordered by water: on the west is the Irish Sea, on the east is the North Sea, and on the south is the English Channel. The weather in the British Isles trends toward mild temperatures and frequent rainfall. The English Channel is about twenty-one miles wide, but it separates England from the continent of Europe. That narrow piece of sea has been important in shaping the country of England. Reason for that is throughout the ages, the Roman Empire, the kingdom of France, and the Anglo-Saxons tried to conquer the British Isles, but they didn't factor in the English Channel. The conquerors made improvements to the British Isles, including England's grid of roads, built by the Romans when the footprint of their empire covered the Isles. The British people use them even today. The Romans were plumbing engineers who inspired large-scale water systems in England that imitated Rome's Cloaca Maxima system for managing areas of flooding. They also built up the ancient hot springs of Aquae Sulis in modern Bath, England. Even today, the British have two huge Roman-built engines at the lake that are used to run water down the aqueduct into London.

I passed by a church and my mind wandered to the oldest church in England: St. Martin's Church, also known as the Canterbury Cathedral. It has an interesting history. The Anglo Saxons made the original structure to worship their pagan gods. Pope Gregory the Great heard about this and sent Saint Augustine as a missionary in 597 AD. The Pope wanted Augustine to convert the Anglo Saxons to Roman Catholicism. Saint Augustine became the first Archbishop of the Canterbury Cathedral in 602 AD. Throughout time, the Canterbury Cathedral weathered many storms created by human conflict. In 1011, marauding Danes traveled in their long ships, killing and raiding, and the town of Canterbury was among many devastated by this rage. The cathedral was set on fire. In 1093, Saint Anselm became Archbishop of Canterbury. He was a quiet, wise and pious man, but it is to him and his scholars that we owe much of the Romanesque architecture and art that survives today. Today, the Canterbury Cathedral is a tourist trap, but some people do not know the history of the Canterbury Cathedral and how it started out as a pagan shrine for the Anglo Saxons.

I saw Aaron's bike parked in front of The Costa Coffee. I opened the door and walked in, and I heard, "Hey, Alex, over here!"

I turned in the direction of the voice and saw Aaron. "Hey, how long have you been waiting for me?"

"Not too long."

"Good. I see you have not ordered. Do you want to order now?"

We walked up to the end of the line and waited. Finally, we placed our orders. "I want a hot, steaming double deluxe coffee, and put whipped cream on top." Aaron ordered a Hawaiian coffee, and once we had them in hand, we went back to our seats. The steam from my coffee enveloped my nose, and its redolence woke up my cold, wet, frustrated body. I felt nice and warm for a few moments. I had blocked out the crowds stirring around in the coffee shop. Aaron said, "Hellooo?"

I shook my head and said, "Yes..."

"Where were you!"

"I was deep in my thoughts. I am back now."

"Good! I must thank you for last night and your fast thinking. I heard her start to open the door, and I froze up! Thanks to you, she didn't catch us!"

"I put you there in the first place."

"Yes, anyone can lead person into a situation, but not just anybody can show the way out of a difficult situation. Very few can, so you—as young as you are—your future is going be great! Did you talk with Della?"

"She talked to me about my future this morning."

"She talks about your future as your teacher. She worries about you, too. What are you going do when you find out who is molesting and killing children? Are you going to chase Robert into the moving car? I hope you decide to give the name to the constabulary... I assume I'm saying it right? The British police?"

"You said constabulary quite well. I will find more evidence when I do that, and then I'll hold the key to justice of all the children who have been violated and killed. They will have power with this abuser, and they need to say what to do with the key. When I get the name of the abuser, I sense they will know what to do with it! I know one clue... Do you remember when Fabron Rahman put down forty-one miles in the ledger book each time after five days children died? I know where he went."

"You're kidding. Where?"

"The Landmark Hotel. It is exactly forty-one miles away from the Eastman mental institution."

"That's right! We went to the Landmark Hotel when we followed the limousine and the gangsters thought the young boy was in there!"

"Propitiously, I might add, Della knows someone who works in the Landmark Hotel. She will meet with her after she stops at Scotland Yard today. I made a promise to Robert that I would hunt them all down, and I will find them to vindicate all the children who have been killed by them! Only then they can their spirits be freed from the legacy of anger that ties them to this world. Okay… This conversation is getting me frustrated. I want to change the subject."

"Go ahead."

I took a sip of my exceptionally warm coffee and thought out what we would talk about. I took another sip of my coffee and said, "I remember you told me that the head doctor during your residency declined your physician's license. Will you tell me now why he did that?"

He took a sip of his steamy coffee, looked down at the cup for a few seconds, then said, "It's still difficult to talk about it, but I have good cup of joe in my hands and a good friend across from me. In 1964, I was in the first year of my residency at South Shore Hospital on the south side of Chicago. It's an African-American community there. My class residency program was made up of all Caucasians, and they made racial jokes to each other. Sometimes a few young doctors used an antagonistic tone when speaking to the patients. I talked with the head physician several times about that, and she told me she would counsel them. My dad taught me that a patient's ethnicity should not matter to a good physician, for if they let it matter, they lose accountability with patients, and most of all, the good doctors who are their peers. Doctors should not be racist, since their work can determine life or death, and if they do that, they choose which patients go on living or not, and that is wrong. Even though my father treated Susan as well as he could have, she still died, so the physicians are not God, but you know that already. So, a few years went by, and the system weeded out some bad apples. The South Shore Hospital's resident staff, including me, worked our behinds off six days a week. We worked on all kinds of patients. You can't even imagine. Young ones, old ones … God made them, and we worked on them and administered care to the best of our abilities.

"Faithlessly, on a night in the dead of winter, February eighth, I was ahead of the residency program at that hospital, at that time, and I worked in the emergency room. In there, I expected the unexpected. And on account of the frigid temperature, which was about forty below zero, people were doing foolish things all the time. It was a skeleton crew in the emergency room. Only the head doctor of residency was working in the E.R. with me, plus one nurse because she could not find anyone else. Fortunately, that night was slow.

"Then, the call came in to South Shore emergency room that two ambulances on east 79th were en route. Two cars had crashed on a southbound exchange, I heard on the hospital's intercom. I rushed to the big doors, and the head doctor was close behind me. She said, 'You want to get the first ambulance, and I'll get the second one.' I nodded and said, 'You take the nurse. I'll ask a paramedic from the ambulance to help me out.' I heard two sirens getting closer, and my adrenaline was pumping in my veins, throughout my brain, putting my nerves on edge like an electric charge, and in my mind I went over everything. I learned over the years, up to this point, how to keep people alive. Outside in the bitter cold, I saw the first ambulance pull in. The driver jumped out quickly and opened ambulance's back doors. The other person inside the ambulance stopped performing CPR and started to push the gurney out the back. Halfway out, the driver released the gurney's front legs and pulled it quickly the rest of the way out of the ambulance. All of that took just ten seconds.

"They pulled that person inside the hospital, and we hurried down the hallway with the lights seeming to flash by me, just like when you drive on the freeway and you look at the headlights flashing past you on the oncoming side. The paramedic relayed her information to me quickly: he performed CPR on her nine minutes, her blood pressure was 77/48 the last time he took it, and her heart rate was 29! Her body was cold to the touch. I asked him to check her blood type and get two pints of blood ready for her. He rushed off to do that. As I looked her over, it seemed to me she was pregnant, and about in her second trimester. I put on my stethoscope to check her baby's heart, and I heard it faintly, so the baby was alive! That was a good thing. I thought she might have become brain damaged because I thought she wasn't getting enough oxygen to her brain, but I know she wanted to keep her body alive on account of her baby. I needed to know where she was bleeding internally, so the first thing I needed to do was put her on a mechanical ventilator.

"We rushed her into a room. I grabbed a laryngoscope and an endotracheal tube! I stood at the head of her gurney and pulled her chin toward me slightly. I put the laryngoscope into her mouth on the right side, but I switched it to the left and moved her tongue downward. Then, I lifted her epiglottis upward and forward and viewed her trachea, and with my other hand, I put the endotracheal tube gingerly into her mouth and slid it through her larynx and into her trachea. I heard a sound like the inflating of a balloon, so I slightly let the pressure off the tube, and air came out from it with a wet screeching noise! I like to hear that sound because it means I put the tube in the right place. It must just be half way in the trachea. I placed the air bulb to the tip of the endotracheal tube and squeezed the bulb. I saw her chest move, so that was good. I asked the other guy to squeeze the air bulb 20 times per minute. The other paramedic ran into the room with two pints of blood at that point, so I checked the information sticker on the blood bags, and I verified it was her blood type. I asked them if they knew how to give a blood transfusion, and one guy said yes. I told him to use an 18-gauge needle because I thought her veins might have collapsed due to her very low blood pressure. I was hoping it wasn't going to be a problem, but I told them that if they ran into a problem, I would be right here.

"I started examining her other problem, the major issue of internal bleeding. I cut her shirt open with scissors, and I started to search her torso. I found black and blue bruises above her navel, but it was difficult to tell if her abdominal cavity was distended or not because she was pregnant. I palpated the contusion and it was rigid. I believed she was bleeding into her stomach!

"The head physician walked abruptly into the room and said, 'What are you doing?' I said, 'I'm trying to save this woman and her baby!' She said, 'Get real! This hospital is not a warehouse for incubating babies after their mothers have already died! Anyway, if that black baby lives, what do you think he or she will make of their life? Do you know what I'm saying? Do you?'

"I said, 'Yes, we do know what you mean, but I thank God that I don't believe same way you do. My father told me that doctors like you seem to be fine physicians on the outside, but inside, you think you are God over the human race. You're only a doctor! Not God!'

"Then she said, 'You are right. You brought up whether I am God. Well, I am God in the sense that I hold your hopes of being a doctor in my hands, and it is fleeing fast! Your opportunity to be a licensed physician still has a chance if you leave this room right now! Or you will give up the opportunity to spend the rest of your lifetime practicing as an excellent doctor.'

"That was the moment when I showed everybody my true colors! I turned away from the head physician, and I said, 'How are you doing with the I.V.?' He said, 'I am in her vein now.' So I told him that I want her rate to be eighty percent! The head physician yelled, as she walked out of the room, 'You are expelled from this residency program right now!' I quickly called up the surgery department, told them the patient's information, and I heard her heart rate monitor starting to beep faster. I told them that she required surgery right away, and that I would be transporting the patient up to surgery. They told me the surgeon was there standing by for the patient. I hung the phone up, and we took her to surgery and worked on her all the way there. I checked her baby's heart again, and it was beating a little bit stronger. I felt comfortable about my actions so far and left her with the operating doctor.

"I waited until that patient was out of surgery, and while I waited, I cleaned my locker out. I folded up my shirts and pants and put them in the recycling bin in the hospital. In the back of my locker, I found a toy that a little girl gave me to thank me for getting her well. I played with it for a moment, remembering that girl. It seemed like just yesterday. I took my coat, and I walked back to the surgery waiting room, where I sat for a half hour.

"I saw the operating doctor, and he told me that the surgery went quite well, and that her baby was well, too. He said, 'I know you did an excellent job on her in the emergency room. And I know what happened between Karen and you. Bad news goes around here fast. Why do you have your coat?' I told him that I was leaving, that I couldn't work for Mrs. Karen.

"He said, 'I understand, but the board of directors of the hospital are meeting tomorrow afternoon, and I am on the board, so they will hear about what happened, the argument and the difference of opinion. Anyway, it's freezing cold outside, and in the dead of night. No one should ride a bike in this weather. Did you ride your Indian tonight?' I told him yes. He said, 'Do you want to go to my office and sleep a while? If you want to leave in the morning, the board will conclude that you left this residency program for personal reasons. It will be written on your transcript that way. They will do that for you,' he continued, as we walked back to his office. 'I promise that.' And he *wink*ed to me.

"The next morning, I walked through the hospital, recalling the three and half years I worked in the residency program at South Shore Hospital. I had learned a lot about helping others who needed it most. I walked outside, and I hopped on my bike. I thought to myself that I would still become a great physician someday, just not this year. And then I rode off.

"I drove for two days until I was at a warm place in Florida, hoping I had left the apoplexy of racism behind me! I couldn't deal with that, and I also couldn't go back home because my pride kept me away. I felt like I'd disappointed my parents. I rode everywhere on my motorcycle for three years. I saw forty-nine states, and each one was different and beautiful in its own way. I met all types of people living across the United States of America, and in each town I stopped, I went to the grocery stores. Inside the stores were community billboards, where I looked to find odd jobs. I mended fences, repaired homes for men who went to war in Vietnam, and I kept my doctor skills fresh by helping a mother who had a child with cancer. At their home his mom and I cared for his needs, but his terminal cancer, after a time, took hold of his body. That little boy taught me lots of different things about life, but most of all, little John taught me humility! After that, I swallowed my pride. I went back home to see my parents. They were sick with worry about me for three years. My mother forgave me first, and after a time my father came around and forgave me, too. I told them about my experiences from the past three years, about my practical knowledge, and how it would help me become the fine physician I'm capable of being.

"A few months went by while I worked in my father's office. I saved money so that I could go to England. My grandpa told me about it when I used to sit on his lap when I was a kid. He told far-fetched stories about the time he grew up in England! I made a promise to myself that if I ever get a chance to live in England, I will. And that's what I'm doing here now."

Chapter Thirteen

I had finished my coffee and set down my cup. "I cannot think anything else to say but WOW! My grandfather said when you listen to people's stories, you can find out a lot of different things about them. Personality, how intelligent they are… Your parents had an honorable son, as your character is exceptional and your intelligence has spoken of itself."

"Thank you… My parents are a little proud of me. I am talking as if I were a kid again, but I don't mind, it actually is fun." He laughed out loud and took a drink of his cold coffee. "I was thinking back to when I was a kid, and it reminded me of something I saw last night when we were on top of hospital's ceiling, and we stood on that steel beam overhearing Jack passionately kissing the nurse. While they were doing that, your blood surged to where it hadn't gone before; you had your first turgescence."

"Very funny. Yes, my hormones kicked in that very minute. Every man has done that before. It is natural."

"Yes, but you must be careful with that! It's powerful connected with your emotions. In other words, you need to think and then act."

"I know what you mean." I absentmindedly gazed into my empty coffee cup. "I am thinking out loud here. When was the first time that a molester violated a child, and why?"

"Your question has too many variables to answer intelligently. Whoever the molester of children is, he is human. Human beings are able to adapt to their environment. What if his parent molested him in childhood, or he did not feel comfortable with adult sexual relationships? He would look at innocent children to meet his needs. Or, he wants to dominate people who have sex with him, but he can't find someone to gratify that desire, and he finds that children are easy to overpower to fulfill his desires."

"I did not think about that, but it is good to know. That is the same reason I cannot tell how intelligent a baby is by looking at her. The baby's environment and the parents' treatment of that baby will determine her smartness."

"True, but a person's intelligence isn't only due to environment and parents. Children's brains, from about three months to three years old, are like the New York Philharmonic playing glorious music together. Their brains are functioning just like the Philharmonic over three years' time, as they're wiring twenty billion neurons together. From the intricate, interconnected system comes their personality, thought process and fine motor skills."

"I am amazed at how bodies work perfectly harmoniously, all managed within our own skins. What are you doing later tonight?"

"I drank lots of coffee. I'm going to study to keep up with the physician's journals of practice, since I'll be awake all night. Why?"

"Well, I could possibly need you to take me somewhere tonight."

"My grandpa used to say, there's only one life to live, and people need to take hold of the adventure. I had a bad feeling for an outcome tonight, but I'm in, so please keep me safe!" He shot me a smile.

"Sure, I will bring you back alive. I have to go now because Della is arriving back at her apartment now." We walked outside, and I asked him, "What happened to the patient who was pregnant?"

"Well, I called that doctor who operated on her, after I went back to my parents' house, and he told me that the patient lived, but she had a severe Cerebral Palsy condition, due to the lack of oxygen to her brain. She had lots of therapy, so she was able to care for her son, who is doing well. The hospital's board of directors fired Mrs. Karen, and the state board of doctors confiscated her physician's license."

"You felt good all over about that, right?"

"I really didn't feel like a hero. It was just the right call for that moment. Any good physician would do that." He put on his helmet and asked me, "You want a ride to Della's apartment?"

"Not really," I said. "I like walking in the rain." And he rode off.

While I walked through the rain that was pouring down on me, I recalled that Aaron had told me about his grandpa and him. I liked it because it prompted my memories of the times my grandfather took me out in the rain. It was so peaceful holding his hand and listening as he told me about the history of how the old world evolved into the new world. I can hear him telling me, "If you acquire knowledge of any country's history, you know what kind of destiny is in that country. Do you know what the reason is, little smart pants?"

And I would say, "No, not really, why, big smartest pants?" He told me that throughout our history, the common denominators are the human beings. Humans are the same as they were since the beginning of time; however, their brains evolved while their animal aggression remained in a primitive state. People keep on doing what they have done many centuries before, and this is the reason for the ability to predict the future of a country a thousand years in the future simply from looking at its history. The old saying is, "If you want to know the future, look to the past."

My grandfather was an archaeologist who did lots of research on Middle Eastern cultures. He excavated their artifacts and worked to bring these discoveries to light. He had to stay there at the sites most of the time, but two times out of the year my grandfather would come to England to see me and my family. We walked throughout London and talked about his research. He taught me that hieroglyphics are symbols of animals or other characters, and that the cultures that used them were the Sumerians, Assyrians and Babylonians, five thousand years ago. My grandfather and I both liked tennis, and each June we went to Wimbledon and saw a tennis match. We had so much fun at Wimbledon. He wrote me two letters each month in code, and in turn, I solved his set of symbols; thus, I knew what my grandfather was doing and where he found his interesting artifacts. All he could do to build my intelligence, he did, even from far away.

I opened the door of the Berkeley hotel and walked into the lobby, dripping on the shining floor again. Whoever the janitors in this hotel were, they should have told me off. If I were them, I would have. I walked down the hall to Della's apartment, took my shoes off, and I knocked on her door. I heard her faintly ask, "Who is it?"

I said, "It is me, Alex."

"Take your shoes off," she called.

"I know. Keep my shoes on your doorstep." I opened the door and walked in, and she was lying on the sofa! "What is wrong with you?" I asked frantically.

"I'm a little tired…that's all."

"Well, that is good, I guess. What did you find out from your friend the assistant commissioner?"

"Well, we talked about the case of the child molester three years ago. It turns out that he had taken children in London and other cities, and they had all ended up dead. He told me that Scotland Yard never even got close to solving the case. Then, as you know, the killings stopped, and the people of Great Britain were eager to forget and return to their normal lives again. I told him about your idea that it could be the same person committing the same crime this year, that he could have gone underground, and that he may have blackmailed the head doctor of Eastman Hospital with his life, as Dr. Fabron Rahman has been missing for about four days.

"My friend said that he'd already heard about that, and he wanted to know more, but I told him that was all I knew so far. He mentioned, though, that he

80

also had a hunch that the perpetrator is in a government position. When I prompted him for his reasoning, he said it's because he thinks he is powerful and intelligent enough to avoid any consequences, and that the best of his police force cannot find even one of the missing children.

"So, I asked him if he had looked for them in the Thames. He foolishly asked me if I knew how long and wide the river was, so I told him that its length is 215 miles, and its width is 60 feet at Lechlade and 328 feet at Teddington. He laughed and said, 'Do you know how many man-hours it takes to dredge the Thames?' He said it wouldn't be done, especially since he doesn't think any of the bodies are there. But I asked him if they had found them anywhere else they spent their precious man-hours, and of course the answer was no. I reminded him that somewhere out there, twenty innocent little bodies are crying out for their families to put them to rest in peace, and that he was only thinking about money while bodies could be floating in the English Channel as we spoke.

"He only said, 'You know this job is political, and that I take care of part of the public. And you know me. You think I don't care for the twenty families who are hurting? Of course I do. You know I have children their age. But this job doesn't allow me to consider my emotions.' And then he asked if he could ask me a question. I smiled and told him of course. He asked, 'How do you know this case so well when you don't have any children? I know you are a concerned citizen, but you know a great deal about this sick man. Why?'

"And then I told him about you: this boy whose own father put him in the mental institution, yet managed to escape just in time. I told him about how this predator rang up Dr. Fabron Rahman requesting that same boy. How Rahman commanded his house doctor to give the boy a shot of a drug designed to stop his heart temporarily, so that another doctor would be witness to the time of death. I told him how the boy had devised a plan using transcendental meditation to break out of the mental institution. And that the boy has told me much about what he's witnessed, and that he's trying to solve this case.

"He wanted me to tell him more about this clever patient and how he connected this predator to the one terrorizing London three years ago. I reminded him that no one had apprehended anyone in the case, and I quoted your thought that this person is surely holding a government seat. I told him you overheard Rahman telling his head doctor about the client: an affluent, powerful political figure in a European country with the power over his servants to make them do anything for him. How his servants are just like his personal gangsters, so when he desires a boy, his servants must find one for him. I also told him about your encounter with these thugs, and that you overheard them describing their attempt to capture your friend, how he ran, and that a car hit him. I have to say that after our meeting, Assistant Commissioner Rockdom is impressed by your ability and intelligence."

"You did not give him my name! Mr. Rockdom knows my father!"

"I realize that, but he can help you. When you find out the names of the perpetrator and his gangsters, then what?"

"I will figure that out, but I need more time."

"I know you will… I also know that they are killers, and they will kill you too if they find out about you. I have an idea for a plan of action, however, and when I talked to Mr. Rockdom about it, he reluctantly agreed. It means you will have to be an informant for him. I know you don't want him to know your name! But if I remain your go-between, he doesn't have to know your name."

"An informant does not have any police protection! They go search out things all alone with no backup!"

"I know that already. Young people…" she sighed. "My plan would include protection to you under Mr. Rockdom. He knows how to get you into parliament undetected!"

I was getting more agitated listening to Della, especially since I didn't have any control over what she had already done in my absence. I had to figure out how to make sure I could control all facets of this surprise plan. "How is he going do that? Parliament is locked air tight, and there are security cameras all over the place."

"He has a way, but he needs to know how you found out about the murderer first."

"Okay. But you already told him everything you know!"

"Yes, I did."

"So he already knows about everything I know!"

"I want to give you a phone number. If you have any emergency, call this number." She handed me a slip of paper.

"I will." And I thought to myself, *Right. If I have a phone that I can use, I will.*

"Mr. Rockdom is willing to take care of Robert here if we have to go to the United States of America."

"What? Why would we have to go to the USA?" I could feel all my plans slipping from my grasp. "I do not want to go to another country! I made a promise to Robert to capture whoever destroyed his life! Not just that, but the child molester has killed innocent children, and I feel their souls crying out to me! *Capture my killer!*"

"I know that already. But one second is all it takes for a life change from good to bad. You can relate to that. You had a normal life, and days later, your father put you in the Eastman hospital. Life is funny, and people can't know when, where or how they will die, but everyone knows it's going to happen at some moment in time. For example, I went to my doctor after I stopped by the Landmark Hotel. My doctor told me that there's a probability my heart could fail on me in the next two months.

"So, I'm sorry. I know you want to find out the killer's name for Robert and those innocent souls, but a couple days from now, your new passport and identification card will be ready, and we are going to Berkeley, California. I know someone who works in the education system out there. I told her about you, and she wants to meet you." I sat staring at her in silence, in shock. She continued, "I know your plate is full already, and I unloaded an extra problem onto your plate, but life is full of problems, we deal with them the best we can. It builds character and teaches us to quickly and expeditiously manage our problems. You have enough intelligence at your young age that you can deal with any problems your life throws at you... Unfortunately, you don't have much time right now."

"Excuse me, teacher. I don't understand. What are you saying? Are you saying that you must go to Berkeley to get heart surgery right away? I don't see why we cannot stay here. Can you not get treated here? We have excellent medical doctors here! I cannot leave now!"

Della remained calm. "I realize thirty days isn't a lot a time for you to solve these crimes, but you are not normal, either. I know you will find out who orchestrated it, who did the dirty work, and who kept it quiet."

"I will solve it soon! I have to! Can I use your phone?"

"Use my phone any time you want to."

I picked up her phone and dialed Aaron's number. "Hi Aaron, it is me, Alex. I hope you cannot sleep tonight because you drank too much coffee!"

He replied, "Well I've been cleaning everything for hours, my apartment is spotless, and I don't want to clean anymore." He chuckled and continued, "I can hear in your voice that you want me to help you in some way."

"Yes, but are you feeling all right to drive the Indian over here?"

"Yes... I'm able to ride my bike around. Why do you ask?"

"Well, you cleaned your apartment three times tonight, thanks to the caffeine's effect on you. I wondered if there were any ill effects on your driving skill from the caffeine."

"No, no...I am okay to drive. I drove halfway across the United States in one night after drinking a quart of coffee, but every forty miles I had to stop to go to the restroom."

"Do me a favor and do not drink too much coffee. Can you come get me one hour from now?"

"Yes. And I know the caffeine influences me, but I like it once in a great while. I'll see you in sixty minutes."

I hung up the phone and walked back to Della. "Do you want anything?"

"I want nothing from you other than your understanding and a promise to me that if you get in trouble, you'll call that number I gave you. What are you and Aaron going to do tonight?"

I tell her my plan on this cold and windy night in England.

One hour later, Aaron walked through Della's door. He said to her, "How are you doing on this cold and rainy night? It seems to me you are not feeling well, lying there on your couch."

"I don't want to talk about it. Alex, you go ahead and tell him."

As I filled him in, Aaron looked concerned. He said, "I am so sorry, Della. I thought something might be wrong with your health, but I never imagined you had cardiomyopathy."

From the couch, Della explained, "I was ten years old when the first doctor diagnosed me with it. At that time, I knew my days were numbered, but all people's days are numbered. Everyone forgets that. My life is exceptional, and I never forgot that. I grew up in a small town in Mississippi in the U.S. I learned about hard work at an early age, which influenced me a lot. I got a great education, and I met a man who I adored, and who I adore even now, though he died four years ago. I don't want to talk about my life anymore. Time is wasting for capturing a child predator in England."

I cracked a smile and told Aaron, "Della convinced the assistant commissioner to make me an informant. What do you think of that?"

"It's cool!"

"One thing cool about it is he told Della he knows how to get me into parliament undetected. I am curious how Mr. Rockdom is going to do that!"

Aaron looked at his watch. "Nine o'clock."

"We have to go now. Della, are you sure you don't need anything else?"

"No. I am not disabled yet. I want both of you to be very vigilant tonight, and if you have any difficulty it all, Alex has a phone number for a direct line to Mr. Rockdom to use at any time for any emergency!"

"I will do that," Aaron told Della, and out of the corner of my eye, I saw him wink at her. Then he turned, and a moment later, we were outside again, latching the door behind us.

Chapter Fourteen

It was cold and wet, and the wind would suddenly push at our backs. Aaron loaned me a pair of gloves and a jacket to put on. "So, Alex, where are we going, and what are we going to do when we get there?"

"We are going to my former neighborhood so we can look inside Robert's house. I also want to visit my house to go through my father's office, and I want to visit Mr. Jesting Heddwyn. I need to see if this links back to parliament."

"Technically, you want to break into their house."

"Actually, I do not break in, as I know where to find the key, but I also know how get in without using a key just as Robert and I have done many times before."

"Just like we got into Dr. Rahman's office?"

"I am going to use their window and back door this time. Ow, what is that thing that just pricked my leg? It is on your front right fender. It looks like a long nail taped to your fender. Did somebody booby trap your bike?"

"Did it hurt you?"

"No, but I am curious why you have that long nail sticking out from your fender."

Aaron smiled. "Well, did you ever watch the cartoon Speed Racer?"

"No, I heard about it. Speed Racer drove into many different adventures that came towards him."

"Right. But I liked Captain Terror. He was the leader of the car acrobatic team in that show. He placed long, sharp instruments inside his tires so he could push a button and have the weapons extend out. He was a villain and you could almost count on him puncturing the other racers' tires. I watched that T.V. show the first year in my residency program, and I was having so much fun watching how Speed Racer outdid Captain Terror that the stress of the day left me for a time. You already know that when I left the residency program, I took a three-year tour of the USA. I was alone out there, and I put that nail on my fender because when I saw it while I was driving, it made me feel safe. I know it sounds stupid."

"No, it is not really stupid. Sigmund Freud said that the unconscious mind is the part of the brain which gives rise to an accumulation of mental and emotional phenomena. It is that manifest of a person's mind which the person is not aware of at the time of their automatic reactions. So, if some person looked at you with an angry expression, let's say, your unconscious mind would pick up that. Your subconscious remembered your emotions while you watched Speed Racer, and your unconscious' automatic reaction was what caused you to put that long nail on your fender. You did that because your subconscious mind wanted you to feel safe."

"How old are you?"

"I am thirteen years wise."

"That's truthful… Well, are you ready to go?"

"Yes! Let us do it!"

Aaron and I got on his motorcycle, and he started it up. It roared into the night. And as it roared, the shiny exhaust pipes pumped out a plume that disappeared as soon as it met the wet night air, just like Della's remaining time on Earth. Wet, dark winds engulfed us as we passed through the streets of London. We went by a familiar neighborhood whose streets I walked through many times with my grandfather. I miss those good times we had, but he always told me to look toward my future, not to my past. My grandfather thought it was facetious of people to think about their past rather than their future. And he was right. People who think about their past try to live in the past, which doesn't exist.

We stopped at the opening to the dead-end street. If we rode past my father's house on the bike, he would surely look to see what was happening out front. I got off his bike and noticed my clothes were soaking wet. My hair was too. I took off his coat, and we walked very carefully to avoid making noise that might wake someone. I knew they were all sleeping in this neighborhood because the neighbors were pretty old! I pointed out my house to Aaron, and then I pointed out Robert's house. Robert's house was very dark inside, but the light was on in my father's office. I thought that was about right, as it was 10 p.m. on my watch, and my father regularly worked in his office about ten to eleven each night. He goes to bed at eleven. I know that parliament's the keeper of Big Ben, and they must set that clock by his routine. We waited until the office light went out, and we waited again for my father to switch off the bedroom light thirty minutes later. I told Aaron to stay where he was and asked if he knew how to make a loud bird call. He whispered, "I do! I just learned the pied-billed grebe call!"

I knew that one as well. I said, "Okay, then you make that bird call if you see any movement or if the lights go on in my parents' house." I started to walk silently, as if my life depended on it, and truly it did. The innocent children's souls depended on it, too. I walked toward the cobblestone wall that formed a fence around my parents' house. As I climbed on the stones, my grip was slippery and my footholds were not very good. I tried to judge the ones that were not wobbly, and then gripped them as well as I could as I climbed up and down the wall. I looked around at familiar surroundings... I was now in my former back yard. It was just as I remembered, except that it was muddy. That was unusual because my father hated mud. He couldn't tolerate it ending up inside his house, and when it did, he went into a towering rage! I wondered what that mud was doing there, but I didn't spend long wondering. I looked for the pathway and quietly walked on the cleanest areas to keep any sludge off of the soles of my shoes.

When I finally reached the front of the hundred-year-old oak tree, it looked antiquated in the rain. Its arms were quivering in the wind, and its strong branches opened up as it tried to shelter me from the weather. I patted its strong trunk and gave thanks to him before climbing up to a low, strong branch. It was shaking from the strong wind, and the rain was going down sideways. To get my long, drenched hair out of my way, I tucked it inside my shirt. This is the same branch that I climbed down on that night that now seemed so long ago. I climbed up the branch until I was next to my window again, balancing on the bough. I tried to lift up my window pane, but it was locked.

A wry smile crossed my lips. I would just have to unlock it, then! I searched for the thin rod that I put up here for Robert in case I wasn't in my bedroom and my window was locked. I had tied it to the tree with a string. Where was it? I lifted up all of the limbs except one, and there it was. It was over there, four feet behind me, dangling like a remnant of a strange wind chime. Very carefully, I got on all fours and balanced carefully on the branch to crawl to where it was tied. I gripped the string and pulled up the rod, which was two feet long and bent at a right angle. Now I could unlock my window.

I moved back to the left corner of the window sill, where I had carved a small hole just the right size for the rod. The lock was in the middle of the windowpane, and I did what I had instructed Robert to do if he ever needed to get in. I put one end through that hole, pushed it until the bent part had gone through. My shadow was cast onto the window, and I saw that inside my room, my furniture was gone, but I ignored it. Carefully, I swiveled the bent rod upward toward the window latch, wiggled the rod behind the catch, and moved the small lever enough to unlock my window. Carefully, I dropped the rod back down, and noticed that my door was shut completely, and that was a good thing. If it had been open even a little bit, when I opened my window, the air pressure in my room would have slammed it shut and woken my father and mother and even the house assistants.

My door was shut, thankfully, so I slowly lifted my window up, and the wind blew rain inside my room as I quickly climbed inside and closed my window quietly. I stood there listening for any noises for a few minutes, but there was only silence. I noticed that not only was my furniture gone, so were my pictures that had been on the wall. I felt strange, as if I had never existed in this room. I began to slip off my shoes, and thought about how my grandfather was right again: People have one chance in life to impact the world, but so many do not get the chance to do that. People forget them after they have gone, just like my father did to me! I shook my head and tried to shake the ambiguity out of me! I thought to myself, *I am still alive, and my mission is to find the name of that child predator in England. When I know that name and the names of his gangsters, I will give the names over to the police. When that happens, I will be vindicating the innocent children he killed, and all of Britain's children will be safe from that pedophile. Most of all, I will pay them back sadistically for what he and his racketeers did to my friend Robert. That was reason I made the promise to Robert that I would find out whoever put him into a persistent vegetative state. I will discover all of them.* I picked up my shoes and walked to the door quietly, opened it silently like a ghost, and there on the other side of the door was a sign. It said 'KEEP OUT—CONDEMNED.'

I made sure to close the door gently behind me, so it did not make a sound. I walked tacitly down the hallway, each step cautious and slow, down the hall past my parents' bedroom. I wanted to open their door so I could see my mother one last time, but my better judgment held me back. Quietly, I walked on to my father's office door. I did not make a sound, and I tried to open the door, but it was locked. *Oh no*, I thought to myself quickly what I might have in my pockets to unlock it. I remembered that when I picked up Della's bobby pin, I had slipped it into my pocket! My fingers found it, still there in my right pocket. By pulling it apart a bit, I created a makeshift set of tweezers. Bending down, I placed my ear near the doorknob, and with my other hand carefully gripped it. The end of the tweezers went slowly into the doorknob key hole. Feeling the pins inside, I pushed one of pins to the right side of the hole but did not hear a click. So I pushed it to the left side of the hole and I felt a click. Then I felt the tweezers hit other one of pins, and repeated the sequence. I did the same with the remaining two pins, and then I turned the cylinder lock a clockwise quarter-turn and turned the doorknob.

Very gently, I pushed my dad's office door open, slipped inside, and soundlessly shut the door. It was unchanged, mostly because I cannot recall my father ever changing his office around. I walked to his desk and sat on his office chair, surveying the exquisite 7-foot maple monolith. It had three drawers on the right side and a small cabinet door on the other side. The top of this desk was beautifully inlaid with cherry wood. And there was his Rolodex, sitting on the left side. A search through it revealed his co-associates in the British Parliament—all of them but one: Mr. Jesting Heddwyn. I found his card in the Rolodex, but my father had crossed his name out.

I pulled out Heddwyn's card to look at it more closely. On the back of the card, he had also crossed names out—and hard, as if he had been angry. Though difficult to read, I was able to recognize one name as Mr. Fitzgerald; I did not figure out the other name. I thought to myself, *What happened between my father and Mr. Heddwyn and Mr. Fitzgerald?* What if this was the key that would unlock the door to the names of the killers? On the other hand, what if my father mistakenly crossed out those names? I had to think rationally. I assumed that I was right about my dad being mad at Heddwyn and Fitzgerald—so then what did they do?

I thought back to that time and probed my memory for any clues. At that time, my father was helping to draft the legislation of Great Britain… Oh… Wait a second! I had my first seizure at the gala… My father hosted that gala with the two houses of British Parliament, the House of Commons and the House of Lords, just three weeks before parliament's Third Reading of his bill in The House of Commons. I did not know whether his bill ever made it to the House of Lords.

My father kept all of the copies of the bills he drafted, and they are here somewhere. But where? That is the question of the hour! If I were my father, where would I put them so they would be safe? He does not have a vault in the house. He worked on drafting them here and in his office in parliament. I know he put copies of his bills that became legislation into some record books. I looked down at the small door near my left leg, and I thought it could be the right size to put the books in there. I looked at that door and thought, *What are the odds, since it has no lock on it*…just as my hand was reaching to open it. I couldn't believe they were actually stacked up in there, each one with the year the bills were authored. I looked for the current year and pulled it out, searching for my father's last drafted bill. It was the bill for the Ambassadors.

Bill C-145 was an act to amend the criminal code. It added a conditional sentence to provide that any international ambassador, committing any criminal act against a British citizen while inside the borders of Great Britain or any of its territories, could be prosecuted by the British judicial system. Additionally, it allowed that any ambassador convicted of such a crime would serve the maximum term of imprisonment allowed for the criminal act.

I slowly and fully read that draft bill. It did not successfully pass the House of Commons. I was wondering why that bill stopped there and did not go to the House of Lords and to the Royal Assent... Was it because my father was mad at two of his associates? I wondered about that. It was odd because any bill must first go to the committee before it becomes a law. They negotiate over the bills and then they make compromises regarding the issues. That bill my father wrote, C-145, was on its third reading when the House of Commons failed it. *Why would they fail that bill? I wish I knew what they were thinking... I guess I will never know.* I closed the book and put it back, then shut the little door very quietly.

I turned my attention to the right side of the desk, and I slowly opened first drawer to reveal his writing pens. My father had a half-dozen pens still in their pen boxes, all lined up next to one another. There was also a stack of blank papers. I felt around the sides of the stack, and there was something... It was a lonely pen hidden in the back of the drawer. I looked at it closely, and my stomach twisted a little. It was the same kind of pen as Dr. Fabron Rahman had, with the Russian flag on the side. In fact, it looked like that flag was on all the pens. Hmmm... I think that someone in the Russian Government must have been handing out pens. It could be!

I tried to keep my focus on learning about the clues, and then after that, I could assemble the whole picture. I replaced the pen in the back of the drawer, in the same corner, then closed the desk drawer as silently as I could.

Now on to the second drawer. On opening it, I saw my father's schedule book. I checked my father's meetings before May 8, and I found that he had gone to France. He had had a meeting with the French Prime Minister on May 4, and he had five meetings that week, including the meeting with the Prime Minister. During the weeks of June 17, July 24 and September 18, he did not have any pattern to his meetings or who they were with. At least, I did not think so, but I thought I would see it if he did.

I wanted to see what my father's schedule was right before he put me in Eastman hospital. I found that he had a meeting with the hospital administrator, Fabron Rahman, on January 28. I wonder if my dad knew of this predator? I know my father knew someone who had knowledge of the killer's name, I am sure about that! My father had played a golf game with Heddwyn and Fitzgerald before the gala, and it seemed strange for my dad to put the golf game on his schedule.

I wished I had been a fly observing their golf game. Wishful thinking, but what I did have in my favor was that my father wrote day by day in his journal. He told me about the journal, as he explained to me that a person needs to write down all of his thoughts and plans because it will help in the long run in life.

My thought when he told me that, was that someone would find my journal and read it. They would know what I was thinking. If I could find my father's journal, if I could read it, what would I find? If I did read his journal, he would never know, so that would be no harm to him. Anyway, I think not. Where did my father put his own journal? I closed his schedule planner and put it back, first looking in the drawer to see if anything else was there. It was clean and empty, so I put his planner back and closed the drawer quietly.

I looked at third drawer down. It was larger than the others, and when I tried to open it up, it was too heavy to move on its rollers! I stood up and silently moved the chair back from the desk. I stood in front of the desk drawers, placed my hands on the bottom corners of that drawer, and lifted it up to ease the weight off the rollers. I slid it out easily. I did not hear any noise, so I pulled the drawer about a third of the way out. I could see seven of his law books in the front and picked up the first one. It had my father's bookmarks in between the pages as if he had been researching, so I opened up a page with a bookmark to see what he was looking at.

Chapter Fifteen

It looked as though it was research for his bill C-145. This page contained part of section 1256, in which the archives of the United Nations declared that foreign ambassadors were emancipated from the rules and regulations of every country if involved in criminal adjudication. I tried to sum it up because that section was about fifty pages long. My father had tried to change that law, but British Parliament did not want that. Very interesting. I do not know why parliament would want ambassadors to be emancipated from another country's laws. Maybe they see a bigger picture? For instance, some countries have governments that treat their people badly. If such a country's president forbade ambassadors from entering their country to help their poor populations, and an ambassador entered that country for anything, that president would have the right to put the ambassador in jail. Another scenario might be one in which an ambassador opposed his bill because he thought he was above the law. It may have been a little of both. I wondered about that.

I had lost track of time, and I realized I needed to work faster. I dug around in the drawer of books and found a box that looked like a small hope chest. I opened it up, and inside was his journal. I felt a rush of adrenalin as I carefully lifted his chronology from the hope chest and laid it down on the desktop. I was not really wanting to read his thoughts, but I had to do it, on account of Robert and the lost souls. I opened this record of my father's thoughts, and I searched for the page where he wrote about the golf game with Heddwyn and Fitzgerald before the gala. And there it was:

December 4th

I had a game with my associates today. We talked about my bill, C-145, but Heddwyn and Fitzgerald told me they could not endorse it this time, and neither would the House of Commons. They said that I need to take the bill off the docket for the third reading in the House of Commons. Why would I want to do that? I told them the whole House would think something was wrong with me if I did that! Heddwyn said, "Yes but there are many nefarious people in the world who want to kill you, or worse, kill your reason for living, your son!

You and I have been friends for a long time, and your son has played with my grandson, so I know you would do anything for your son." I said, "You are threatening me, and I do not like that. Yes, it's true that we've been friends for a long time, so you know that I do not back down to anyone!" Heddwyn let me know that a certain powerful group out there does not like my bill, and that they will do anything to get their point across...including killing my son. He made sure I understood that they would indeed do that if I didn't withdraw my bill.

My father stopped writing there. It made perfect sense now. My father was angry with Heddwyn and Fitzgerald, and they knew about the child predator and his gangsters.

Wait a minute. Mr. Heddwyn said my father would do anything for me. I wondered why my father put me in the mental institution, then. Was it because I was having the seizures, or was it something else? I knew the answer was lying here within this journal. I turned the page.

December 5th

I was talking to my associates about bill C-145, and they told me they would not pass my proposed legislation. One of them told me he had heard rumors that it was a powerful individual wanting to stop the bill from going to the House of Lords. He told me that he thought it was the person who had raped and killed children in England, the same person who is now pressuring the House of Commons to vote against C-145 for that very reason. I was driving home this evening and thinking out loud whether it's true. Is he right about the man trying to block my bill being the infamous child predator of England? Suddenly, my fear overcame me and I had to park my car somewhere. I was thinking wildly of a way to keep my Alban safe. He can't know anything about this, but I do not know how to do that. My boy is intelligent enough to figure out something is wrong. He is just like my father was, just as ingenious. I see my father in Alban every time he explains something. He creases his nose the same way and says "the reason for that is" just before he explains something with his great knowledge. I would always smile inside when my Alban did that, but I did not show that to him. I remember hearing about the tragedy of the innocent boys three years ago. It was all over the news for a time. Is it really the same person who is trying to stop my bill? I need to find out. But to do that, I need to talk to the one person who truly knows the pulse of England.

I do not crease my nose... I thought to myself, *but I do say the reason for that is, like I had said many times, and my grandfather's nose wrinkled when he was thinking about big information.* I was lost in memories for a moment, but the seriousness of my situation didn't allow me to drift for long.

My Father did not know that the child predator was blackmailing Dr. Rahman. His still does egregious things to children even now, but the British citizens do not know much about the mental institutions. He was blackmailing the head physicians of these hospitals for access to innocent bodies to use for his diabolical desires.

I did not know that what my father did to me was for my protection. So much was happening that I was not aware of, even when I felt that I knew. How could all of this be happening? How could my father have had to do such a thing for my protection? That is so wrong! I did not want to turn the page, but I needed to, so I did.

December 6th

I reached my contact in England, and that person will find out some information for me soon. When he does, he will contact me. In the meantime, I hired a private investigator today to watch over my Alban and his friend Robert for a few days. I am so worried about my son, but also Robert because Robert is Alban's best friend. If Robert is killed or injured, my boy would hunt that person down no matter where they fled, even to the ends of the Earth. He is the same as his grandfather. My boy does not know what his abilities are, not yet, but soon he will. I feel frustrated that I lost an entire year working on that bill. A whole twelve months, and I cannot figure out why someone would want to stop my bill from going into law. My C-145 legislation acts only on the ambassador. I'm wondering if the blackmailer could be an ambassador for England from somewhere. I hope I have a better lead on this person, the one who wanted to block my bill, a couple of days from now. Four days from now is my gala. The lawmakers always have a gala at their house for the members of the House of Commons and the House of Lords to talk about it and determine if there are enough votes to successfully pass or not, or if more negotiation is needed. Only, my gala is pointless because I know my bill is not going to be voted on. I wrote six articles of British legislation, and all went to Royal Assent. On the other hand, this bill C-145 does not have any chance to make it to the Queen of England so she can royally sign it into law. I cannot try to reach a compromise with parliament, as my associates have heard rumors, just like Heddwyn and Fitzgerald did. Some of my associates have children, and they won't have anything do with C-145. I really do not blame them.

December 10th

I just got back from the hospital. My boy had a seizure at my gala. In the hospital, Alban told me he was sorry for crashing my gala. He was being sweet to say that, but if the truth were known, my gala was crashed a long time before that. The doctor who saw Alban said he had a seizure, and he wanted to do a few tests in the morning because he wanted to know what kind of seizure Alban had. My wife and I walked with the doctor out of his room and into the hallway as we talked. Claire asked the doctor why Alban had a convulsion, and asked whether his life would ever be normal. He responded by saying that our son would never be normal, but only because he was very intelligent. That made me proud to be his father. So much happened today that I forgot that someone handed me a note early this morning. I had put it into the pocket of my suit jacket so I could concentrate on the gala, and then my boy had an epileptic seizure. I had completely forgotten about that note, but it says that my associate was right. That man who wants to stop my legislation is indeed the predator. He scared England to death three years ago, but Scotland Yard didn't capture him. I wonder if they wouldn't capture him because he is an ambassador. What if the British judicial system did not have right to prosecute him? I wonder about that. But right now, I am most worried about my boy and how to keep him safe from this evil man. I hired the private investigator, but I know this malevolent man is going to outsmart him. I can take my bill off the docket from the third reading in the House of Commons, but if I do that, this predator will win. I know that the British citizens do not want him to have influence over our legal system! I cannot do that. I will find a way to keep Alban safe from the man who would rape and kill him as payback for my refusal to withdraw the bill. I won't take my bill off the table, even though the House of Commons won't pass it anyway. At least my conscience will be clean, knowing that this sick individual could not pressure me to withdraw my power to help make the laws in Great Britain. I have an idea, but my boy would not like my idea. I am sure he wouldn't like that sick person molesting and killing him! If I make my plan work, Alban will be safe until I know the predator's name. I searched for the name of the head doctor of Eastman hospital in my Rolodex, and here it is. Tomorrow I will call this Dr. Rahman to see if he can act on my idea.

Wow! I could not believe that my father worried about me all my life. I thought my father did not feel affection for me, but it looks like I was wrong. But wait a minute, why did he not check out the death certificates in parliament for Eastman Hospital? Maybe he did not think about that. I thank my God for my intelligence! If I did not have my intelligence, I would not be alive now! I would have gone to be with the lost, innocent souls crying out for justice.

Possibly, I had found my destiny. My grandfather told me that all people have one unique skill that will either contribute to a better society or be responsible for destroying a little bit of our civilization. Could my destiny be to weed out evil people from all of our societies? I looked at the clock on the wall... Two o'clock. I had to go. I put my father's journal back into his hope chest, and I placed it back just as it was before. Silently, I placed the seven law books back in their spots, lifted the front of the drawer a little, and pushed the heavy load in quickly and quietly.

I walked to the office door in silence. I opened the door, walked out into the hallway, and closed the door so gently that I did not hear any sound when it latched. I walked through the empty hall with my steps as stealthily as I could manage. I looked at my parents' bedroom door, now knowing the reason my father put me in the mental institution. I will not forgive him, but I love my parents. I walked past their door and opened the one that used to lead into my architecture room. It brought up so many memories with Robert. We built England's and Europe's great architecture together with laughter and learning about the styles of historical structures in Europe. I closed the door again quietly. I walked down the hall to my bedroom, again stepped inside the empty space where my furniture had been, closed the door, and walked toward the window. But I stopped this time to kneel down on the wood floor. I touched the unfastened oak plank and lifted it up. I saw a piece of my wool blanket there. I picked up the blanket, unfolded it, and there was my grandfather's 18-karat-gold Rolex watch. I looked on back of it, where it said, "When you look at this watch, remember me. Every move you make, I make with you." I kissed the watch and put it in my pocket, zipping it up carefully, and fitted the plank back in place.

I went to the window, waited a moment or two, and lifted the window. The wind blew into the room as I climbed over the sill onto the branch. I quickly shut the window and climbed down from my old room for the last time. Now for Heddwyn's house. The fence that separated my parents' back yard from Robert's grandparents' was high, and although it was hard climbing it, I made it over. I knew that the Heddwyns had been gone for a long time because their yard had not been mowed. I was not able to walk through the grass because this grass was too tall and wet. I saw thick clay on top of the path, and I had to walk through that mud and mire to get to their back door. I looked around for the rock that Mrs. Heddwyn used to hide the key to their house. As I reached for one behind the hedge, I had my other hand on the doorknob to steady myself as I bent down. The doorknob inadvertently turned with my hand, and it was unlocked.

I was in shock! I was thinking to myself, *The last time I went inside an open gate in the burg, the police captured me, but I am lot wiser now.* I pushed the door open more, I listened to the house for any noises, but the wind ripping through the house was all I heard. I walked inside quietly. I could not believe my eyes! Someone had plundered this house. Their fine furniture, all the chairs and sofas, it was flipped over and the cushions were torn up. I looked around and found the cushion stuffing all over the house. Their hutches had been turned over, and their excellent porcelain china was broken into bits and pieces. I cleaned my shoes off, and I carefully walked through the house. Someone needed something in this house. Reason for that is every square inch in the home was investigated and looked like a few bulls ran freely in this place.

I went upstairs next. I saw that someone had split open Mr. and Mrs. Heddwyn's and Robert's mattresses, and they emptied out all of the kapok fibers. It was everywhere and it was still in the air. I know who did this! Evil gang killers of innocent children executed their rage here in this home. Once it was a beautiful house, but not anymore! They slashed all of the wall boards, checking to see if Mr. Heddwyn had a wall safe. They were looking for something, but I do not know what, and they did this recently. I walked on Mr. and Mrs. Heddwyn's clothing, even their underwear, as I stepped on all of the rubble that was once all their possessions. I finally reached Mr. Heddwyn's office, and it was messy, but I knew it would be. I saw that this room was trashed, too. His desk was turned over and the desk's drawers were emptied out! They had broken these drawers up, and they cut all of the walls up. I went over to his desk and looked around on the floor. There were lots of papers strewn around here, and out of the corner of my eye, I saw a pen underneath his bookshelf.

I went over there and picked up that pen. It had the same unique Russian flag symbol on it. Eureka! That is it! I remember I saw a Russian flag in the Russian Embassy when Della and I went there about six months ago. There, they had the same pens as my father, Mr. Heddwyn and Dr. Fabron Rahman had in their offices. That could be a coincidence, but if not, it could be that the Russian ambassador is HIM. He wants to stop my father's bill, and reason for that is he wants to be an ambassador only if he can be above the law in any of the countries he visits. He raped innocent boys and did not want to face consequences for his actions. If it is not him, I know one of the ambassadors in England is involved in these same crimes.

I heard a pied-billed grebe! That was odd, as this bird lives in the woods. Oh, I just remembered that I told Aaron to let me know someone was outside by using that bird call… which he did! Maybe there is some action at my parents' house. I looked out Heddwyn's office window at my parents' front yard. I saw two men put on black masks. Oh no! Where is the phone? I found it! I dialed up my old home number, while fishing around in my pocket with my other hand, and my father answered the phone. I hung up the receiver. I retrieved a slip of paper from my pocket: the one Della had given to me with Mr. Rockdom's direct phone number. I unfolded it, and though it was little wet, I could read the digits and started dialing. *I hope it works.*

Chapter Sixteen

A man's voice answered, "Hello, who is this?"

I said, "I am an informant for you—Della told you about me—can you send the police out to Sir Alban II Christopher's house immediately? Some guys with masks want to kill that family!" I hung up the phone, picked it up again, and I dialed my parents' house: "Hello? Who is this? It is late at night!" I put the phone down while my dad talked, and I ran fast downstairs with the kapok and the stuffing material flying as I ran by. As I opened the front door, I heard police sirens.

I ran after one of those men, and I was behind him about one hundred yards, so he did not see me. The police sirens had stopped. I assumed that they were on foot. I was being extra cautious. Reason for that is if police saw me, they would think I was there to kill my parents. They did not know that I was an informant. I saw the man who was there to kill my parents running ahead of me. He ran through someone's back yard, and I climbed their fence as fast as I could. I ran through their back yard and saw his head just as he climbed down the far side of another fence, and a few seconds later, I climbed that fence, thinking, *I hope these homeowners do not have big dogs in their back yard.* I felt the mud fly up and hit me. I saw his head while I climbed up their fences. He turned on a dark road, and I turned on that road just a few seconds later. I did not see anything—it was as if someone had covered my eyes up with blindfolds! I listened to that man's steps as he ran, dead ahead of me. A few moments later, I saw that lights were coming from behind me.

I jumped off the road as a car screamed past and splashed water on me. Without hesitation, I was up again, and I started to run after I saw that man in their head lights! He slowed down as the car cruised beside him, and then he leaped in and slammed the door as the car drove off and turned on another street. My adrenaline pumped into my bloodstream just like gasoline pumped into an engine. Suddenly, I heard a motorcycle coming from behind me. I was running as fast as I could go, still only halfway to the street that the car turned on, when the motorcycle cut me off. Aaron said, "Hello! You want me to give you a lift..." But before he could even finish speaking, I shoved him to the back and grabbed the handlebars. I turned the throttle and drove off after them, going fast. As we turned on that street to follow them, I shouted, "Hold on for your life!" Soon, I was shifting to high gear and we were doing eighty miles per hour! And then, I saw that car dead ahead of me, as the raindrops hit my body like tiny wet bullets. We were flying on that road, and we were catching up to them. We had good providential reason to speed, as it was the middle of the night, and I didn't see any cars on the streets. Before long, we were doing ninety.

When we were three cars' lengths away from them, the passenger in the car saw us tailing them. They knew we were following them. Then I saw the passenger push a gun out his window and aim it toward us. I slowed down, and he started to shoot at the one thing I imagine he could see, which was the motorcycle's headlight, but we were right behind it! I weaved to the left so we were just behind the driver, but then the passenger climbed into the back seat. I was terrified and out of ideas, so I braked hard to slow down and create distance, even after all the work I had done to catch them. He broke the back window out and shot at us, but now we were ten car lengths away from them, and I was zig-zagging to avoid the bullets! I was hastily analyzing our situation: I had counted his bullets. He had shot twelve rounds then stopped for a few seconds. I thought he probably had two guns. When he stopped shooting at us to reload, I heard sirens wailing again, and coming closer. I told Aaron, "Cover up your license plate! I do not want police to know this is your bike!" I felt my blood energetically pumping to my brain, just like my deliberation!

I was thinking about how this would end. I wanted the killer to know that I was looking for him, but while driving this bike, there was no way for me to overtake that Ford Capri. If it were different, I would overtake them in a heartbeat. But at that moment, I knew what I had to do. I shouted to Aaron, "Time to decide how much you trust me! If you do not want me around after this, I understand, but you have got to trust me a little longer! Take two deep breaths with me: breathe in, hold it, now exhale! One more deep breath, and I will pass them! Ready, wait, wait, wait—deep breath NOW! I accelerated quickly, and the pump in the bike's engine filled the wet air with its screams! We were two car lengths away from the Ford Capri. I saw that the man was still in back of the car, determined to load his gun quickly, and I was determined to get ahead of them before that happened. The driver was weaving radically in and out of the lanes, making it hard to pass them, but I had to pass them now or never! I turned the throttle harder, and now we were right up on the Capri, even with its back tire.

In a fraction of a second, something blew out from the Capri's left rear tire and hit the bike's gas tank! The Capri lost control! I heard the car's tires burning on the road, but I kept my focus on keeping the bike upright on its wheels. Without hesitation, I squeezed the brakes gently, and all of a sudden, the car's front end slid around counterclockwise, and I saw out of the corner of my eye the gunman's body catapult through the Capri's gunned-out back window. The Capri continued to spin, and the passenger side of the car almost touched this bike's front fender! The back end of the car then somehow slid away from us and the front end came toward the right side of the bike! I saw this man's eyes filled with fear by the grim reaper! He felt the same as the innocent children did when the child predator and his gang raped and murdered them. Though, the innocent children's souls were touched by God as their spirits still cried out for justice. That man's soul goes to eternal damnation, and his spirit will be raped over the eternal flames forever. The Capri's front bumper scraped my right leg as it passed, and it threatened to unbalance the bike, but I was able to control it and we drove on.

A few seconds later, we heard an explosion and saw enormous flames that lit up the rainy sky this early morning. The flickers of red were reflecting everywhere from that blaze, but we kept driving on. A couple minutes later, I parked on the side of this street, got off Aaron's bike, and I walked into a patch of grass. Aaron walked toward me and said, "Exceptional driving skills. Who taught you to drive?"

"My Grandfather. He taught me while I was visiting him in the Middle East. We camped near his archaeologist excavation site and we rode his old motorcycle there and back again. One morning he asked me if I wanted to drive his old bike. I said yes, so that morning we fell down a few times, but luckily we were wearing our helmets. My grandfather dusted himself off, and he got on the bike again, and I drove it again. After a few times, I drove that motorcycle like it was second nature for me, and that was four years ago." I walked away from Aaron, but he followed me.

"Hey, what is wrong with you?"

"Nothing I guess." I walked away again from Aaron, but he continued to walk next to me.

"I do not know what is going on inside your head, but I will walk with you anyway."

We walked for a few hours and stopped on top of a grassy knoll. I asked him, "What are your thoughts about the sanctity of life?"

"Well, I think life is special, but most people think that way because it is in our DNA. Some people ignore that."

"I caused the loss of their lives. I do not want to become like some people who disregard all human life. I do not want to get pleasure out of the killings!"

"Look at them! Those guys went to your parents' house to murder them, and they might have even murdered Mr. and Mrs. Heddwyn! Those guys were going to continue killing children for their boss! You saved many innocent children's lives. Children do not get raised equally—it's a shame, but true. Society created those guys and their bosses. God made special people to watch over societies because God wanted them to be safe. You did not kill them. Their faith killed them with a nail, or something like that. You almost killed me! You told me to take two deep breaths with you, and then you instructed me to take another deep breath, but you forgotten to tell me to breathe out! Two and a half hours later, you still have not told me to breathe out!"

"Well then, I order you breathe out completely now!"

"Thank you for restoring my life to me. Are you ready to go to Della's hotel?"

"I am."

"Good. But I am driving."

"Okay, I guess so. It is your bike."

I woke up later that morning and walked out to Della's family room. Della said, "Good late morning!"

"Good morning to you. How are you?"

"I am fine, although I did read the newspaper this morning, and it said a couple men tried to kill your parents last night. The police got an anonymous tip but when they got there, two men were making a run for it in two different directions. The person who ran after that one man ... how tall are you?"

"Same as the newspaper reporter reported it!"

"I figured that!" She gave me a motherly look of concern. "The newspaper said that ten minutes later, the man driving the Ford Capri picked up another man on foot. Here is really interesting part! Someone on a motorcycle chased the Ford Capri in a high-speed chase at over eighty miles per hour. That driver was excellent! The Ford Capri went out of control and did a one-eighty in front of the motorcycle doing around seventy, and then it flipped over three times and the car exploded in flames! The driver died, and the crash threw the other man onto the street, where he died, too, and the motorcycle went on."

Della looked at me as if she could see through my soul! She folded up the newspaper, saying, "I imagine that some genius person drove the motorcycle, since a normal person wouldn't drive a motorcycle so close to a car going so fast..."

"True, but normal people do not know how to handle abrupt things like being only three feet away from a car when it blows its tire? The car driver himself was killed! The motorcyclist is a genius, and reason for that is he is quick-witted. You read that in the newspaper."

"So I did. Intelligence is good, but that instance, in large part, was due to luck, and only a fraction of the outcome can be attributed to any quick-wittedness from that driver…whoever the driver was." Della smiled at me.

"Can I have one of those fresh bagels with cream cheese, and one of those hot honey buns, please?"

"Please do. Help yourself. So, what did you find out last night?"

"I found out a lot of different things. My father was working on some British legislation. His bill includes wording to prevent ambassadors from committing criminal acts against British citizens, or rather that the judicial system would have the right to institute legal proceedings against any ambassador. Somebody wanted to block that bill from going to the House of Commons for one more reading, and someone told my father that it was the child predator who struck panic into the hearts of British citizens three years ago! We know that person raped and murdered children then, and he has kept on doing it.

"I saw that my father, Mr. Heddwyn and Dr. Fabron Rahman all had the same writing pens—they had the flag emblem of Russia on the side. Now, it could be a coincidence, but my instincts tell me that the Russian ambassador is perhaps the one. He has the means. That is, he is wealthy, he is well connected to people in high positions in British Parliament, and many people around him are willing to fulfill any desire he has. Those pens link back to Mr. Heddwyn and Dr. Fabron Rahman. They were both assassinated, I think. I know that last night, two men went to my parents' house to assassinate them too! Those pens— there is only one place to buy them, and that is at the Russian Embassy. Their ambassador works there, too. My thesis is simple. The Russian ambassador was the child predator in England three years ago, and also today."

"I see where you're coming from," Della said. "Your observations are good, but peoples' animal instincts are difficult to observe. A case in point: either your father, Mr. Heddwyn or Dr. Fabron Rahman may have given the pens out to the other two. If their friends gave those pens to them, it is circumstantial evidence, and then there would be two ways to look at the evidence. However, you are correct. You knocked on the right door, and I have the key to unlock that door. I forgot to tell you yesterday—I went to see my friend who works at the Landmark. Remember that?"

"Yes, so who is it?"

"Mr. Wehczeslaw Ezajasz. He is an ambassador to England from Poland. He worked out of the Russian Embassy, though. We have a big problem now; in that he has free range."

103

"I know about ambassadors. None of the governments can prosecute them, but my father tried to write the bill to eliminate that law. Someone didn't want that bill passed, and they spread threats and rumors in the House of Commons: whoever has children, look out if that legislation passes. And then, that bill did not progress to the House of Lords. It is unfortunately true. I want to know who in the British Parliament knows this man."

"Right, but it is difficult knowing who. We know what department he or she worked in: the one with the death certificates."

"I can look there if Mr. Rockdom lets me into parliament undetected. When you call him, see when he can do it. The sooner the better. Reason for that is Mr. Wehczeslaw Ezajasz realizes somebody knows he is the criminal."

"I will do that for you. What you are doing today?"

"You do not want to know what I am planning to do. But the fresh bagels, cream cheese, and hot honey bun were so good! They filled up my stomach so good, too!"

"Do not change this subject."

I smiled at her while I wiped my mouth. "Well, I am going to try to meet with the ambassador of Poland. I need to see if this is the right man or not."

"I see. Well, I am coming with you to see Mr. Wehczeslaw Ezajasz because he will know what you're up to if you meet him in his office all alone. I will tell him I am your teacher, and I will ask him if you can pose questions to him about your government. It is better if I come with you."

"Guess so. I will let you go with me." I smiled at her, then I wandered down the hallway to the back of the apartment and took a long, hot shower. I felt ready to face the world, even though it hurled many obstacles in my way. I put my clothes back on and walked out of the bathroom.

Della said, "I called Mr. Rockdom. He said we are good to go tonight. I will call him again at 10 p.m., and then I will tell you the details!"

"Great. I am ready to go tonight. I hope when we're done, I will know who is involving parliament in the disgusting crime of molesting innocent children. When I do, the spirits of the children who were taken, abruptly raped of their innocence and murdered will finally be at peace by the hand of God."

"You are a young boy who stumbled onto an evil crime. Unfortunately, if we were to capture all the men who ever committed this diabolical crime against British children, some of them would do it all over again the next day!"

"True, but there is an old saying: one bad apple in the barrel spoils the whole bunch. This is because the bad apple's rot eventually affects the healthy apples. It's the same with societies. A corrupt person exerts an influence on the other people in that society. Someone needs to take the bad apple from the barrel because it will keep the other apples healthy. It's the same thing I'm trying to do now."

"I did say it before, but you are young boy, and young boys do not think that way. They would not go to talk with a child molester if they knew that person was a child predator."

"You said I was not a normal boy. I am intelligent enough to be cleverer than a normal person is."

"You are, but I did say it before. The way people contemplate thoughts is difficult to tell. I mean, you could not tell what a person's thoughts are going to be as long as you are not immortal!"

"True. But all people are mortal. That is, I am their equal and when people look at me, they cannot tell whether I am intelligent."

"We were arguing about ignorant nonsense. I am sorry about that."

"It is okay, and I had fun."

"I think you should consider that he might be responsible for Robert's condition. Did you think about that? You're going to meet him face to face soon. I called a cab."

"Yes, I thought about all the things I would like say to him, but my emotions will not be on my sleeve. You taught me good timing skills. Now is not a good time to convey what I want to do to him. I need to know for sure that he is guilty of these crimes. That is the reason I need to see him, okay?"

The phone let Della know that the cab was waiting outside. "Are you ready to go?"

"Yes I am. Let's do it."

Chapter Seventeen

Our cab began moving through the streets of London to take us to our destination. I wanted to take her mind off her worries about me, so I asked, "How has London changed since the first day you moved here?"

"Mmm. It has been nineteen years since I came here from Laure, Mississippi. Did I ever tell you where I came from? Lots of people have moved here since that time. London is getting crowded and the city needs to make some changes to allow for the population to live comfortably. Like beautiful high-rise apartment buildings. All of the cities have to build them to accommodate growth, or they dry up. I remember back when I was growing up in Laure, my hometown. My family lived on the poor side of town. Racism was commonplace then. When my mother and I would walk through town, white people would stare at us and make negative comments. My mother never learned how to read, but she knew that reading would be a powerful thing for me to learn at an early age. I remember my mother and I would go out at night to dig around in the white people's garbage cans. She kept her eyes open for a book for me to read, and after a while she found a book with torn pages that someone had thrown out.

"After that, we would learn a word each night, and in two years we had finished that book. I loved to read to my mother. She was so happy and believed that reading was my ticket to a better place, and I studied hard in school, too. At seventeen, I wrote letters to the admissions offices for the colleges I wanted to attend. Those colleges denied me because I was black. Other colleges, though, didn't care that I was black or if I was smart or accomplished enough to attend. Many did accept me as a person with initiative, and I accepted the invitation from Stanford. I accepted a lot of their scholarships, too. I cannot believe this, but thirty-two years ago, after a lot of very hard work, I became a teacher. Life goes on, and so much has happened since then. Time does not stop for anyone or anything…only death."

The cab was quiet all of sudden, and I knew she was thinking of her imminent death. I told her, "You have accomplished excellent things in your life." She smiled at me weakly.

The taxi cab stopped in front of the Russian Embassy. Della and I both got out of the cab and shut the doors. I was walking by her side, and her arm reached over my shoulders and she gently offered a hug. She whispered to me, "My greatest accomplishment has been teaching you and observing the fine young man that you have become. My life will not have been in vain. Now, are you ready to go into the lion's den?"

"Yes, and there, you will see my abilities firsthand," I said, as I unlatched the Russian Embassy's front gate.

We walked up to the front of the building in silence. Della opened the door and we walked in. I got nervous for a moment and became aware of my breathing. We walked over to the desk of the office clerk, where a uniformed young man was seated.

Della asked, "Where is Mr. Ezajasz's office, please?"

"Yes, of course. Just, uh, walk down this hall, take the elevator to the seventh floor, and turn right. Then at your next opportunity, turn left, and the second door is Mr. Ezajasz's office. Do you need an escort? I'd be happy to walk you there."

"Thank you, but it's not necessary," I said. With a polite nod to the clerk, we followed his directions to the elevator and found his office on the seventh floor. It all felt surreal, like I was in a dream.

Della opened the door with the nameplate that said 'Ambassador's Office,' which opened into a reception area where his secretary sat behind a dark, heavy desk. I followed behind her and shut the door. Della said, "Excuse me... is the Polish Ambassador in his office?"

"Yes, he is. May I help you?"

"Yes, you can. I hope to see him, although we're here without an appointment. I'm a teacher from the east end of London, and I've brought one of my students with me. He has a school project to do, which involves interviewing an important person, and I am standing in for his mother, who is working two jobs and can't be here. My student would like to ask the ambassador some questions. Can you see if he can spare a few minutes to answer his questions?"

"Wait here. I will go ask him."

Della turned around and winked at me. I walked over to their waiting area, where I saw a rubber ball on the floor under one of the chairs. Although there were other people waiting there, I got on the floor and fished it out of its hiding place. Then I started bouncing it around, trying to annoy the other people waiting in the room with us.

The secretary came back to her desk and said, "Sorry, Mr. Ezajasz is in a meeting right now. It will take up to two hours before he's available."

"Okay, may we wait here?" Della was so good at making people feel at ease. The secretary said that she didn't mind. Della walked toward me in the waiting area, and we sat down next to each other.

My grandfather was right again. He told me that people's basic emotions are animal instincts, but humans evolved for millions of years, allowing some people to develop an analysis of facial features to guess at their underlying emotion. In this office, if looks could kill, these people would have killed me many times over!

We waited two and half hours for Mr. Ezajasz. I made sure to talk to as many of the visitors near me as I could, and now they all thought that I was hyperactive. The reason for that was they saw me as a boy getting on their nerves. I think the child predator likes children who are that way; if he does, he will surely love me. I was ready to play my next move. I walked up to the secretary's desk and bounced the rubber ball off his door. I caught it on the rebound, and it had the desired effect.

"Stop it right now! He is in an important meeting. Can't you see his door is shut? Don't disturb him!"

At that very moment, he opened his door and walked out. With a commanding voice of authority, he said, "Mrs. Buttwiner! Who disturbs me while I'm in an important meeting behind this closed door!"

"That antagonizing boy right there," she said, pointing to me.

He walked over to me and grabbed my shoulder with a strong grip. "So, I see you found my blue rubber ball for me. Are you the student with the school project and a few questions for me?"

"Yes, I am the one. My teacher came with me because I don't like school and homework, so for homework she gave me this project."

"Hello. I am Della, his teacher."

"Hello. I am glad to meet you and your student today. Wait one moment right here, as I need to check my appointments. Mrs. Buttwiner, do I have any appointments this afternoon?"

"Your afternoon is free."

"Well, you came on the right day, Della… And young man, I am sorry. I did not get your name."

"I am Alex Ottoman."

"Okay, Alex. Come with me to my office."

The three of us walked into his office, and Mr. Ezajasz closed the door quietly. "Your office is huge! And beautiful, too," I said as he sat down behind his desk.

He said, "Thank you. I like it. And if you work hard at school, you can be up here, too, working behind a large desk just like mine someday. Do you want that, Alex?"

"Well, I'm not intelligent enough to sit down behind a big desk like yours."

Della said, "It doesn't hurt to dream big dreams, right, Mr. Ezajasz?"

"Della is right about that. This is a dream that I once thought was impossible, and look at me right now. I am the ambassador for Poland in Great Britain. My life is glorious."

I walked around his office. "Your paintings are interesting. The artist is Michelangelo?"

"You are correct. That painting is called *David with the Head of Goliath.* I like Michelangelo's paintings because he incorporates his emotions within his paintings."

"I had to take the dumb class where the teacher told us Michelangelo's paintings have home… what is it called? Homo-erot-i-cism. His paintings of the male's beauty, I mean… which attracted him both aesthetically and emotionally."

The ambassador fumbled for words.

I walked towards his desk, and I saw his personal pictures framed on top of it. It looked like pictures from a boys' club, I thought. "Did you work in a boys' club? Because I saw your pictures there."

"Yes, I did in my youth. I liked it well enough that I thought I wanted my career to be helping boys out in life. But I went to college, and there I found out it's a big world out there. Why, I am here now, far from that life, but I look at my pictures and I recall my memories. Great memories. Any more questions about my life?"

"I am sorry about my questions."

Della said," Alex, do you not have any manners?"

"Well, it's not all that bad," the man said.

"Any child without manners may as well not have parents," Della sighed.

"Alex has an inquisitive mind, Della. You should like that quality in a child, yes?"

"Sir, I have thirty-nine students in one class. There are only so many inquisitive minds one person can take and enjoy it… Alex, do you do have any final questions for your school project?"

"Yes, I do have some questions for Mr. Ezajasz."

"Okay, you ask them," he said. "Kids today… they have too much time on their hands!"

I then asked a few questions of the ambassador, and he answered each of them. As he framed his responses, I thought to myself, *This man has performed despicable acts against innocent children and destroyed their bodies to dispose of the evidence.* If I followed my gut feelings about him, I would have tried to throw him out the window. But I had to restrain my emotions. The children who were killed needed the world to know about him and the dirty secrets that he hid from the world. The longer it dragged on, the harder it had to have become for him to keep his secret from the world. However, I believed that he had become overly confident. In a few days, all the people of the world would know about him and his atrocious secret! Britain's judicial system could not do anything to punish his crimes against humanity because of his title, but the population would torment him forever. A proud man would feel more hell on Earth this way. *When he finally dies, his spirit will feel its punishment. Then, and only then, the children who were murdered will finally get their justice.*

Chapter Eighteen

In spite of that, my friend Robert's life will never be the same. I hate this man because he turned Robert into just a shell of who he was. I can't believe I am talking to him right now in his office.

If Robert could speak, he would say, "You remember when you picked me up from my school and we walked to our houses? The boys followed us, and they taunted me to no end, they said my life was a sack of shit and that they would squash that sack in the ground, just like my life… Stuff like, 'I forgot you don't have any brains because your mother was on drugs while pregnant and it fried your brains out!' You wanted to hit that guy so badly you could almost taste it!" I remembered that day.

I whispered under my breath, still there in the ambassador's office, "All dogs have their day."

The ambassador spoke sharply, bringing me back to the moment, "Looks as if you had a daydream."

"No, I listened to your answers. Your information about Poland's school system was great, and now all I have to do write my school project. Yippee… I'm going have so much fun writing it!"

"When do you need to turn it in?"

"I have to write it tomorrow night because I'm going somewhere tonight."

Della interjected, "I see that you have today's newspaper on your desk. Did you happen to read the front-page story?"

"Yes, I did."

"Do you think Britain's unsafe now because of the assassination attempts? Can I see your newspaper please? I want to check the name of the family that was targeted."

"Go ahead."

"Here it is… Mr. and Mrs. Dillingham. He's in British Parliament. He makes British laws, and the newspaper said his next-door neighbor has been missing for one month. He was in parliament, too. It's a little odd, don't you think?"

"Yes, I do think so. But he and his neighbor, they are in the political arena. It's not strange that some corrupt person wants to kill them. I have a few men who protect me from criminals who want to murder me because something made them mad. People in the political realm are the scapegoats for criminals at times. And his older neighbor? I do not know where he is, but political work is stressful. Maybe he is traveling somewhere and he doesn't want anybody to know where he and his wife really are."

"Good points you made. On the other hand, what about the average citizens of Great Britain? They aren't safe either. The murders, the missing children... And Scotland Yard doesn't know where those children's bodies are, or whether they're still living."

I saw the ambassador's body stiffen.

He said nothing, so I continued. "I heard about that story in the newspaper, too. Two of the men who wanted to assassinate that family were from Poland, by the way. You are the ambassador for Poland. And how did you know Mr. Dillingham's neighbor is older? The newspaper didn't include that information in their story."

Now the ambassador was dazed and angry. It showed clearly on his face. He looked at his watch and said, "It is time for me to leave. I have to go now!" We could feel his strong energy push us back as he stood up from his desk.

"What happened to your meeting earlier?" I said, as he hustled us toward the door.

He ignored me and flatly said, "Thank you again for finding my blue ball."

He opened the door, and Della followed me out to the reception area. We heard his door close as we exited to the hall, and we said nothing at all until we got on the elevator. I said, "That man is evil. I know he is the murderer. Do you think so?"

"I know so," she said quietly. "But we have to be very careful. I know his friends are going to follow us now."

"You drop me off near some poor apartments on east side of London, and then go to the store. Keep watching for someone following you."

"I know that. I am not so ignorant that I would just go shopping. If somebody follows me, I will cause a diversion and find a place to hide. And you... what are you going to do?"

"I hope his friends follow me to Aaron's apartment."

"What do you mean? Oh no. I hope you aren't going to do what I'm thinking," she sighed.

The elevator doors slid open and we walked in like nothing had happened. Della calmly called a taxi cab as we walked. We waited outside like we were tourists on holiday until the cab came. We hopped in, and Della said, "Tower Hamlets borough, Southern Grove E34."

"Sure. You got money for the fare?"

"Of course. Drop him off there and I'll be going to a second location."

"Sure, lady. My pleasure."

The cab drove off, and I turned my face toward Della so I could peek out the rear window. A couple minutes later, I saw a car, and I had no doubt that it was following us. I whispered, "I see one."

Her hand squeezed my hand, and she took a notepad out of her purse, wrote on it, and gave it to me. It said, "Be very careful. If you think of anything, act on it. I know you will."

I took the pen and wrote under it. "Call Rockdom 4 me! Ask him 2 send secret police 2 watch over kids at Southern Grove bldg! Then call Aaron. Hang up after 1 ring if Rockdom said yes, 2 rings if no. Be careful—get lost in crowd. Wait til bad guys leave. Meet at yr apt. 5 pm." I scribbled as fast as I could on the small page.

Just as I handed it to her, the driver said, "Here we are. Southern Grove E34.

I opened the door and turned to her, still sitting in the taxi. She looked worried, and I have rarely seen her anything but calm. She was like a mother and a best friend to me now. "I am going be all right, and you be careful." She nodded, and I closed the door.

I watched the taxi drive away. Reason for that was to see if the same car followed her. I did not see that car, so that was good. They were following me... Good. I would enjoy surprising them with my intelligence.

I walked up the path and inside the hallway. It was dirty and palpably sad. I walked to the other end of the hall and opened the door to the stairwell, listening for footsteps. I heard the door open again, and the footsteps of one person entering the place. I nimbly propelled my body up the stairs to the second floor, and I waited to hear if the stairwell door opened. It did. I opened the door to the second floor, closed the door quietly behind me, and then scooted down the hall quickly.

I looked at the room numbers for #223 as my hand searched around in my pocket for Aaron's key. I found it. Quickly, I put his key in the keyhole and turned it just as the stairwell door opened! I yanked open Aaron's door just enough to cram myself inside, and I looked back down the hall and saw the bottom half of a person wearing a nice blue suit. I immediately closed the door and walked in to Aaron's room. Aaron was in the bathroom when he realized I was there. "Hey! Where'd you come from!"

"From outside, of course. Sorry for busting into your apartment that way. Why did you leave the bathroom door open?"

"Because I'm the only one living here? Because I didn't expect someone to just walk in out the blue?" He pushed the bathroom door shut with his foot.

I walked to his window and saw a man in a business suit in the parking lot. I guess he was waiting for something. *Me, I guess.* I saw his face as he looked around, and I realized it was the guy who wanted to snare me in the hearse. The same guy who wanted to capture Robert. I thought a lot about how Robert must have felt that day while these men chased him for his life. He must have thought about me and wondered where I was because he really needed help. I could feel his fear even now. I whispered under my breath to that Robert, back on that day: "I am here, Robert Zachary."

I am not violent, and I hate guns, but if I had a gun at that moment, I would have used it. I imagined aiming the gun at the top of his leg to hit his femoral vein. The reason for that is I wanted to watch him in agony as he bled to death for the sake of the children, who he undoubtedly watched as he tortured them.

"Hi, Alex. So, what are you doing here?"

"Well, let me tell you. Della and I met with the murderer earlier today. The ambassador for Poland! And when we left, his goons followed us! I asked the cab driver to drop me here, and Della went to a big store to mix with the crowds. Look outside yourself, and you'll see a guy wearing a blue suit."

Aaron leaned toward the window and peered out over the parking lot.

"The other one is in the hallway."

"Well! We are stuck again! Unsurprising for you! Okay, have you thought of a bright idea for the next step in your grand plan?"

"I do not have a bright idea for now. We will wait for Della to call us."

"Okay. Can I ask you a question? What did the ambassador seem like to you if you didn't know he was a child molester? When you met him for the first time, what was your impression?"

"He seemed to be an intelligent man. I felt a strange sensation when he touched me… as if I felt all of the children whom he killed. I also felt like he liked talking with young boys because when Della talked with him, his voice changed. When he talked to me, his voice was more controlled. Another thing about him was that he did not shake Della's hand the whole time we were there. Most of all, there was a blue rubber ball that I found in his waiting area. I know those rubber balls are popular with adults for reducing stress, and an adult could use one to win a child's trust." I paused to think some more, as Aaron waited. "We cannot know what other people are thinking. We can only see their actions. Just like the head physician of your residency program. You did not know she was such a racist until she showed it to you. Just as my father eventually showed his true feelings with his actions toward me..."

"We know about your father and what he did to you. He put you in a mental institution because you had a few seizures... I am right? What does that have to do with the Polish Ambassador?"

"Yes. My father put me into the hospital for the seizures, or at least it seemed that way at the time. But then, I read his own words in his journal that explained everything. I don't know how much you know about British law, but the current law protects all foreign ambassadors from prosecution. It's a very odd law that allows them the freedom to commit crimes. So, my dad wrote Bill C-145, the one that would give judges the right to prosecute ambassadors up to the maximum the law allows. It caused a grisly backlash, and it was rumored that if the bill passed, the children of those in the House of Commons would be murdered. There was a great push from the House of Commons against my father, insisting that he kill Bill C-145. He refused, not only because he believed justice should be meted out equally, but his pride wouldn't allow him to withdraw it. He knew I would be at risk of a mysterious death, however, and his idea was to put me into a mental institution. The rest of the story, you know."

Aaron took a deep breath. "My, my... Your father's life is complicated for sure, and you escaped the mental institution, but what you are going to do after Della passes away?"

"Hopefully we will get to California before that happens!"

"Okay, then what will you do after that in the U.S.?"

"Get my diploma from a high school, and after that, well... I am an intelligent young man, you know that."

"Nevertheless, in the U.S., children need an adult to watch over them until they're eighteen. You're only thirteen now. You can't get around their laws for that long. So, what are you going to do?"

"Della has a friend living over there. I could stay at her house and she could look out for me. Della told her about me."

"Of course she did. What was I thinking?" Suddenly, he walked to his desk and pulled out a piece of paper. "I want to give you my parents' phone number," he said as he fumbled around in a drawer for a pen. "If your circumstances change, call my parents. I told them about you."

He handed me the scribbled lifeline, which I folded carefully and put in my pocket. "What did you tell your family about me? I hope you didn't tell them about all our excursions!"

Aaron laughed. "You think I'm crazy? My mother would have been on an airplane over here immediately. She would have found you, sat you down and had a talk with you. I told my parents about your bright personality and your smart brain."

His telephone started to ring, and I listened for a second ring, but it didn't come. "That's good," I told Aaron. "One ring means Della got a hold of Mr. Rockdom, and he is going protect the children living here. Now I need to get out of here."

"Have you masterminded a good idea, now?"

"Yes. I have a plan. I open your door, walk through that stairwell door to the ground floor, and I go to the Tower Hamlets Cemetery. I am going to try to lose them in there. There are lots of trees, and there are many hiding places in the trees. Then, I am heading to Victoria Park. Can you pick me up there at the fountain?"

"Are you sure you want to go to the cemetery?"

"Why not? It is the perfect place. Reason for that is only a few people are there visiting their loved ones, and the grounds are so quiet that if they captured me, I could scream and someone should be able to hear me."

"When do you want me to pick you up at Victoria Park?"

"In half an hour. If I am not there at that time, can you wait for me?"

"Sure."

I walked to the front door and grasped the doorknob, thinking to myself, *I have to do it for the children of Great Britain.*

Chapter Nineteen

I took a deep breath and opened the door. No one was in the hallway. I slipped out and walked down the hall, nerves on edge and ready for anything. I descended that stairwell as nimbly as I could. I did not want the other guys to sandwich me in there. That would not be good. I made it outside and walked down Southern Grove for two blocks. I held my breath and turned my head… and I saw that the two men were a block behind me. I walked a little faster. My plan was to give the illusion that I never noticed them, but how could I stay safe at the same time? I reached the entrance road to Tower Hamlets Cemetery and calmly went inside via a one-way road. I was still keeping firm control of my physical reactions, slow and steady. I turned around and I saw them walking toward me briskly, about forty feet away now! My heart was really beating fast now. Too fast. I walked as quickly and calmly as I could through the middle of the cemetery.

It was a cemetery from another time. This cemetery was created around 1840, and in those days, it was in favor with the East End residents. In its first two years, this cemetery's burials were 60% in public graves. Public graves were those of poor people who could not afford a funeral. Within 10 years, this percentage increased to 80%. Those graves were purchased and dug by a company who offered to bury the dead of poor families who could not afford a plot. The company realized before long that several bodies could be buried in the same grave, and they began a habit of opening a grave again and again to bury other dead in the same grave. The company owner behaved like Adolf Hitler with his disregard for the Jews, and I know where he is right now. He is with the Ford Capri's driver in the lake of fire.

After the Second World War, London's government bought these plots from the company, and then the ground was closed to burials. The intention was to create an open space for the public and make it into a park, but the public did not want create a park out of this land. I knew how they felt, too. I felt a little odd as I walked through this place. With each step I took, I felt dead bodies underneath me, but I needed to go on. I turned around again to see how close those guys were. I saw one guy, and I thought the other guy flanked me to the left because of the road a few exits to the left of me. I needed to veer to the right, and fast.

I ran through some graves, then zigzagged through the trees and more graves—I was looking behind me to see if I was out of their view. I did not see them anywhere! Did I lose them? I looked at the trees to see if one was right for climbing. I scraped the mud off my shoes and climbed up the tree quickly. I managed to get four limbs up, and from there, I looked around. I didn't see them anywhere, but I wanted to wait longer to make sure. Perhaps they got lost. *They are so ignorant,* I thought to myself.

I climbed back down the tree, and I headed toward the southeast end of the cemetery. I walked along the train tracks, watching the sky as black clouds gathered for a big thunderstorm. I could feel it coming, and soon. I rushed to get Aaron, walking southwest to Bow Common Lane. I took Burdett Road from there to Grove Road, and from there I walked to Victoria Park.

Aaron was there with his bike near the fountain. Perfect! He waited for me. And now I am almost there. As I walked toward him, I wondered why he was wearing his helmet. Maybe it was to remain anonymous? He never wore it before. He never wore those leather pants and that coat, either. I yelled at him to start the bike, but he did not move or make a sound.

I started to feel strange, as the small details bothered my intuition. It is little bit odd, so I checked my surroundings. Aaron was about fifty feet from me, the lake was on my left, and there were a few bushes and some trees to my right. From somewhere behind me, I heard the sounds of a car door closing and an engine starting up. I kept my composure and emotions in check so that I could think, but I couldn't help the adrenalin rush—I sprinted to his bike. Halfway there, I saw that the helmet was his, but there were no hands or feet! It is a decoy! *Aaron must be in one of the cars… it is a good thing!* I kept running, unhesitant now, to just get to his bike. I hoped Aaron kept the key in the ignition!

I reached the bike, grabbed the helmet, and I put it on while I kicked the decoy and clothes off the seat. Jumping on, I reached for the ignition, but the key wasn't there. I heard the car grind to a stop on the gravel, and I could see them getting out of the car, only ten feet away! My eye went to the key in the dirt right next to the front wheel… In one motion, I grabbed it and shoved it into the ignition and turned the bike on. I revved the throttle all the way, and I kicked them away from me just as their hands reached out to grab me! I took off quickly on the small walkway and gained control of the steering. I could see, just ahead of me, the other car that had left the cemetery, and I knew that Aaron was in that car. It turned on Old Ford Road.

I drove his bike as fast as I could, crossed the little bridge and turned off at Sewardstone Road heading southeast. There were people on sidewalks and cars parked on each side of the road, so I had to zig-zag between cars driving slowly and ignore the people who were staring. I made it to Ford Road and turned west. I was looking for the black Sedan. Where was it? I drove even faster now, but I couldn't speed up much due to the stop lights. But that car cannot go through them either! I sped up as much as I could between the lights, but I didn't see the car anywhere.

I began to worry that the car had turned off somewhere, when I glimpsed the back end of a black sedan. I kept going and got a good look at it—that was the car that had Aaron! I slowed just a bit, so I was barely able to see the car, and then I searched my rear-view mirror for the other black sedan behind me. I knew it was somewhere behind me, still looking for me. I was a mouse caught between two cats, so I needed to keep my wits about me. One eye was looking at the sedan ahead of me, and other eye was looking in the rear view for the sedan that was in Victoria Park.

There was a lot of traffic at this time of day... I did not remember there being this much traffic on the roads... Well, I did not notice. Reason for that is I had never driven anything before. It was harder to negotiate in traffic than I expected. My plan was to get behind the sedan in front of me, and at the next traffic circle, I would get off the main road and wait for the other sedan. I figured it would go by in thirty seconds or less because of the timing of the traffic lights.

I could see the next traffic circle ahead of me. I turned off onto Kenning Halt Road, made a U-turn, and then parked on the side of the road. I observed each car carefully as it went through the traffic circle, about fifty cars every ten seconds. The next group of cars passed by, and I still did not see that sedan. The same thing with the next group of cars.... Did I lose Aaron?? It could not be that I was going to lose all my friends at once! A few seconds later, that sedan whipped around that traffic circle as quick as a hummingbird! I took off after them, and we flew down Watermead Way. They caught up with the first sedan, and with each traffic circle they passed, they went faster and faster. By the fourth one, they had nearly reached 50 mph in a city zone! A couple minutes that seemed like an hour passed by, and they slowed and turned onto South Ordnance Road.

I felt a foreboding about this area. This was the bucolic agricultural countryside with a canal that flowed back into the Thames River. The car's route led us twisting and winding around some lakes, and finally slowed to turn off at a farm, where they opened and closed an entry gate.

Once they were out of view, I parked the bike behind a hedge, and I hiked to where I could have a better look at the farmhouse. I could view the front entrance of the house from their fence line. People could drive past this house, and with just a glance, think nothing of it. I was lucky there was a tree by their fence because I needed a place to conceal myself. I barely had the strength left to climb it, but I managed without drawing any attention.

The sedans were parked right out front, and they were empty. I assumed that Aaron was in that house, and that he was alive, but I needed to know. Suddenly, two of the men walked back outside and got in one of the sedans. They drove to the gate, which opened up for them, and they drove off.

Two less men in that house, but I do not know how many were inside to begin with. What I did know was how many cameras were in this section of their yard and what they were aiming at. There were three cameras attached to this side of the house: one camera was at the back side of the house, one was in front, and the third camera was in between. It was a very long house extending toward the back, and I guessed it was about one hundred and twenty-five feet. There were four large windows on the side, all of them closed with heavy drapes. That meant no one was likely to hear or see me, as long as I could avoid the cameras. All of the cameras were pointing toward my location, but it seemed they angled down a little bit toward the ground. I was still in the tree. The lenses were focusing on the middle of this section of the yard, for some reason. But I had to do something fast, as it was around 4:30, and Della would worry about me if I was late.

I hopped from my branch to the top of the fence, and then jumped down to the ground with my back against the bricks. I sprinted along the wall to the halfway point between the middle camera and the one at the back of the house. I had calculated that there might be a two-foot dead area there, and from there I ran to the side wall of the house. I made it, but did anyone see me? And if they had, would they come out from the front or back door? I put my back against the wall and bent my knees to slide past their windows toward the back of the house, moving under the angles of the cameras. As I reached the back of the house, I turned my head to face the back yard. I saw no one so far. I moved my body around the corner so I was facing their back yard. In the middle of that yard, there was a good-sized building, like a low barn.

The back wall of the house had a couple of windows in it, so I couldn't just walk toward that barn. I turned my attention back to the house. One window was right next to me, and the other window was at the other corner of the back wall. There was a sliding door near the middle. As I scanned the back side of the house, I noticed a basement window, too. It was about 18 inches square, and it was pushed open. I got on the ground to slither under the window as low as I could go. When I had wriggled next to the window, I looked inside. Nothing was out of the ordinary. I pushed open this window even further to get in the basement, and luckily, the wind from the big thunderstorm approaching was rattling the other windows and giving me some cover. The rain would be here very soon, too.

I climbed into the cellar and dropped myself down to the floor. It was a little dark, but I could see. The first thing I noticed was the row of bricks stacked up along the wall, and I recognized them from the fence. There was a large tank used for the oil heater, too. A pump would take the oil up then ignite it through the use of a step-up transformer. A lot of pipes went into the house, just like the organ pipes in a church. Near the other side of the room there was an electrical box with fuses and breakers. I began to form an idea as I walked toward it, but then I heard their phone ringing through the heater pipes.

A man picked up the phone, and after a pause, he said, "I understand. We will do that," and he hung up the phone. He said, "We have orders to kill him and cut him up in the barn. He'll go through the meat grinder and into one of the bags with some bricks. Then, into the canal to join the children."

Now my brain felt as if it were hit with a bolt of lightning. Just then, a gale of wind from the storm came into the cellar. "What was that?" the first man said.

"I think it was the wind in the cellar."

"Okay… you check that out."

I was still stunned by what I just heard, but I quickly found a place to hide among a pile of wood next to a broken wheelbarrow. I found a couple of long ropes and one short rope there. I grabbed the short rope and then ran to the other side of the bookcase next to the stairwell. The doorknob turned, and the man opened the door and leaned in. He stopped for a few moments to listen at the landing. My heart was beating like the drums of Africa, and I grabbed the ends of the rope in my fists as tight as I could!

He stepped down off of the landing and walked toward the open window. His back was only three feet away from me. He was taller than me, but I was ready to fight! Fueled by adrenalin, I took a step toward him, jumped up and threw the rope over his head, and aimed it for his mouth, just like a horse's bit. He had grabbed the sides of the rope to pull it away, but I kicked his legs out from under him instead, knocking him onto his knees. I had my knee in the middle of his back, and I pushed his chest to the ground! Then I tied the rope in a knot on the back of his head. I reached for the long rope while I kneeled on his back, grabbed his arms, and wound the rope around his wrists. I tied that end of the rope with a tight sail knot, and the other end of the rope, I tied up his feet. I struggled to drag his jumping body around the corner and behind the stairs.

While I was pushing his body out of sight, I heard the other man say, "Are you okay down there, Jigs?" and I heard steps near the cellar door. With Jigs tied up and out of sight, I knew what I needed to do. I quickly and quietly positioned myself in the cellar about twenty feet away from the stair landing, and I waited until I saw the doorknob turn. I felt a river of blood rushing into my muscles, just like how water crashes into an island and gives and takes nutrients as it moves, that's what my blood was doing right then in my muscles and brain!

I saw the doorknob turning, and my muscles were called into action! I started to run toward the door that was opening, and with my foot planted on the upper landing, I leaped up! I aimed all of my strength on the middle of the door. The door's hinges broke as the door hit the guy, and it thrust him backward with the old door on top of him! I quickly took the door off him, checked if he was breathing or not, and he was unconscious.

I turned my attention to finding Aaron, but I was careful. Reason for that was I did not know how many of his gang was there. I moved cautiously in the house; I was in their kitchen, then I walked in to the living room. I did not find anyone else there. I did not see Aaron, either. I went down the hall carefully, and I saw five doors down this hall: two on the right side, two on the left, and one at the end. I thought I heard water running. I walked toward the first door and cautiously opened it. This room was a traditional bedroom with a bed and chest of drawers. Everything in the room seemed all right. I went to the nearest door across the hall from this one, and that was the same as the other one. I opened up the third room, and there was nothing in it. The floor did not even have a rug, just a plastic cover on the floor. I walked to the fourth door and was about to open it, when I saw something glimmer in the crack at the bottom of that fifth door. It was at the end of the hall. I walked toward it, and I heard water. It was coming from the fifth room. I opened up that door to see a plastic curtain hanging around a bath tub and water overflowing onto the floor.

Chapter Twenty

No one was in the room, so I stepped through the water and pulled back the curtain. Aaron was drowning! I turned off the water, put my arms around him to pull him up, and I dragged him out of the tub and onto the wet floor. His arms and legs were tied with rope. I felt his carotid artery but felt no pulse. His chest was not moving, either! I lifted his neck slightly and quickly started the cardio-pulmonary resuscitation right there. Two of my breaths into his lungs, and two compressions at the right spot on his chest. During the second round of compressions, I heard a gargling noise, so I immediately turned Aaron on his side. I hit his back, and he threw up water onto the floor. He gasped for air and his eyes opened. If I could see the cells within his body, they would be coming back to life again. Then he started to cough as I untied the ropes on his hands and legs. I heard his waterlogged voice say, "I knew you'd come save me. Why'd you take so long to get here?"

"I do not know how to drive in traffic, and I almost did not find your bike key!"

"Well, thanks anyway," he said. We smiled, but in the back of my mind I knew we were not out of danger.

"How does your body feel now?"

"Much better, since I almost ceased to exist!"

"Do you want me to help you to sit up?"

"Yes. I'd like that."

I sat Aaron up against the bathroom vanity, and I told him I was going to tie up the guy that almost drowned him with the wet rope. I went back to the kitchen dragging the rope behind me, and the man on the stairs was still unconscious. I tied him up tightly. I looked into the other side of the house, where there was a large family room. It felt cold in there. I saw a small telly on a little table in a niche, and on another table, I saw eleven knobs with buttons on top of them. They were installed in a panel, and there were words below the knobs. The buttons were switches for turning cameras on and off, and the knobs were for focusing the cameras outside the house. I assumed that the television set was for showing the camera feed. I wanted to turn on the television, but I did not want to leave my fingerprints on anything. I used my fist to turn it on and read the titles underneath the buttons on the panel. With my fist, I turned on the camera for the left front corner of the house. I turned the knob, which focused it on the gate, and then just a little more to focus on the box at the gate. I saw that it had a key pad on it.

I looked at rest of the knobs on the panel: three cameras for the left side of the house, three for the right side. I turned the knob for the right side of the backyard of house with my fist, and I saw that barn on the screen. I saw it was a traditional barn.

The #11 knob said 'INSIDE BARN.' I pushed this button, but felt a chill in my bones… I felt something helped me push the button. The camera in the barn came on, and I could see stark white everywhere. There was a large white machine, with a smaller white machine near it. It had an electric hoist with a white chain going through it, and the chain went up to the barn rafter. From there, it went through the white pulley, and at the end of that, the chain had foot cuffs in it. Underneath that was big, white steel drain. A few feet away from it, there was a table about seven feet long, and on it was a white plastic table cover with knives in a nice row at the end of that table. As I stared into the television monitor, I started to go into a trance again. No, not now! I'm not in a safe place…

I am in a hollow building, and I cannot see anything at all. I am standing up, I think. It is pitch darkness. I can hear the rain forcefully hitting the rooftop, and the noise is pulsating through the building. My body feels a bitter chill, as if somebody was there, but not a human! I hear someone walking toward the building from outside, and I hear somebody struggling. The door unlocks and then the lights come on. I can see now that I'm inside the stark white barn. I can see children's spirits standing around me, and I am with them in a large circle inside the barn as a witness. The circle is open in only one spot, right inside the door. I see two men come in the door carrying a large white roll of plastic with a person struggling inside. As the men pass the electric hoist, one man turns it on by pushing a button. The men walk toward the foot cuffs that are coming down slowly and surely.

I see one man's face for the first time: it is Jigs. The men unfurl the white plastic and reveal a boy who was inside. He tries to fight them, but Jigs punches him in the head and knocks him out, growling, "He's dead meat anyways!" I want to stop it but I cannot move, and I have no voice. I wonder who the boy is. I feel a little tug on my shirt, and I look down to see a boy spirit. He tells me, "It is my body. All the children in this circle died this way."

My eyes look back to Jigs roughly putting the cuffs on the boy's feet and the other man pushing the button on the hoist machine to reverse direction. The chain is lifting up his feet while his head is dragging on the floor, bouncing and rolling like a ball. His body is naked and lifeless now, and the top of his head is four feet off the ground with the white steel drain underneath. His blood is rushing to his head. The other man reaches up and slits his neck, draining both his carotid arteries, just as normal to him as eating morning breakfast. I feel his life force gushing from his neck onto his face and through his hair, as it drips down into the drain, now covered with red.

I am helpless to do anything for him. I feel in my stomach that time shifted before me. Now the floor is dark red and the blood is discharged from his body. Those men are taking him down... they are tossing his body on the table. I watch as Jigs pushes the button for the meat grinder and picks up a hammer, and I see the other man pick up knives. The boy's spirit asks me, "Do you want to see more of this savagery against us?" I shake my head with sadness. He continued, "We around this circle can leave Earth in peace now, since you are finding our killers. We ask one more thing. Tell our families what happened to us, and most of all that our parents could not have prevented the incidents that took place."

Like a snap of the fingers, I woke up out of the trance. But where am I? How did I get in the barn with these machines! It was stark white and calm, but I do not know how I got here. It was freakish to see those machines, now that I knew they were used to pulverize innocent young bodies to destroy the evidence of an atrocious man like Wehczeslaw Ezajasz!

I had forgotten about Aaron. I turned to see if the barn door was open, and it was. My legs were screaming to get inside that house as I ran across the yard. I saw that the man in the kitchen was still tied up and unconscious, so I ran to Aaron in the room in the hallway. "How are you doing?"

"I feel great. Could you help me stand up?"

"I am sorry for taking a long time to tie up that man," I said as I helped him up, "but you know me, I found out what happened to all of the children the ambassador killed."

"Great. You took only two minutes."

"That's all?"

"Yes, because I looked at my watch when you left."

Bewildered, I asked, "How are you feeling? Are you ready to try and get out of here?"

"Yes I am."

I helped him to stand up, and we walked to the front doorway. It was evening now. He looked things over for a moment, and I pointed to the direction where we'd have to climb back over the wall. With no idea how much time we would have to linger, we used up our last bit of adrenalin running across the front lawn and climbing back over the rock fence, and then we walked to Aaron's bike where I had hidden it. I handed his key to him. He took it and hesitated for a moment, and at that instant I knew Aaron was all right.

As he put on his helmet, I asked, "Are you cold? Your clothes are all wet."

"Very funny." He smiled at me, and he said, "We are in the United Kingdom! There is always a raindrop or two coming down from the English sky, and my clothes got a little wet as I rode my bike. Are you ready to go?" I nodded, and as Aaron started up the bike, I climbed on behind him.

It seemed like it took far too long to leave that countryside and the farmhouse behind. We rode into London, straight to Della's apartment. During our ride away from there, I remembered what I had seen in that barn. My soul will never forget. It was chilling reminder that human beings want to control others—and for a few, even at the cost of other people's lives.

Chapter Twenty-One

We were almost at Della's apartment when we saw that police officers were blocking off the street in front of the Berkeley Hotel, and my heart dropped. Aaron cruised slowly over to a police officer, who asked us what we were doing there.

Aaron shouted over the noise of the motorcycle, "My friend lives in that hotel! What's going on?"

The police officer said, "It's another murder. Someone was killed on this street, and we're looking around for the people involved."

I asked, "Who is the victim?!"

"I can't reveal any more information to the public, but another officer found an eyewitness to the murder, and we caught a guy who fits the description. So you guys pass on through."

We rode up to the Berkeley Hotel parking lot. On the way in, I saw a white sheet draped over a dead body. We kept riding until we reached the lot.

I jumped off the bike and ran to the hotel entrance. I took the stairs, leaping up seven flights as fast as I could. I ran, panting, to Della's front door, opened her door, and I saw Della cleaning her apartment. I ran up to her and gave her a big hug.

"Thank you for the hug, but can you clean my rug again? You didn't take your shoes off at the front door!"

"My apologies. I will clean it up. You need to call Mr. Rockdom! I know what happened to all of the bodies!" I reached into my pocket and pulled out the piece of paper with the address to that house and handed it to her. "Wehczeslaw Ezajasz and his men, they killed the children and desecrated their bodies at this place! Can you ask him also to begin dredging the canal on South Ordnance Road? Tell him to follow that canal to the Thames River. He is looking for eighteen bags, each containing a brick and the ground remains of human bodies...." I panted as I stared at her, trying to catch my breath.

Della said, "Are you sure about that?"

"Yes! I am as sure as my heart is beating right now!"

She said, "That is sadistic! People who are living right here with us?" She stared at me in shock for a moment, then walked over to her phone and placed the call to Mr. Rockdom.

I had already slipped off my shoes and was putting them at the front door, when Aaron walked in. "Take your shoes off. She just cleaned."

"Okay," Aaron said. "Is Della all right?"

"Oh yes… she is great. I forget to take my shoes off, and now I have to clean her rug."

Della was talking to Mr. Rockdom on the phone. I heard her say, "I will…" and then she dropped the arm holding the receiver and rested it against her leg. She said, "He wants to know if you're able to go break into the parliament building tonight."

"Tell him I am willing and able! If he goes to that house, he will find a few sadistic men who I tied up. One of them is in the kitchen, and the other man is down in the cellar behind the stairs."

Della told him what I said, and she hung up the phone. She straightened her posture and took a deep breath. "Are you hungry after all that? I'm famished. I only ate with you this morning…. Aaron, what is wrong with you? Your face is so pale, and all of your clothing is drenched, even the bottom of your socks! Let me get some men's pants and shirts for you both. Change your clothes, and I'll call in an order of food."

***

We devoured a lot of great food after it arrived, and between swallows, I told Della what happened to Aaron and me. She said that two men had followed her, but she was able to call Mr. Rockdom. After that was when she called Aaron's phone and let it ring one time. I told her I got the message from the ring, and that soon after that, the men following me left the apartments, but I had wondered where they went. Now I know they had captured Aaron. "Hey, Aaron, do you want to go to the hospital now?"

"Oh, I really feel fine. I can thank Alex T. Ottoman for that."

"Both of you were fortunate," Della said. "You, Alex… If the police officer had pulled you over and found you had no license, Aaron would be dead now."

"Yes, but they didn't. And Aaron is alive. Luck is part of every person's life, true, but to balance out good luck, there is a counterpart… and in this case, it points to the innocent children who are gone. I realize that I am not God, so I do not know about every murder that occurs in the world today! I did know about Aaron, though, and I rescued him. So, umm, I am like God to Aaron!"

"Well, who is arrogant now?" Aaron joked. "Can I throw my two cents in?"

"Sure, go ahead," I said.

"Well, I see each human being as a little God here to help out. For example, a person who gives water to a dry plant is a God to that plant. I will give one more example. New parents are like God to their newborn baby. The parents have so much power over their baby. They have a choice to be good parents or not, and the world hopes that they nurture that baby. In time, the baby becomes who God wants that person to be. Or, if the parents are bad parents, and they do not nurture that baby, it will be unable to function in today's world. Worst-case scenario, the parents kill their baby after it has been born."

I said, "I knew that already, I am just messing around with you Aaron. Don't you know that?"

"Sure, I knew that!"

I asked Della, "Why do some people choose evil? Do you know why some people want to murder other people?"

Della was already clearing the empty plates from the table. "I can give you my opinion on why, of course. Early in the history of the human species, we were gregarious animals. We formed groups, lived together, hunted together, and produced offspring. However, we were dying fast. So one man would respond by using dominance of his group to form a small tribe, and the population grew after generations of this hierarchical structure. Each tribe had a leader, and the leader tried to grow his tribe. Unfortunately, through time, conflict erupted between tribes. The leaders did not want their followers to leave their tribe to join up with a bigger tribe. Over tens of thousands of years, it gave rise to racism, beginning in the Middle Ages. The kings used racism to control their people. The kings wanted their men to fight in their war and help gain supremacy over other people and gain their land. You know that already. Two thousand years passed, and our bloodline was no longer pure, since the Vikings and Romans and others were creating their empires by attacking other countries, men were pillaging their goods and raping their women. Offspring from these unions introduced other bloodlines, and I think it is a good thing, since all of the people in the world are equal! We have the same blood flowing in our veins. On the other hand, the predominance of aggression and competition people still have as their frame of mind, even now, each and every man, woman and child... it affects our actions."

I said, "In modern societies, people do not have the chance to crusade and pillage other countries. Our aggressive tendencies have no outlet, so some people carry out unscrupulous crimes toward humanity. Just like the Polish ambassador's crimes against the children. Aggression in people causes murder, rape, and other abuses against people each day. That is the kind of thing the warriors did in the history books, but they do it in the modern age, today."

"Yes, and it is not going to end," Della said.

"I was afraid it would not." I took a deep breath, and we paused for a few moments. I thought about my grandfather and how he wrote me two letters each month in code. I knew he was trying to train me to think about details, just like he was searching for!

Aaron said, "Mmmm! The food was so good! I am full of cottage cheese pie!"

"I am too," Della said. "I will tell the chef about your positive review of his food next time I see him. Can I change the subject, though?"

"Sure?"

"What are your plans?"

My eyes lit up: "Which one?"

"Your plans for searching the parliament offices. You didn't forget about that already, did you?"

"Ah, okay. First, I will start in the office with the death certificates. I want to find records of all the people who died in England in the past five years. I will search for children who died in Eastman Hospital in the last year. I know many children died in there, and I want to know who signed the death certificates. After that, I will go on from there."

She said, "Do you know where the office of archives is located?"

"I do not know, actually, where that office is in there, but they have an index of offices at each floor and what kind of offices are on that floor. There's a main directory on the first floor, too. I will do fine when I get in there."

Aaron said, "I'm worried about the cameras in that place. People watch all the video cameras throughout all the government buildings. Especially parliament."

Della said, "I know, but Mr. Rockdom knows that too, and I think he must have access to the cameras. Why would he put you there tonight, otherwise? Are you afraid that he wants to capture you?"

"If he wants to see my face on the cameras at the British Parliament, then he can."

"Yes, he could," Della said, sounding frustrated, "but I don't think he is the type of person who would!"

"The first time you met Mr. Ezajasz, you did not know about him. You would not have thought he raped anyone, and least of all, innocent boys. You would not have thought he would destroy their bodies, just as if their bodies were a piece of a paper to throw away in the trash."

"Wait one second, young man! I've known Frank Rockdom since before you were born! After thirteen years, I think I am able to judge his character!"

"You think so?"

"Yes, and you are intelligent enough to know people's personalities, but I did not mean it that way. I know Mr. Rockdom, and I think he is good, but you are right. People are strange…What is the old saying? Do what I say and not what I do?"

I said, "I know what you mean. You are right."

Della continued, "My mother said, people are good in this moment, and in the next moment, they are sinning! Now I don't know what to think. We should be careful. I understand why you don't want Mr. Rockdom to see your face. He may tell your father about you. What if you wore a mask?"

I smiled, and said, "Okay, I will look like I am a robber! If Rockdom sees me, he will put me in jail! Can you bail me out at the police station, please!"

We were laughing with each other, and for a moment or two, my brain forgot the souls in the barn. But my spirit did not forget it. I looked at the clock, and I saw it was already seven o'clock. I was feeling a little tired, so I told Della I wanted to lie down on my bed and take a few z's. As I took my dishes to her dishwasher, I asked Aaron how he was doing.

"I am feeling awesome right now! Can I stay here? I want to take you to wherever you need to go tonight."

I said, "Great! Can someone wake me up at nine o'clock? I want to take a long shower."

Della said she would. I walked into the bedroom and fell asleep immediately.

Chapter Twenty-Two

Della woke me up from a deep sleep. My eyes opened, I slid my legs over the side of the bed, rolled upright, and I walked over to the bathroom. I opened the shower door and turned on the hot water. The steam filled the bathroom and it filled my lungs with the warm vapor. I felt tranquillized and I stepped into the shower to let the hot water flow down over me. I thought to myself, *A few hours from now I will be breaking into the British Parliament.*

All English people have high regard for parliament. It has been Britain's treasure since 1066 when the Anglo-Saxons created it for Britain's laws and taxes. Our kings and queens have always been the head of the Imperial Parliament. In 1707, another enormous change in Britain's Parliament was the treaty of Union. Acts of Union were passed in both the Westminster Parliament and the Parliament of Scotland, which created new Kingdom of Great Britain. The Acts dissolved both parliaments, replacing them with a new Parliament of the Kingdom of Great Britain. Scotland joined of the Parliament of the United Kingdom. Since that time, no one had ever broken into our treasure of the British Parliament. I had never heard about it if someone did.

I remember my grandfather told me, "If you ever need to find a mole, you have to get dirtier than he is. Also, you have to dig a lot deeper than him. If you can do all that, you can throw that mole out of his comfortable place, and then that mole will be exposed so all the world can see his dirty deeds!" My grandfather found many types of moles in his lifetime. Unfortunately, it is my turn now, and the wisdom my grandfather, Della and my father all gave to me, I must put it all into practice it tonight. If I do not, the mole will go free and the spirits I need to vindicate will not get free from the world! I will not let that happen. There is a man who is just as guilty as Mr. Wehczeslaw Ezajasz and his men. I must and I will find that mole and deposit him aboveground, so the sunlight can shine on him and people can look at him and they can see his true colors. I am able to do that. I wish I could do more, but I can't. My grandfather also told me, "Life will throw stuff at you, little pants. You deal with it whichever way you can, but some things you cannot deal with at the time, and you need to let it go."

I heard Della calling me through the white vapor filling the room. "It is nine forty-five... Are you done steaming up my bathroom?"

"I will be right out!" A couple minutes later, I walked out of the bathroom, clean and dressed, and I asked Della if I could make a cup of coffee.

"Yes, but you'd better fix half a pot for us all. Tonight, I feel I will not sleep at all."

"But your heart... that is not good for your heart."

"My heart will keep on beating whether I sleep or not."

"I hope it does," I offered, "but the caffeine... It does raise your blood pressure."

"Well, I am a big girl now!"

"I am intelligent enough to know that. Is that okay with you!? Fine. I will fix half a pot of coffee."

We were all drinking hot coffee within minutes.

Della's doorbell rang, and she got up from her chair and went to the door with her coffee. I heard her say, "Okay, thank you," and she walked back to me and gave me a big yellow envelope.

I looked at whom it was from: Mr. Frank Rockdom. I opened the envelope quickly, and inside I found a small camera, a map, and the letter to 'my informant.'

The letter said: I did order to dredge the canal in on the Ordnance Road, and my men are halfway through to the Thames River. My men found two bags. In each one there was a brick and something else. I sent it to the coroner's office to have it tested and to see if the material in the bags is human remains.

I also ordered the detective inspector go to that farmhouse. They found the two men you captured, and they also found about fifty items of boys' clothing in the closet of the master bedroom. I think it is a little odd that a grownup has young boys' clothes in his closet. Also, the detective and his men went into the barn.

Della told me what you told her about that barn. Wehczeslaw Ezajasz and his men did dispose of children's bodies in there. I didn't want to believe Della, but I believe both of you now. A couple of undercover police officers watched Mr. Ezajasz's every move tonight, and I hoped Wehczeslaw Ezajasz was not ambassador, but he is and tomorrow morning two of my police officers will deliver him to Poland and I will write a strong letter to Poland's Government to put him in jail. I will wait for you. I sent a camera for you to use on the indictable documents that you are going to find in somebody's files. After you find them and you photograph those documents, send that camera back to me immediately, and I will piece together the killer's puzzle and arrest all of the parties involved in this horrifying scheme! I promise that to you and those parents who are without their children now.

You will want know how to get into the British Parliament without being noticed! Here it is. During the Second World War, the queen commissioned the construction of a bomb shelter for the House of Commons, the House of Lords, and the lawmakers of the Great British Parliament. They built it underneath the Imperial Parliament, but they did not use it. Now, the House of Commons, the House of Lords and the lawmakers all know about it, so if a *catastrophe did happen, they know to go to that shelter.*

Tonight, you will go through it and access parliament. The five tunnels in that shelter grant access to all of the floors of the Westminster Parliament building. I sent you the map of where you need to go in order to access that shelter. One other thing: the electricity in the parliament building will shut down at 11:05 p.m. tonight, and will come back on at 12:12 a.m. You do not want to be in there when the power is on, as the alarm system will be on. It is the best in the world, and it will find you. It will lock every door and *call me automatically.*

Good luck to you, and I hope that in the parliament building, you find the person who knew what Wehczeslaw Ezajasz did to the children.
Assistant commissioner for London,
Frank Rockdom

***

Della asked, "What does the letter say?"

I handed the letter to her and said, "I need to go now!" I slammed the rest of my coffee to let the caffeine pulse throughout my blood, and I said, "Ready to go?"

Aaron nodded his head yes.

I picked up the camera and put it in my pocket. I carried the map and small flashlight, and on my way to the door, Della handed me a pair of gloves. I asked her, "Do you have a cheap watch I can use?"

"Sure. I'll get it."

By the time I had put on the gloves, she was walking out of her bedroom. She held in her hand my grandfather's gold watch. She gave it to me and said, "I took it to my jeweler and had adjustments made to the band, so now it's small enough to fit your wrist."

I took the gold Rolex from her and put it on my wrist. It felt all right, and checking the clock, I saw it also had the right time.

Della looked at me and said, "You are becoming a lovely young man, and your grandfather would be so proud of you, just as I am right now. You go save the world from those killers. I know that you are a shining beacon in a dark world tonight." She hugged me, and she whispered in my ear, "You be careful."

"Well, I need to go now."

"Okay," she said, and she opened the door.

***

Aaron and I walked out into the hallway and ran through the Berkeley Hotel to get to the lobby. Outside, I grabbed the map out of my pocket and looked to see where we needed to go. I told Aaron to drive to the Albert Embankment just off Westminster Bridge Road.

We got to his bike and we jumped on it, just like we had so many times before, and we rode through the damp, windy night. I hoped that this part of our journey would turn up conclusive evidence for the sake of those innocent young souls detained in this world because their lives ended so violently and quickly, watching as their killers went on to kill again. Tonight, I am finally ending that cycle, although my friend Robert's life has changed forever because of Wehczeslaw Ezajasz and his men. My promise to Robert is half completed, but what's in my hands now is not entirely within my control. Tonight will be pivotal.

We turned off the Westminster Bridge Road, and we rode along the Albert Embankment. We were near the St. Thomas hospital. I told Aaron to stop, and we jumped off the bike.

We were not in complete darkness as I'd hoped. There were lights mounted that lit up an area about ten feet across. In the center, there was a trapdoor made of copper, with more copper surrounding it in a twenty-feet circle on the ground. Outside that boundary, grass extended about 15 feet out in all directions, and surrounding that grass, twenty feet more of pavement.

"I want you to leave me here, Aaron," I said as I slid off the seat. "I do not want you involved in this part of the operation. It only takes one person. I thank you for helping me escape from the Eastman mental institution, and for saving my life in more ways than you can ever know. But now you need to go."

"Okay. I am going to the St. Thomas Hospital's coffee shop to wait for you. When you get through, you will have the information you need to nail those evil bastards."

"That word is a little word, coming from a smart man."

"Well, I am American."

We were laughing at each other, and for a few moments, I forgot that this night would be throwing obstacles at me. Aaron started his bike up, still laughing. He smiled at me and drove off.

Now I looked at the map … it had directions written on it. It said, "Stand at the middle of southeast corner of this location. Face north. Walk toward the third planter box. There is a stone in upper left corner. Turn the top of the rock ten degrees to the south."

So far so good, and it seemed straightforward enough. I turned the rock.

Chapter Twenty-Three

I felt the ground vibrate and heard rumbling underneath the trapdoor. Astonished, I ran to the door in the ground, and it was opening up slowly, propped by a megalithic rusty arm. I felt air rush down into this underground cell, and I was chilly all of sudden. I breathed in the old air that had been trapped in this cell for a long time, I assumed. The door was halfway open, and now I could see the dilapidated stairs that ran down into the blackness.

I reached down into my pocket, got my flashlight, and grabbed it extra tight. I pointed it down into this darkness that had not seen daylight for eons. I could tell because there were about ten thousand spider webs in the shaft, and as far down as my light reached, I could see the webs.

I was apprehensive about this plan tonight. I did not know what was going to materialize inside this underground building. I remember my grandfather told me about fear, and how some anxiety is good, but abnormal anxieties will manipulate your life and hold you back until your existence is nothing at all. My grandfather was always right.

I took my first step on the stairs and suddenly the heavy, thick metal door began to close. I quickly descended the stairs, and soon that door had shut me into total darkness, except for the beam of light that guided me through the blackness. The air felt dense, and a thought disturbed me that this might just be a big tomb for me. The metal door clicked shut behind me, and I was stuck underground. I felt cobwebs hit my body with each step I took. I pointed my flashlight so that I could see to the bottom of the stairs, about fifty in total.

I reached the bottom with what felt like a couple pounds of the spider webs stuck to me like glue. I tried knocking them off my hair and clothes, but I could not get all of them, and my skin started to itch, but I minimized that with my brain focus. I took the map from my pocket and illuminated the map.

The first instruction was 'Look for the door.' I shone the light onto the walls and saw that they made a circle about fifteen feet across. I could see the door on the far side, so I walked to it and brushed off the webs as I went. The door had a number pad bolted onto it.

The next instruction on the map said, "

You must enter the code precisely at 11:05 p.m. or the parliament's alarm will go off and they will notify security! Also, their system locks the doors automatically, and they immediately stop the six-month routine that shuts down parliament's electricity. Enter the code at 11:05 pm, and travel the passageway under the river. You will find another door like this first one that needs a second code. You need to unlock that door thirty seconds after you unlock this door. The first code is 576582 and the second door's code is 843156."

I looked at my watch, and the time was already 11:04 and forty-five seconds! I thought to myself, those young boys' spirits are counting on me for a little justice for the brutality of their murders. My grandfather told me, "You have responsibility to the human race because you were born with phenomenal brainpower. It is a gift for you. Use it wisely, my little smart pants."

I looked at my watch... five seconds before 11:05. My adrenaline started to pump through my blood now, my heart distributing it to my muscles with every click of my second hand!

The Thames River is 200 meters wide right here. I calculated that I needed to run about twenty-five miles per hour to reach the other door before that half-minute ticked down in the world's history book. I placed my fingers on the right numbers on the door pad, and I watched my second hand until it was pointing up and down. My fingers put that code in the door panel with lightning speed and unlocked it.

I threw open the door and pulled it shut behind me, and as I ran, the walls of the small tunnel echoed my steps back to me. That was ironic. Reason for that was I was underneath the Thames River, the artery of England, and all conquerors in the history of England sailed on the river above me... the Vikings and Romans... I had goose bumps, but I didn't even notice. I pointed my flashlight on the walls from one side to the other as I sprinted to the other end of this tunnel. It had not been used for a long time, and it showed on the walls.

This air was suffocating me because it had been closed in for years. Air loses some of its oxygen atoms, and I tried to fight beyond that, as I was half way through the tunnel already. I could sense the water on the other side of the walls. I saw the second door ahead of me, and I sprinted faster. This air was asphyxiating me, and I could not breathe anymore. I was only about ten feet away now! The cells in my body cried out to me for more oxygen.

I almost fainted, but I managed to look at my watch. I recalled my grandfather telling me to never give up! I thought about those young spirits trapped in that deathly barn, with no peace there, and without their parents, either. Those young spirits were counting on me for little peace! I had four seconds to enter the second code.

My body wanted to pass out, but my firmness of purpose got hold of me. I reached my hand out to the number pad, and I slowly and determinedly put in the code. I pushed the door's heavy lever down, fell against the door, and I hit the ground gasping for air. I needed to know where I was! I pointed my flashlight on the walls beyond the door, and I was in their bomb shelter.

This part of the shelter had clean air with four slow-turning fans to circulate it. Then I realized they were turning slowly because the electricity was off. I hoped that the fresh air would stay that way. I looked around while my cells started to breathe once more. This bomb shelter was a good size and well made. Thick concrete blocks made up the walls, and a couple of long tables were along the walls with benches. I estimated that it could hold about seven hundred people. I pointed my flashlight across the room and noticed a large storage space for canned goods. I noticed that the cells in my body felt well, my blood had lots of oxygen in it, flowing to my brain, and I felt intelligent again!

I stood up and walked over to one of tables. Why do human beings need to dig large holes and put in thick blocks to keep the people safe from another country's evil rulers. They shoot the bombs toward the other countries, and they want to be in control of other nations, same as the conquerors in the Middle Ages. There is an old saying that "the times will change, and the technology will change in time," but peoples' thinking did not change.

One case in point is this bomb shelter. It was created for one purpose only, and that was to protect the British officials. The queen did not want to interrupt the British government during World War II. Adolf Hitler wanted to control the United Kingdom to have access to the Atlantic Ocean, and he directed air raid bombs into London because he wanted to obstruct Britain's government. Then, his troops marched into London and captured the United Kingdom, for he wanted to make his own warships for sailing out of UK harbors. It was the same as in the Middle Ages, when the conquerors wanted to capture the countries that had access to the oceans for their ships and food. It is a shame that evil people exist, but they do, and I am going to find an evil person tonight within parliament's walls, that is for sure!

I pointed my flashlight to the wall at my right, found the door I was looking for, and climbed up its stairwell to the top of the landing. There, I found a door, which I assumed was the door to the British Westminster. I looked at it to see if it was locked or not, and that door was not locked. That was peculiar. But of course, both doors were not locked in case of emergency. If people ran down to the bomb shelter and both doors were locked, it would not be a pretty sight.

I opened this upper door and walked in. My flashlight was on the walls and sweeping across the center to see what things were in there. This room was huge. This room was the basement of British Parliament. My flashlight was now shining on one of the massive cast iron curved columns, one of eight altogether, to take the weight of the floor of the Central Lobby above. These columns enabled architect Charles Barry to span the width of the Central Lobby without needing any pillars inside the lobby of the British Parliament. My flashlight could only guide me through the maze in the long-established parliament basement; above me, a thousand wires were going everywhere, and there were air ducts going to the east, west and south of me. The tubing started big, then got smaller and smaller, for my light could not reach the end of it. As I walked through the basement, my back was against the wall because that way I would not get lost.

I was looking for the elevators up to the British Palace of Westminster, the meeting place for the House of Commons and the House of Lords. The building is so large that it uses four elevators: the south elevator for the 1st to 3rd floors, the east elevator is for the 4th and 5th floors, and the north elevator is for the clock tower. The fourth one is private, only for the queen and her V.I.Ps. They used that elevator only.

I saw an elevator, and I walked toward it, but as I walked faster, I could see that this elevator was the east one, and that was the wrong one! I was looking for the private elevator because it would go to all of the floors. I found three elevators, but I was not finding the isolated elevator the queen used.

I thought for a moment. The queen never walks in the front door because the crowds will swarm around. The Queen would always go in the motorcade whenever she goes anywhere. That is it! That private elevator is at the private parking lot, located at the lower left of this basement. I remember that the elevator does not stop here. I looked at my watch: the time was ticking away, and I had to seize the moment!

I was back at the first elevator I found. I grabbed the door to this elevator and pulled it open. Inside, I checked the ceiling to see if I could see the trapdoor, and there it was. I stepped on the elevator's railing, I reached up for that trapdoor, and my fingertips pried it open. Before long, I was in the shaft space on top of the elevator.

On my left side were the gigantic pulley and its enormous cable that rose up to the attic. It was same as the Eastman Hospital's attic and its elevator shaft. I pointed my light upward in the shaft, and I could see the door to the 2nd floor. I climbed up the rungs on the wall of the shaft, and I was able to reach the 2nd floor doors. I stepped on the door's narrow ledge and balanced on it carefully. My fingers were placed on the right and left sides of the crack in the middle. With all of my strength, I pulled both sides apart to break their seal.

I sucked in my breath and squeezed tightly between the doors. I pulled my flashlight from my pocket and aimed it onto the walls. I was in the central lobby of the parliament complex. I always liked the lobby's chandelier because it was developed by Sir Charles Barry in 1854. This chandelier was connected to a winch mechanism which allowed it to be lowered to the floor of the lobby for cleaning. I love how intelligent people look at a problem and then rectify that problem.

I ran toward the stairwell door, flung it open and lunged up the stairs. I opened the door to the third floor and stepped out into the hallway. In the darkness, I turned around to the wall and pointed my light on the information guide for the names and offices. I saw that the office for death certificates was on this floor, but at the other side of the hall. The parliament building was constructed in a semicircular shape, and the death certificates office was on the other side of this semicircular hall. I ran along the slow curve as fast as I could, using the little flashlight just to keep me at the right angle. As I ran, its light bounced off the walls, and the artifacts on them were beautiful. If I walked these halls every day, it would empower me to do right by the British people. My father had feelings like that.

I know one person does not feel the same as my father and the rest of the people working here. Reason for that is that most people, if they noticed a pattern of boys dying at an alarming rate in one place, like the Eastman hospital, they would tell the appointed person so they could investigate. This person did not do that. This person was callous to the situation, or was involved in the murders of innocent boys.

I found the death certificates office and went in to find the archives room. I tried opening the door that was labeled 'Records and Archives' but it was locked. Luckily, I knew this wasn't much of a barrier. I reached into my pocket and grabbed my trustworthy tweezers. I put the end of the tweezers in the doorknob key plug, wiggled the tweezers and felt the pins. I pushed the front pin to the left side of the hull, and I felt a click. I felt the tweezers hit the second pin, and I placed that pin to the right inside the hull. I positioned the third and fourth pins in the correct position to unlock the door, and I knowingly turned the doorknob and pushed the door open.

I walked in and shut the door gently. The room was pitch black. I shined my flashlight around the room and found two desks and eight large file cabinets. Although I was in the very place I had hoped to be for so long, I held my breath and started the search for the names of the innocent boys. I searched all the file cabinets for the names Joshua G. D'arcy, Harry B. Rogelio, Daniel

I. Zackary, James William S. Wahchinksapa, Oliver F. Mabsant, Thomas W. Edmond, Harry B. Rogelio, Jack L. Saith, Samuel A. Easton and Charlie H. Radbourne.

I did not find any of those names in the death certificate archives. It was a little peculiar. I pointed my flashlight onto the desk. The plaque on it said 'Head Clerk.' Nothing on the desktop seemed abnormal, so I walked around it and pulled out the drawer. It was empty. I did the same for the rest of the drawers, and found only a few papers and pens.

I pointed my light across the room toward a second identical desk and walked quickly toward it. The plaque on this davenport said 'Clerk.' I pointed my flashlight onto the expansive walls. Within these walls were the names of ordinary people who lived and died in Great Britain, and the room felt cold to me! I went back to the Head Clerk's desk, and I looked at her phone. It had names to the side of the digits, and the name at the top of the list was Dr. Fitzgerald.

Chapter Twenty-Four

I remembered that name from somewhere... Dr. Fitzgerald was at my father's gala! I didn't look to see which physician had signed their name on all of the death certificates, so I looked inside one of the file cabinets to investigate. Something gave me a feeling that I would see his name scrawled there on the bottom. I looked at the line for the doctor's signature, and it was indeed Dr. Fitzgerald!

I put back the files in the cabinet quickly with nervous hands, and left the office, opening and closing the door quietly in one swift motion.

I ran to the stairwell and descended the stairs to the second floor. I pushed open the door and ran down the hall with my beam of light bouncing off the walls. The directory containing the names of all the offices is on this floor. I could see it dead ahead of me. I ran down this hall as fast as I could, and finally, I read the names of the offices.

I searched all the names on that directory, found Dr. Fitzgerald's office, and ran toward it at the other end of the semicircular hall with my light bouncing off the walls again. I looked at my watch: the time was 11:26 and 17 seconds, and time was still ticking away.

Finally, I reached Dr. Fitzgerald's office and pulled out my trustworthy tweezers. In my other hand, I had my beam of light pointed at the doorknob. I reached for the doorknob and turned it, and surprisingly, it turned freely. I dropped the tweezers back into my pocket and slipped into the room quickly and silently, closing the door behind me. I pointed my flashlight around the doctor's office and saw one desk and a few file cabinets. On the desk, there was a plaque that read 'Secretary of the Commissioner of the General Register Office.' The desktop was spotlessly clean, just like the other two clerks' desks were. I saw only a phone and a calendar in the middle of the desktop.

I opened the drawers, and one drawer contained the Rolodex. I took it out and looked through it quickly. It only had names of the registry offices in Great Britain, which didn't seem unusual. I closed this drawer and looked into the other two drawers. One had a cup holder full of fountain pens.

I looked through them and found that one had the Russian flag printed on it, the same as Mr. Jesting Heddwyn, Dr. Fabron Rahman, and my father's pens did. It leads back to Mr. Wehczeslaw Ezajasz… the reason for that is, although he is the killer, maybe he did not rape the innocent boys? If another man committed the rapes, and that man asked Mr. Ezajasz to murder the boys after he violated them, then who is that man? Does he work here? If he does, the British Parliament will have the largest scandal since 1483.

At that time, there were two princes: Edward V of England, and his brother, Richard of Shrewsbury. He was the first Duke of York. In May of 1483, Edward arrived in London for his accession to the throne. Richard, at that point, was with his mother in safety, but joined his brother in the Tower in June. An Act of parliament of 1483, known as Titulus Regis, pronounced both princes illegitimate of being the king of England. Richard Duke of Gloucester was crowned as King Richard III, and the new king was the uncle of the princes. There were reports that some people saw the princes playing in the Tower grounds, but there are no recorded sightings of either of them after the summer of 1483. Many historians hypothesized that they either died or were murdered in the Tower. Their fate remains disputed, and to this day, historians call them the princes in the Tower. That was a very big scandal at that time, and everyone who lived in that kingdom was intimidated by whoever did that to the princes. If my grandfather lived in that time and place, he would have found out who murdered them and told everyone who would listen to him. But he did not live back then. He taught me his knowledge, and it lives today through me.

It is a fact that I will find whoever knew about these atrocious murders of innocent boys, and it will be tonight! My flashlight searched the walls, and my beam of light landed on a door. The door had a plaque hanging on it, saying 'Mr. Fitzgerald – Commissioner of the Hospitals and General Registers.' I walked over to that door and I tried turning the knob, but the door was locked. I reached down into my pocket for my trusty tweezers. I pointed my light on that doorknob and put the end of my tweezers into that key plug, then joggled for the pins to unlock the door. I immediately turned the knob, opened the door, and closed it silently behind me.

I searched this room, too, with my flashlight, and once more I found a desk. Mr. Fitzgerald's large desk was messy with papers stacked up on top. His papers overflowed even beyond the sides of the desk. I walked toward his davenport and stood near his chair. I tried opening the center desk drawer, but this one was locked. I had to find something to unlock that drawer.

I know what… a letter opener. I started to search for a letter opener on his desktop… my hands felt underneath all of the papers, and I eventually found it. His letter opener was small, and that's a good thing. I tried to put the end of the letter opener into the drawer's crack near the lock. First, I needed to bend the letter opener, so I had to be careful not to break it. I put the letter opener into this crack and moved it to the lock cam. I felt the letter opener hit the mechanism, so I added more pressure to move it. I moved the cam north to south, and I opened the drawer up.

I found a mess in there, too. It seemed there were about 100 of the pens rolling around on the bottom of this drawer. My hand moved through those pens to feel for the bottom of the drawer. If something else was in here, I would surely find it. I pulled out the drawer a third of a way, and then I shined the flashlight in there. I saw piece of tape on the rear wall of this drawer. That masking tape surely secured something, and I pulled the masking tape off.

Removing the tape revealed a key… an old skeleton key. I wondered if that key unlocked the door to his skeletons… I did not know what this key went to. I knew my time was ticking away. I opened the rest of his drawers up and they were empty. Running out of ideas, I pointed my beam of light onto a picture across from his desk. Something seemed abnormal about it, but I couldn't put my finger on what. So, I walked toward it while shining my light on another picture, which looked coated with dust. I changed course and went to see if my eyes deceived me. I glided my finger over the picture frame, and there seemed to be an inch of dust on my finger! I looked closer, and saw that these walls have dust coated all over them. *This man does not act like my father and Della… he needs someone to clean up his office, like Della, that is for sure.*

I continued over to the first picture I saw, the one that looked unusual, and it was not dusty at all. This picture was pushed out from the wall a little bit, too. I tried to pull on it, and the picture opened like a cabinet on hinges. Behind this picture was a safe.

I felt cold, but I knew what I was searching for was close. I had to figure out how to open his safe, and quickly! I felt those boys' spirits encouraging me. The safe had a dial, so I knew it must have three numbers, just as any combination lock, but I did not have any idea what they could be or how to remove the bolts from his safe door.

I checked my watch… I had less than thirty minutes until they turned the electricity back on! My heart was pumping fast, pushing the adrenaline into my veins, but I could not let it keep doing this. Reason for that is, I needed my body calm and fluid, not jittery. My brain commanded my adrenal glands to halt the production of adrenaline into my bloodstream. My mind controlled that and my body was calm and collected again. My brain then went to work on ways to crack the code of this safe.

I turned the rotating dial… it turned rough. The gears inside this safe were pretty old, and that was a good thing. Reason for that is, all gears create friction teeth when they're turning. In time, after continuous use, the gears' teeth get little bumps and fissures on them. That is how I knew I would be able to find out the combination to his safe. I hoped so! I put my palm right underneath that dial as I turned it, so I could feel any grinding or bumps. My other hand gently and slowly turned the dial to zero. I started to feel the dial's gears as I turned it slowly. I felt that the gear's teeth were hitting the other one. I turned it all the way back to zero again. This time, I turned it stopping at each number and moving it back and forth until I felt the bumps on this gear's teeth.

The reason for that is, when people are entering the three numbers for the combination on their safe, they normally slow down the movement of the dial a few numbers before each number of the combination. Using this same principle, and assuming Mr. Fitzgerald used his combination lock in the same way, this lock's gear teeth would have gained bumps and fissures, and I would be able to feel them. My theory was that the first gear on the inside of the safe was fastened to the turn dial on the outside, and that its teeth were synchronized with the numbers on the dial. His three numbers for his combination must be clear of bumps and fissures, because he would have slowed down at each number. That is the reason I was confident I could figure out his combination lock and open the safe door.

I turned the dial to zero again. *I think I have it…his three numbers are 73, 45, and 86…* But I had another problem… What order do they go in? I would just have to try. I needed to get this safe open to reveal his dirty secrets, if Mr. Fitzgerald had any in his safe. I would find out in in a moment or two. I tried the three numbers in different combinations, and none were working until I tried the last one.

Eureka!

I had it! I turned the dial to the last number, and while I turned it back at zero, every movement I made with the dial stiffened it up. It was a good thing that when I turned it to ninety-five on this dial, I could not turn it anymore. I pulled the safe handle down, I heard the bolts retract, and I finally pulled open the solid, heavy door.

My beam of light was filling the interior of the safe, just like the sunrise illuminates the morning. My light shined on his darkest secrets inside that safe. In this safe I saw a shoe box and a hope chest, and I picked up both. I took them to his messy desk, and I cleaned an area off his desktop for them. The hope chest was locked. I looked at the key plug on this hope chest… it took a skeleton key.

I went instinctively to get that old skeleton key from his desk drawer. I put it into the lock of the hope chest … Is it the right key? … I turned this skeleton key, and it opened his darkest secrets to the light! His journal was inside. I took his journal out from its hiding place and began thumbing through it. I stopped at a random page in his chronicle.

Chapter Twenty-Five

In his own words, Mr. Fitzgerald wrote:

Tuesday, 24 October 1972
   I am a powerful man around the world and exert influence over the British people. The presidents of other countries and important people around the world come to see me to seek my recommendations about each of their problems in their countries. Just as my paterfamilias held discussions regarding the First World War with elected heads of the countries for their military action with the head of Germany, my father was great helping people out in past generations.
   I am sitting in the formidable chair in parliament's Head of British Medical Hospitals, and the mental institutions too. The Queen asked me to look over all of Britain's hospitals, and the physicians in those hospitals as well. I pay attention to recently developed medical technologies and techniques, and then I research them. I understand how to perform operating procedures with the new medical technologies, and then I command each hospital to implement the new technology. I oversee all of the physicians in Great Britain, and every two years they get training for new medical advancements and technologies of saving lives. If any hospital or physician in Great Britain doesn't perform within the current operating procedures, I will know about that because I am the commissioner of the General Registers. I sign all of the death certificates. If I see an unusually high amount of deaths in a hospital, I will fire the head of that administration and hire another administrator to take their place immediately.
   In the event that any person reads what I wrote above in my chronicle, they would think I was an incorruptible man, just as my father was to past societies. My paterfamilias was an excellent lawyer, and he did nothing wrong through the eyes of those who knew him. I know him in a different manner, however. Seventy-three years he has haunted me, and still he tortures me, and I'm sure he will for the rest of my life. Every day, I saw in his eyes his domination over me in my bedroom mirror, as he molested me repeatedly. I

did not tell anyone about this because who would believe a little child's story over a very powerful man like my father was? But I told my mother. She would not believe me either. Finally, he had a massive heart attack while molesting me. That day ... I can smell it, and I can see it, even now. It is abhorrent to me.

I only went to school and back home. I liked being isolated a large amount of the time. But my mind was sharp, and I wanted to go to a good college. My teachers told me, why not send a letter to Admissions and Applications offices of the colleges you want to go to? So I applied, and they accepted me.

I went to the Complutense University of Madrid, since my father hated that college. I did not have a goal in mind. After being there a while, I figured out what I wanted to study: human anatomy and science. After two years, I took the MCAT test for Medical School at the University of Göthenburg, and they accepted me. I am as intelligent as my father was, and I loathe myself for that. I had to repress my emotions for many years about being a whore to my father because I wanted to be a normal young adult in my environment. Sometimes it was hard for me to do that, but I did. After eight long years in medical school at the University of Göthenburg, I graduated in there in 1930. Then, I went into the residency program at the Addenbrooke Hospital in England. It was hard for me because I saw what I was eighteen years ago. I still have that raw emotion inside of me toward my parents. On top of everything else, I have an added problem blazing inside of me, with evil thoughts going through my head while treating the children in the hospital. I tried to keep them from interfering with my work. After all, it was only my thought, I told myself, all people get immoral thoughts through their heads once in a while. Only a few people ever act on such thoughts, and I am not one of those people.

I finally finished my residency program and started up my private practice. My execution of becoming a physician within ten years was good. One day, I was driving near a school playground and saw many children playing there. Instantaneously, my blood raced with lots of testosterone, just as if I had puberty again! I tried to ignore it, but I couldn't. My body was driven by my emotions. I drove away from the playground that day, and after that I was thinking about boys twenty-four hours daily. I tried to repress those feelings, but I was failing at that. Cold sweat poured from my body all of the time, and in my practice, I did not do as well, since I could not keep my focus on my patients.

It had to stop, and I made up my mind up for better or worse. After I made the decision, I felt much better, and it would protect the children here. I went on a trip to Romania with a plan. I tasted it, my body had wanted it for so long, and it felt to me just as a lion hunts for his prey. I quenched my sexual appetite with a young boy. After that, I asphyxiated him and immediately knew what I had to do with his lifeless body. I must drain his blood. As I cut his carotid artery, his blood flew up to hit my face, and it felt so perfect to me! Then I tilted his body, with his head facing downward. Finally, his blood finished draining, and then I split that body open and I cracked his ribs wide open until I could see his heart. His lungs were lying flat, his stomach was empty. I disemboweled the boy and placed all of his vital organs in a large garbage bag. I took off all of the skin from the body, and then I started to dissect the muscles off the bones. I hammered his skull to pieces, took the brain out from his cranium, squishing between my fingers! I put it in this trash bag, too. I need to conclude that I broke up his bones and put them in another garbage bag.

I went to my hotel to take a shower. The water felt very vivacious to me. I cleaned up my body and I felt alive again! I packed all of my stuff, and I went back to my home to do the same things I normally did. The next day, I went to my office and I saw a lot of patients that day. I was up to speed. A week later, I got that itch again. I tried to control it, but it was stronger than I was... I fought my urges for three weeks. I was not able to fight it anymore. I had to take another trip as the month before. Again, again and again, for twenty years, monthly I have to take a trip to different poor countries, as I alleviate my urges for innocent boys as my father had done to me.

During that time, I did so well at my private practice, the Queen of England Her Majesty asked me to become Head Commissioner of the Hospitals and General Registers. I felt so nervous as I sat in this powerful chair. I was too busy, and I did not know if my urges had left me or my subconscious was afraid because I was now in the spotlight. Important people watched my every move. It lasted for ten years, and then I met Mr. Wehczeslaw Ezajasz on the golf course. We clicked, which was unusual for me, since I like being alone much of the time, but I did like to talk to him. I felt that he was similar to me, and we talked for a few hours every night for one and half months.

I did not know how the discussion started about my urges for undefiled boys... it just did. I told him about my hunger for young boys for sexual intercourse, and killing them, and how I then disassemble their bodies to make them disappear forever. Their bones and their insides I put it in my little crushing machine and deposit it in my garden.

My subconscious was not apprehensive of him. He will not tell anyone about that, I hoped. And he did not. A few weeks later he asked me, "Why did you stop hunting young males?" I told him that since I work in the British Parliament, everyone wants to know my personal business. That's why I cannot show my urges any more. Even if I could, I would not do it again because my body is seventy years old. I cannot lift the bags of bones and the innards and all of the vital organs any more.

150

A few days later, I talked with Mr. Wehczeslaw Ezajasz again. He said, "I have the perfect plan for you. I am capable of capturing young boys for you, and you can play with them all you want! When you get finished with them, I will kill them and their bodies will evaporate and no longer exist on Earth. I am able do that, due to my barn which contains a large meat grinder and equipment with it on my property. I'm willing and able to do that for you, but you must pay up for your pleasure, one hundred thousand pounds for one innocent boy."

I said, "Why would you do all that for me? Are you hard up for money? Tithe ambassadors make a large salary. I know you cannot be hard up for cash. But there is something about you. I do not know what is going on in your head... I cannot put my finger on it, but I like it!"

"Let's say I like to hunt, and most of all I love to kill something. I love to see the light in the eyes fade to blackness. I get goosebumps down my body when I see it!"

"I am a physician. Any doctor would not like to see lifelessness in somebody's eyes, even me, but I killed as an afterthought because I did not want them to feel just like me, as I did when I was a little boy. Where is your place?"

"At the end of South Ordnance Road. I can show you, if you want."

And he did show me. His house was nice, but his barn was eccentric because he had set up a sterilized environment for slaughtering animals of any kind. He had a drain in the floor for draining blood out of the animals' bodies and plenty of butcher's knives that would remove guts out of anything and skin everything, and then cut a variety of meats from them. All I was saying was that Mr. Wehczeslaw Ezajasz likes indigenous meats.

I like it as well, and as I was viewing Mr. Ezajasz's barn, some old feelings revived. I needed to accept Mr. Ezajasz's proposal, and I did. Three months later, Great Britain had three children missing. Scotland Yard investigated it. I got in a panic about that, and I called it off with Mr. Ezajasz, which made him angry toward me.

A couple days later, Wehczeslaw called me and said, "I have another plan that is going to work better. Do you control administrations for the mental institutions?"

"Well, yes, but I do not regulate them so strictly. Why?"

"That is excellent, since this plan demands that you regulate the mental institutions so stringently, they will be afraid to lose their exceptional jobs. You want them to think that because you command the administration of the mental institutions, you ask that they must give me an innocent young boy out of their institution. And if they do not do that, then someone will capture their children

151

and kill them first, and then they will lose their own life if anyone mentions something to the police about this. You need be authoritative, because you must have the position to cause people to fear for their lives, as if you are god to them."

"I understand," I said. "I am forceful within other administrations, and I know what I have to do in order for it to work. The doctor needs to give an injection of a cocktail to those boys, and their heart will stop working for a few minutes, enough time for another doctor to declare the boy dead. Minutes later, his heart will start working again, but his body will be unable to move. Then, the hospital will call the funeral director, and his employee will drive the body to his funeral parlor. You are going to hijack that body and coerce the funeral director not to tell anybody. You pay extra money for him for go on with the funeral ceremony without a body in the coffin. If the public knew the coffin was empty, they would not care if the boy was an outcast of our society. They would be outraged. But otherwise, they are happy the mental patient is gone because they as citizens pay for the child to live in that mental institution. That's a win-win situation for us!"

"I couldn't have said it better if I tried, but it is going to cost you more: two hundred thousand pounds for one innocent boy."

"I cannot turn it down." I accepted his proposal. It worked perfectly for three years.

One day, my colleague wrote a bill for the UK legislations... bill C-145, I think it was... That bill was going to add a regulation for the ambassadors that live in the UK. If they committed any criminal acts in Great Britain, our judicial system would have the right to sentence that ambassador to prison for his crime.

Mr. Ezajasz heard about that bill. He called me, infuriated, and said, "I am commanding you to annihilate that C-145 bill immediately! If you don't do that, I will expose you for molesting and murdering boys, dismembering them and crushing up their bodies to feed your garden with them! Your good legacy would be all gone, and your corrupt legacy would then start!"

I replied, "Well, well. You sure are in a bitchy mood tonight. You don't remember that you told me about your experiences in the boys' club where you worked? If my legacy comes down, your legacy comes down with mine! Now, can we work together?"

He replied, "I am worried about that bill. I can be volatile and explosive sometimes, but now I am calm."

"Much better," I said. "I have a plan... You need to capture a young boy on the street for me first out, and it must be free. I will handle the rest."

"I do not like anyone pressuring me to do anything, including you, but I am a reasonable man. You stop that bill first, and I will capture two innocent boys for you. It will of course be free!"

I said, "I accept your scheme, although it leaves a bad taste in my mouth."

The next day, I went into my office and talked to Mr. Heddwyn first, since he is the circulator in here. I started a rumor that someone does not like our friend Sir Alban II's bill, C-145, and that this person knows the molester who was raping and murdering the boys in Great Britain. Three years ago, Scotland Yard could not find him. If this bill goes to the queen, then that person will call on the child molester to defile and kill all the children whose parents are working on this Legislature in the Commons and the House of Lords. You can be sure about that.

Mr. Heddwyn walked away from me, and I had a big smile inside of me. I did my job, and now I had only to wait for my rumor to circulate in here, which it did. But Sir Alban, his will is strong. He did not believe my rumor. I asked Mr. Heddwyn and Sir Alban II to play golf with me, because I wanted to talk with Alban II at length, but Mr. Heddwyn did all of talking to Sir Alban.

He told Sir Alban, "I won't back C-145, and I'm afraid the House of Commons does not endorse that bill, either. But you still have time to take your bill off the docket for a third reading in the House of Commons."

To which he said, "I did write a few bills, and they made it to law in Britain. This one will protect many people, but a few people do not like my laws because they are criminals. I keep on writing them anyway, since I am working as a representative of the British people. I do not work on behalf of the malefactors of our country. You are not working for them, either, but you sound like you are."

Mr. Heddwyn replied that everyone was afraid for their own children.

Sir Albin Christopher appeared not to believe it, since he hosted the gala for his C-145 bill. All of the people working in the Commons and the House of Lords came to his gala, as did I. I wanted to see if Sir Albin Christopher worked his political magic on them. He did not have a chance to, because something happened to his boy... I think his boy had a seizure. Too bad. I had talked to him thirty minutes before he had a paroxysm, and I would have loved to be better acquainted with him! A couple weeks later, the C-145 bill came up for Third Reading in The House of Commons, and it did not pass.

Mr. Wehczeslaw Ezajasz was happy about that. A few days after that, I got a call from him. He said, "I have bad news for both of us. My gangsters captured a boy, but he got away from them, and as he was running away from them, a car ran over him. I do not know name of the boy, but I am going to check the newspaper in the morning for his name.

Mr. Ezajasz called early that morning and told me that the name of the boy was Robert Zachary. I said, "This boy is Mr. Heddwyn's grandson! Of all the boys in London they could have captured, they chose the one boy whose grandfather is a colleague of mine, and is the one who started my rumor. Now his grandson is on his deathbed. If Mr. Heddwyn is any kind of man, he realizes I am the notorious child molester of Great Britain. And as he is great talker, if he knows about me, then other people will know about me, and you do not want that."

"If Scotland Yard apprehends me," he replied, "surely I will tell all about you and your hunting of people for your food, and that it's the reason you became the ambassador of Poland. You wanted to be emancipated from your crimes on humanity. If I talk to Scotland Yard, and then they talk with our intermediaries about you, your information will be floating in people's heads. Some people ignore it and keep on living their lives the best they can, but other people will be so angry with you, they will want to kill you, even though by their nature they would not kill a fly. Most people, if they got a chance, would kill you. It will not be pretty."

A week later, I dialed Dr. Fabron Rahman in my tenacious voice and said, "It's me. What do you have for me today?"

"You called the Eastman mental asylum, not a restaurant. You can't order anything here!"

"Don't get smart with me. I realize now that you do not care for your undemanding job. I will take it from you so damned easy and put your life six feet underground faster than the one heartbeat's worth of a second it would take to do that to you! Your children will pleasure me nice and slowly after I finish with them, at which point my friend will take their bodies, cut out their internal organs and place them into the meat grinder. He will grind them into hamburger meat which he will use to prepare dinner. Then he will eat them immediately after they sauté. Alternatively, you can simply give me what I lust after. Do I make myself perfectly clear?"

"Yes, Mr. Fitzgerald, you made this quite clear to me. I have a boy who is the perfect age for you."

"I am not harsh with you when you see things my way. Now...this little boy, what is his name?"

"His name is Sir Alban III."

"Not THE Sir Alban III, son of Sir Albin Christopher?"

"I'm afraid so."

"A rumor has circulated in parliament that his son was killed by a pack of wolves while he hiked north of the York."

There is also a peculiar rumor that began as if someone knew Sir Alban III was still alive, yet they did not want to tell anyone. I know who it is, quite frankly, it is I! I won against Sir Albin Christopher, yet again. I thought about that while I conversed with Dr. Fabron Rahman. I informed him that I want Sir Alban III tonight!

"Does any degree of remorse run in your veins?"

"How very amusing you are. Are you aware that I have lived for many years before you were born? I survived two world wars, and I listened to my father's communication with the presidents. He was forced to fight Germany's military forces. I witnessed details of many killings of these soldiers, their life blood flowing to fend off the German military's world invasion. In addition, by the end of the 1920s, the American stock market crash spiraled despairingly into the worldwide Great Depression. I managed to come out of all of this tragedy as a successful physician. I realize I did not answer your question regarding any remorse from my dealings with children. The answer is, simply put, no. My father did not hold any level of guilty conscience towards me, either. Now, while I don't believe you shall be convinced by me anyway, I accept this with no concern, as I plan to impose my will upon you. If you do not give me Sir Alban III tonight, I will do all I said earlier, and even more than your placid imagination can conjure! Goodbye!"

I telephoned Mr. Wehczeslaw Ezajasz to inform him that the shipment was coming that night. Wehczeslaw replied that he would alert Haritian. I told him, "Tonight will be an exceedingly special night, as I shall call in a reservation to the Landmark Hotel to arrange for a penthouse. If one should be available, I shall meet the package over there."

I anticipated that Sir Alban III would show signs of life after I would gift him a necessary but shocking awakening—he would see me first wearing only my boxers, and then, only then, would I feel in heaven! On the other hand, Alban may be conscious of hell on Earth. I love seeing children feeling that way! I see the emotion in young boys' eyes the first time they gaze upon the devil as me, the moment their frightened eyes realize that this will be the last time they see anyone alive.

As I waited excitedly in the Landmark penthouse, my longing mind conjured all things I could possibly do to him. In anticipation, I waited, waited and waited until they brutally arrived, but without my package! "Damn it!" I implored angrily. "Where is my lovely package?"

His goon responded, "We managed to intercept the hearse, and as we retrieved the coffin, it was heavy. We then placed then coffin into our car and drove to a vacant parking lot, as we do every time. Then we opened the coffin.

We were surprised to discover just some tools inside! We came here to inform you of this, but we have not told our boss."

I called Wehczeslaw right away to give him a piece of my mind. I lifted the phone from its receiver. *"Hello?"* he answered in a bored tone.

"You ignorant bastard!" I screamed angrily. *"You cannot deliver my package? Twice I've waited for my packages only to have them never arrive! I have reserved a penthouse for tonight in which I should be joyfully enjoying my intelligent package. Instead of a young boy for my great pleasure, I received your two gangsters! And please, allow me to disclose the best part: they do not even have the boy! I do not know where Sir Alban III is, but I do know he is not here. That is beyond any shadow of a doubt!"*

Wehczeslaw interjected impatiently, *"Can I talk to Mike?"* I handed off the phone. Mike shared the same story given to me regarding the empty coffin. Mike handed me back the phone. *"I am here, but I believe your guys are telling us a pack of lies!"*

"Can you hold a few minutes?" Wehczeslaw uttered. *"I understand your anger, but we need a cool head as we logically consider this unfortunate situation. Someone placed the tools there in the coffin, and they did so proportionally as if a boy of the same weight were lying inside. Do you think my men are smart enough to consider the level of intelligence required in this plan?"*

"Well, no!" I replied.

"Could this person be a physician or administrative person? Could Fabron Rahman be involved?"

"You think so?" I pondered curiously.

"He has a motive, but my guys do not."

"It is true. He would not want to give up the boy to me, the stupid bastard. His life is going to end in a number of days! Will you capture him and hold him in your barn so that I may torment his body in only the way a mad physician could!?" I angrily implored.

"I will ensure that it will be done in a couple of days. I will call you then."

A few short days later, I commenced to Mr. Wehczeslaw Ezajasz's barn. I did indeed do to Fabron Rahman's body more than a deserving amount of painful excruciation. Finally, I asked, *"If you shall have me cease, you must answer promptly one question: why did you place tools in Sir Alban's III coffin?"*

"I didn't do that!" Dr. Rahman cried. *"I told my head physician to give a shot to Sir Alban III, but he died prior to receiving it. Two doctors made great*

156

attempts to revive him, but it was to no avail. The head doctor then wrote out his death certificate. I know this, as I myself witnessed his death certificate and personally sent it to the registry office in my district. That is the honest truth! Now will you kill me and stop tormenting my body please?"

"I am not finished with your deserving torment, as I am not convinced that you speak the truth. Once more, I repeat that only your truth can stop me," I stated coldly without meeting his pleading gaze. He repeated his story incessantly until finally, his gray ghost left him. I want to believe him, but my primary aggression took over. I never knew if Dr. Rahman told the truth or not. As I exited the barn with his bloody organs splattered across my body, I considered his story. What happened to Sir Alban III? Did he disappear after he died? What happened to his body?

"I finally saw his death certificate in my office, only to realize Dr. Rahman told me the truth regarding the date and time Sir Alban III died. Yet still, I hold no clue as to the whereabouts of his body. Mr. Ezajasz considered the possibility that Sir Albin Christopher somehow found a way to hijack his son, as he did not want people to know his son was alive in Eastman Psychiatric Hospital.

"On the other hand, if Dr. Rahman told them about you and me, then we have a problem again! What do you think about the possibility that perhaps Sir Albin Christopher was responsible for this? If it were not for his boy's body, I would not figure out where the body was located. This possibility is contingent on Sir Albin Christopher being responsible."

Wehczeslaw then replied, "It's so damned easy for a body to evaporate into thin air… you know that already."

"Yes, I definitely know that, but it would be difficult to divide his son's body into nothing at all. Is Sir Albin Christopher a sociopath? Ten years in my past, I knew him. He did not show me one sign of characteristics of the sociopath. I do not think Sir Albin Christopher has done this," I responded.

"I can tell you my fresh proposition about why he may have wanted to destroy his son's body. If you have ever covered a lie, you do everything: cheat, lie, steal and kill. However, he did not kill him. Dr. Rahman told him that you wanted his boy for a sex toy that very night of the boy's death. He then saw his son's lifeless body as he opened his coffin. He thought it could not possibly be real. Over time, he knew his son was really dead, and in that moment he snapped. His unconscious took over his body as he considered his lie of the pack of wolves mutilating his son. As he kept his lie alive, he realized that his lie had turned into a bleak and terrifying truth!" Wehczeslaw explained. "By the way, if Sir Albin Christopher told that lie to me, I think it is a little odd because it is common knowledge that wolves cannot climb trees. In your forest, there are many trees. You told me Sir Alban III was intelligent, and I thought the boy was smart enough to know this. Sir Albin Christopher is not yet talented enough to create believable lies."

"That is a good point, but where did he capture Sir Alban's dead body? The doctor escorted that body to the hearse. The hearse driver ushered Sir Alban's body in until your gangsters apprehended a casket full of tools."

"While this is very true, consider that people are easily able to lose their concentration. Perhaps as the doctor walked to the hearse with the casket, he left the coffin for a few minutes… only a couple of moments would be needed for Sir Albin Christopher to switch an identical casket for another. Sir Alban's dead body lied! Or perhaps you think Sir Alban's body resurrected back to life again, as all of the ministers are saying Jesus did. If you think this is what occurred, I need to make a call to the white coats to take you away to the mental institution," I offered to him without dismay.

"Hold on there. My faculties are quite good, thank you very much! I am convinced that you need to kill Sir Albin Christopher, but I want you do it assassination style, as he requires being in control. During his final breath, he won't be self-disciplined any further. This will cause his hell to confine him considerably longer!"

Chapter Twenty-Six

I put this evil book down and I rubbed my eyes. I was thinking about every detail I had just read, and it made it very hard to have any positive thoughts at all. In a couple of hours, Mr. Fitzgerald and Mr. Ezajasz would have a date with the sunlight. No more hiding. The evidence of their evil deeds right here in my hands was screaming for me to put it out in the light where all could finally see their deeds toward humanity. Only then would the spirits of the innocent children be at peace.

That thought made me happy. Reason for that is, those souls are more powerful than Mr. Fitzgerald and Mr. Ezajasz and the men who worked with them. I looked at my grandfather's watch: the time was 12:07, which meant I only had five minutes to get out of there.

I thought to myself, *Plenty of time left.* I glanced over at his shoebox, and my brain told me not to open it, but I needed to... I reached for it. All of a sudden, I heard someone opening the door to his main office! I quickly picked up the journal and the shoebox, put them back in the safe, and shut the heavy door. I replaced the picture frame silently and calmly. I looked around his office for a place to hide, even as I heard the key hitting the door lock to this room. I went to his coat closet and quickly swung the door closed.

I heard somebody open the door to the adjoining office. They walked in and closed the door. Whoever it was turned on a flashlight. I heard the picture frame swing away from the wall, and then they must have known the combination because the heavy door to Mr. Fitzgerald's safe was being opened. *That person could be Mr. Fitzgerald, and I cannot figure out why he is here.* He walked over to his desk and put something on the desktop. I heard it hit the papers that were on the desk. *Great... Only three minutes left until they throw on the electricity. Wow, what should I do?* My heart was beating so fast that if Mr. Fitzgerald listened hard, he could hear it beating.

I once asked myself what I could do with my life to help out the planet, to propel change for the betterment of society. All of a sudden, I knew what I needed to do, so I took a deep breath! I kicked the closet door down, ran to the desk, pushed Mr. Fitzgerald down into his chair, and pinned both his hands against the arm rests. I was squeezing his bones to death. We looked eye to eye at each other, and he gasped for breath. He said, "You are Sir Alban III?"

I was enraged, and my voice conveyed it. "Yes I am. I assume you are Mr. Fitzgerald, the molester and killer of innocent children around the world! I am disgusted with your old face close to mine! Today, all people on Earth will know your name as the molester of our deprived children! British society will see you put in jail, and the inmates will love you in the same way you loved the innocent children around the world. Too bad I cannot see it happen, but those you murdered will see it, as they go on in peacefulness and tranquility. Reason for that is, the children murdered by you and your friends want justice, they want you to understand suffering as you tormented their little bodies. They want you to feel the same as they felt when you raped them. Also, you put a knife into their necks to cut their carotid arteries. Today is justice day for you, so you get ready. I am kind to you for telling you that, as you did not tell those children you murdered what you wanted to do to them."

"I am not a child molester; I am a physician! I am head of all of the doctors in the United Kingdom because our queen commissioned me to look over our physicians in the British Parliament. That's why I'm here tonight. However, I don't know why you're here tonight!?"

"Mm, mm, mm… How do I explain this to you quickly, as your time as a free man fades away? I have an idea. I will explain it perfunctorily to you, and you will comprehend me. Do you remember when your friends almost captured a boy for you? 'Almost' is the significant word."

Mr. Fitzgerald sat motionless.

"Okay, as you will not respond, I believe you do remember that the boy's name is Robert Zachary. He is my friend. Your friends chased him to a parking lot, and a car hit him and left him unconscious. He is in a coma right now in the basement of the Eastman Hospital. I know this because I was in there. You know that already because you called up Dr. Fabron Rahman for a boy from the Eastman Hospital. He did not want to give a boy to you, but you blackmailed him. Did you tell Mr. Fitzgerald that you were going to sexually molest and murder his children if Dr. Fabron Rahman did not get a boy for you out of that mental institution? Well, he responded to that threat, and the boy he tried to get for you was me! However, I am little smart, as I faked my own death, and that physician thought I died. Reason for that is he gave me the cardio pulmonary resuscitation. He broke a rib and I almost died. He laid me in that coffin, and that driver put the coffin in the hearse with me in it.

"Mr. Ezajasz was wrong. My father did not sign to have my body taken away, and he never would have allowed someone to destroy my body. You and Mr. Ezajasz were mistaken about my father. I do not know why serial killers think that other people think the same way as the killers do, but for some reason, they do. Don't you, Mr. Fitzgerald? Of course, you do. Now where was I... I was inside that hearse. I opened the lid of that coffin quietly, I removed myself from inside it quickly, and I searched around. Did you know that hearses have a trapdoor in the floor in the back? I did not know that until I searched, and that is where I found some tools. I lifted them out, and I put them in that coffin to weigh it down. I hid out in back of the hearse, after I did all that, until the hearse stopped. I heard car doors open and slam—it was one quick motion. I heard two men walk up to the hearse. Your men opened the back of the hearse, and while they pushed that casket out, they talked to each other about Robert Zachary. They said it was very cool to see his head hit the street and described how his brain shattered inside his head!

"When I heard that, my blood was boiling. I hunted you and your gangsters as a lion hunts for his prey. You put it elegantly in your words, in your personal journal, which is on the desktop now. Your chronicle has your actions and thought of substance throughout. You are right. I did read your chronicle. And a few minutes from now, the whole world will know of your evil actions on our society's children. Why I am here tonight? It is the end of your monstrosity over the progeny of Mother Earth, and I am ending it right now!"

He laughed in my face, and then he said, "How old are you, now? About thirteen? There's something about that age. I like you, really I do. Sir Albin Christopher... he really loves you because you are intelligentsia. Nevertheless, you did not think through this predicament you are in now. In less than a minute and a half, parliament's electricity will be back on, and their cameras will be working, too. Parliament's security guards are going to see you running away from my office, and they will call the London police to capture you! All of the people in Britain will see that you're alive, and then people will know that your father told a huge lie. They will not trust Sir Albin Christopher anymore! I see the emotion on your face... I suspect your father doesn't know you're alive! It is wonderful for me that he doesn't know, especially if you get away before parliament's electricity comes on. You have my journal, and I know you won't show it to the police because your father would go to the same jail as me. In my journal is the criminal evidence of your father. Scotland Yard is going to have a field day with your father if they read my journal.

I smiled at him, and then I immediately let go of the chair, grabbed him by his arms and lifted him up sharply to standing position. Quickly, in one motion, I turned him around, yanked both of his wrists to the center of his back, and kicked his knees out from him! He quickly fell to his knees, and I kicked him squarely in the back. I let go of his arms, which barely prevented him from hitting the floor face first. I immediately stepped on him, and his face hit the

161

floor hard. I quickly reached for his phone and dialed Mr. Rockdom. I heard, "Hello?"

"I have an old nasty package here with plenty of stamps. Can you take it to the jail? The package is in Mr. Fitzgerald's office, and his stamps are going be in a chair outside the front door to his office. I'm going to lock the door to his office because I do not want that package to get away from you."

Mr. Rockdom said, "I understand. I am sitting two blocks from the parliament buildings. I waited until you called, but now I am going there at once! You have one minute and forty-three seconds before the electricity is back on in there. If you need to go, it's all right by me."

I dropped the phone receiver onto his desk, picked up his journal and shoebox, and shifted my weight onto the one placed in Mr. Fitzgerald's back. Then, I ran to the door. I turned around to face him, and he started to get up... I said to him, "By the way! You wrote in your journal that the evidence against my father is circumstantial. You have a nice night!"

I opened the door and shut it behind me. I put his things on the secretary's chair, turned on my flashlight, and jammed the back of it under the doorknob. I sealed his fate, as he had done to countless innocent children around the world. If I could see the innocent children in spirit, they would all be smiling right now. My heart was beating happily.

I ran to the other door, threw it open, and ran like lightning through the hall full of the rich history of England. With each step I took, I went faster! My beam of light was cavorting around the historic artifacts that made England what it is. Right then, what Mr. Fitzgerald had done in parliament did not hurt. He stained our history a little bit for a while, but after some time, England will be a little bit stronger. Mr. Fitzgerald did hurt families, but most of all, he hurt our world's environment. I think all people affect the world's ecosystem, both good and bad, but if men kill as Mr. Fitzgerald did, then they are not living as intended: they become malfeasant of all humanity. I believe that it is true.

I skidded to a stop at the elevator and took a few deep breaths. I pulled its doors open and jumped! My hands grabbed hold of the large cables, and it ran between my legs as I slid down almost as fast as free falling. Then I squeezed my legs together against the cables, which acted as a brake, and I stopped just above the elevator's large, steel pulley. I jumped off, and my feet landed on top of the elevator's roof. I stumbled but got my balance back quickly! I opened up the trapdoor in the elevator ceiling, jumped down into the elevator, and placed my fingers between the two door panels. I noticed my left hand was bleeding, but I ignored it. With all of my force, I pulled both sides apart to break the first seal. I needed to break the other seal, and with all of my might, I actually opened the door. I squeezed through the small opening and ran through the basement. I tore my left sleeve out as I ran, and I put it on the deep laceration on the inside of my left hand. I wrapped it around tightly to stop the bleeding! It was not stopping my hemorrhage though… blood was flowing into my makeshift bandage. I made a tight fist out of desperation, knowing I lost precious seconds by wrapping my hand up.

I went through the double doors, and I remembered this hall. About ninety feet away from me was the other door, and on the other side of that were the stairs down to the bomb shelter. In a blur, I sped across the hall and opened that door up. I leaped down the stairs rapidly and nimbly, with my beam of light searching for the other door I needed to go through.

I found that door and on the other side was parliament's Westminster bomb shelter. Frightened people had gathered there in the 1940s. My light hit the fans, and I saw that they were not working, and that was a good thing. They had not thrown the electricity on yet. I ran up to the door and pushed in the code on the keypad. My watch said it was 12:02 and thirty-five seconds… I took few deep breaths, and I closed this heavy door behind me. I flat-out ran through the enormous tube underneath the Thames River. The middle of this tunnel does not have enough air to keep a bug alive. Nevertheless, I needed to go through it anyway.

As I neared the middle of this tunnel, its dead air encompassed me. The air going into my lungs did not have enough oxygen, and the cells through my body were burning from an insufficient amount of it. I knew I must moderate my heart rate while running hard because I did not want my brain and my legs to fail me. I felt my heart racing for the lack of good oxygen. I could not faint and die in here! I tried to moderate my heart, and I slowed down my heart little bit, but not enough. I felt my brain become deprived of oxygen… my mind was going dim. I heard the Thames River… it was surrounding me… but I knew it was in my mind! I had to reach the other door and unlock it as fast as possible. I needed to climb up that ladder… and only then I would breathe some good oxygenated air.

Wait… there it was. I saw the door dead ahead, about thirty feet away from me! I could not feel my legs at all, but I was running normally, and finally I reached that door. But faced with the keypad, I realized I could not recall the code for unlocking this door. I needed to remember that code! In a split second, the right cells in my brain with some good oxygen remaining pulled up the right numbers! I pushed the code into the number pad, and as I pushed last number, I exhaled what I hoped was the last thin breath of the night.

I felt a reverberation as the machine came on, and I saw the megalithic rusty arm move the heavy thick metal door above me. I saw my first glimpse of a lovely raining night! Good air rushed in, and I started to climb the disintegrating ladder. With each step I took, I breathed damp, cold, fresh oxygen into my lungs, and my blood cells came alive again! I reached top of the ladder, and I climbed out of the copper box and crawled onto the lawn for about ten feet. I heard the metal door close behind me, and immediately after that, the electricity in the parliament buildings went on, both inside and outside, and I saw the police's red and blue lights flashing into the dark sky at the parliament's parking lot. I heard the ambulance's siren, and I knew then it was there, too. I crawled onto the sidewalk and sat there because I needed my blood cells to recharge with good oxygen. I turned my face toward parliament and the Thames River, which was flowing red and blue as police lights surrounded it. It seemed to me that this river flowed underneath the House of Parliament.

***

The Thames had flowed aside British Parliament for many years before this night, and in my heart, I knew the Thames was touching it lightly. They will see it in generations to come as I see it tonight, but I hoped without red lights flickering on the water. Our United Kingdom will go on forever, and this situation won't prevent this country from going forward. Not at all.

My blood cells recovered. My lungs filled up with a lot of good, fresh air, and oxygen rushed through me like a freight truck out of control. I tried to get up to a standing position, but I was still weak in the legs. I walked slowly to St. Thomas Hospital, which was not far from where I stood.

I walked into the hospital and saw the Information Desk in the lobby. "Can you tell me where to find the coffee shop?" The nondescript woman behind the counter pointed me to the left. It was right there down the hall, and I thanked the lady and walked to it. I saw Aaron in back of this coffee shop, facing the wall. A couple seconds later, my bleeding hand touched his back and startled him. He said, "Look out, man," and he looked at me. Then he smiled and said, "Hey, did you catch that child molester? I know you did because I heard sirens across the river just after midnight. Did you have any problem catching that S.O.B?"

I sat down and started to tell Aaron about what happened just a few minutes earlier, but Aaron interrupted me. "What happened to your left hand?"

"I slid down the elevator's steel cables and slit my hand open. I ignored it because I needed to get outside the parliament building before they powered on the electricity. You know that already."

Aaron took off my shirtsleeve bandage that was drenched in my own blood. My hand was throbbing in pain. He said, "My God—I need to suture up this laceration. You need it quickly. I know you're thinking about how the physician and nurses will need your personal information, but we are in my town. These days, every hospital is its own town. They need the physicians and nurses to run them, and I am almost a physician. Come with me."

I wrapped my hand again, made a fist, and followed him through the lobby. We walked toward the emergency room, and a few seconds later, we opened the large double doors and walked right into the middle of the emergency room. A lot of nurses, physicians, and a few the residents were hustling and bustling around here, but we went directly to the main desk. Aaron interrupted a nurse who was talking to another nurse and told them, "I am a doctor from Stratford-on-Avon. I saw this boy hurt in the middle of the street, and I examined him. He has a large laceration inside his left hand. I need to stitch it up for him now!"

The older nurse said, "How can we trust your story? Do you have a physician's license?"

"Of course, I do, but it is in my car. Do you want me tell you the numbers from my medical license?"

"Yes, that would be fine."

Aaron gave her some random numbers. "Can I help this young man before he bleeds to death, while you check out my medical license?!"

"Yes, of course, doctor." She told other nurse to get the sterile sutures, and she took us directly to their cubicle. A couple minutes later, the nurse gave Aaron the sutures.

He put my left hand in the tray with my palm up, unwrapped my blood-soaked shirt sleeve again and asked me, "Do you want me to numb it up for you?"

"No thanks."

He whispered, "Okay." It was time to get it over with quickly. Aaron started to sew up my wound, and the pain was rushing through my body as a tsunami would rush into the coast!

A young nurse asked me, "What happened to your left hand?"

I opened my eyes at her, and using my most refined British accent, I said, "Well, I was walking around in the parliament square, when I stumbled and I caught myself with my hands. My left hand caught on a sharp rock and started bleeding, so I quickly tore my left sleeve out and wrapped it around my palm. Immediately after that, this gentleman saw me on the ground, and fortunately he is a physician. He looked at my wound and told me to go to this hospital. I did not want to go to a hospital, but he persisted and talked me into it, only because he told me he would take care of it himself. My skin feels like someone's sewing a quilting patch out of my hand." Aaron raised his eyebrow at me. I smiled sideways at him with a glance, and I asked this young nurse, "May I ask you a question?"

She said, "Yes. I like your sophisticated British accent! Shoot away!"

"How long have you worked here as a nurse?"

"Actually, I have only been a nurse for three days. I graduated from nursing school, and my mother works here as a nurse, so she got me a job here. I like it so far because I love to help people in their hour of need. Most of all, the emergency room needs to know as soon as possible when a bad case is arriving by ambulance. While I was getting the sterile sutures for you, I overheard our dispatcher communicating with the driver of the ambulance. The driver said, 'My helper and I are in the British Parliament right now, with five police officers. The assistant commissioner is with us. A police officer told me this crime scene was little strange because the door was blocked with a chair holding a logbook and a little box. Inside the office, the commissioner had hung himself from the ceiling. The assistant commissioner has his logbook, and the other officers are searching for any evidence that this may not be a suicide. His body is going to come there after the officers search his office.'"

Aaron started to tie a knot in the suture. I looked at my six stitches, and they were tiny. I told Aaron he did great job. He said, "My hobby is quilting!" Aaron smiled and wrapped gauze around my hand. When he had finished, he added, "We have to go right now, quickly!" His eyes pointed to the front desk, where an older nurse was on the phone. I knew what he was getting at. Immediately, we jumped to our feet, and I thanked the young nurse for talking to us, but this physician had to leave, and so did I.

She asked me if I had a ride all the way back to Stratford-on-Avon. I said, "I am staying at my friend's apartment these days."

She reached into her pocket to get a card, and she wrote her number on it. "Call me." I thanked her and put the card in my pocket.

Aaron and I walked quickly through the large double doors just as the ambulance stopped in front of the emergency room. I stopped to watch the ambulance driver and his helper as they opened the rear doors and pulled out the gurney. On it was Mr. Fitzgerald's body. Even though it was covered, his hand had dropped below the white sheet covering his body. Mr. Fitzgerald's spirit had now taken up residence in a new realm, and his soul would now stay forever in darkness! I knew that what he did to innocent children around the world was going to be heard about and read about today in the media. They will be talking about him around the world and describing what he and Mr. Wehczeslaw Ezajasz and his friends had done. I thought, *That is a good thing.* The driver and his helper pulled the gurney through the double doors into the emergency room, and the doors closed unceremoniously behind them.

Aaron tugged at my coat and whispered, "Let's go." I nodded my head, and we walked to his bike.

Suddenly, we heard the older nurse shouting through the double doors at the security guard. "Arrest that man with that boy—they are right there at the end of the parking lot! He was impersonating a physician!"

We took off running toward Aaron's bike. He jumped on first and started it up, and I jumped on behind him. As soon as my feet were off the ground, we took off fast. Our clothes got drenched by the time we were a mile down the road. I told Aaron, "I don't think that guard had time to see your license plate." He nodded his head. All of sudden, I got a warm feeling, and I thought, *My grandfather is joyful in nirvana with the children who suffered the loss of their lives and dreams by the hands of Mr. Fitzgerald and his friends. My grandfather is playing with them and they are running around in heaven in euphoria.*

I needed to know that. At the same time, I felt sad that Mr. Fitzgerald's life was cruel. Because what parents teach their children becomes integrated in their young minds, and then they grow up to imitate their parents' actions in some way. In Mr. Fitzgerald's life, his father molested him repeatedly, and after his father died, he continued raping him through the feelings his father had caused to fester in him. Nevertheless, Mr. Fitzgerald did not have the right to rape and massacre innocent children around the world and destroy their lives and dreams. My grandfather said, "You reap what you sow," and that is the best metaphor for what is happening to his life.

We stopped at Della's apartment sopping, dripping, wringing wet again. I asked Aaron, "What you have planned for tomorrow?"

"What normal people do... they go to work." I smiled at that. Aaron asked me the same question.

I said, "Well, I will wake up, hope my name is not in the newspapers, and then I will figure out how to tell all of the children's families who the murderer was and what happened to them. I have to tell them they could not have prevented that incident! So, a day not like a normal person's."

Aaron smiled at me and said, "You're not a normal person."

I said, "Everyone I meet says that. I do not know why! Reason for that is I put on my pants same as all people do... one leg a time." Aaron laughed out loud! I continued, "What are you laughing about? Surely not me..." I smiled at him. "Okay, I need to get out the rain now because my left hand is wet and hurting a little bit."

Aaron asked me if Della had any gauze. "I do not know, but I will find something else if she does not have it."

Aaron said, "I know that only you could find something better than gauze."

"Can you drop by Robert Zachary's room and visit him? I also need to go visit with him. Maybe I can go spend time with him tonight."

Aaron swung his leg over his bike again and said, "I'll do that at my lunch break." I nodded. He started the engine and said, "I'll see you later," and he sped off through the driving rain.

Chapter Twenty-Seven

I walked in the entrance to the Berkeley Hotel and I saw the towels for the use of residents and guests if they got wet in the rain. I went over and I dried my long, wet hair the best that I could with only one hand to work with. I blotted my clothes and put the wet towels in the big can. Then I walked over to the elevator and pushed the up arrow. It opened right away, and I was soon rising smoothly to the level of Della's apartment. I walked down the hall to her apartment at the other end, took off my shoes and put them on the doorstep. I searched my pocket for her key and then turned it quietly in the lock. Tacitly I stepped through her kitchen and den. Her Persian carpet felt great between my toes, and I felt safe.

Della was lying down on her sofa. "Hello," she said, "and thank you for taking off your shoes. I don't want to read the newspaper this morning... I would rather have you enlighten me on what's on the front page!"

"Okay, now after all this, you are interviewing me? Are you going to call it in to the newspaper office?"

Laughing, she replied, "I have to get my money wherever I can! But what happened to your left hand, there?"

"Do you have any gauze in your apartment?"

"Yes, I do. It's in my guest bathroom, in the third cabinet to the right of the sink."

While I fixed up my hand, I told her about my dealings with Mr. Fitzgerald, and how I discovered that he was the molester we had been looking for, and how he had been perpetrating crimes for about forty years. The police in each country did not know about it because he visited impoverished towns in countries around the world.

"I do not know how, but the queen placed Mr. Fitzgerald in the role of Commissioner of Hospitals and General Registers. The queen's staff went through his history with a fine-toothed comb—they did not find out that his father molested him habitually, or that he made trips each month to poor towns in other countries. For ten years, he had stopped violating children, but after that, he met Mr. Ezajasz, and their evil spirits clicked. Mr. Wehczeslaw Ezajasz talked Mr. Fitzgerald into resuming the molestations, but this time getting the boys from the mental institutions. Fitzgerald had power over all of the hospitals, and Ezajasz promised to dispose of the bodies for him. You know rest of this story now. I am so tired… I will go to bed without further ado, and I will see you later this morning." I moved to get up from my chair and head down the hall.

But before I could leave the room, Della asked me, "Where is Mr. Fitzgerald at the present time?"

"I think he's in the morgue. Mr. Fitzgerald committed suicide a few minutes after I left his office and locked him inside."

Della saw the disturbed look on my face and asked me, "Do you feel like you caused Fitzgerald to commit suicide?"

I reflected for a few moments, then replied, "I have mixed emotions. I am happy he is gone because his actions caused too many young lives to end, but those spirits are delighted now because he got the justice he deserved. Yet, I think about his life, and I wonder, if my father had done to me as Fitzgerald's father did to him, would I have acted in just the same way?"

Della said, "You sit down by me. Individuals have the right to think uniquely and act on their ideas. Most people do that, and they do it in right ways. People have the right to choose. We saw that in history in 1774, when the forefathers of America, the leaders of the thirteen colonies, rejected the legitimacy of parliament to govern them without representation. In 1775, they organized a boycott of British goods.

"They were ignored by the British soldiers that were barracked in Boston, but by later that year, the Provincial Congresses had formed the Second Continental Congress and authorized a Continental Army. Additionally, the Congress announced them traitors and the states to be in rebellion. The Americans responded in 1776 by formally declaring their independence as one new nation—the United States of America—claiming their own sovereignty and rejecting any allegiance to the British monarchy. The founding fathers of America chose rightly to choose freedom in that new country."

I asked her, "But those forefathers had the slaves, is that correct?"

"Yes, nobody is perfect. Those men thought of a perfect idea in spite of the fact that they had the slaves, and across the pond, that decision has blood stains on it even now. History has abominable people, too, like Napoleon Bonaparte, and in this century, Adolf Hitler. They are two of many throughout the ages. I could not speak of all of them because I would be talking to you about them for five days straight. The individuals need to choose a path, whether morally correct or diabolical. Most people choose a path somewhere between good and evil. Mr. Fitzgerald chose a right path for about thirty years, but after that, he chose to become his father and pursue a straight path to nothingness—his choice! If my mother and I didn't take an hour per day to learn when I was young, I wouldn't have known how to read so well, and I liked to read to my mother. My mom and I knew reading would be important to my future. If I didn't love to read, I wouldn't be in here in this rich hotel, and I would never have taught you. I was definitely on the right path.

"You are a fine young gentleman," she continued. "You knew how to sort out the evidence of the two diabolical killers. Scotland Yard didn't discover one of the killers, but you hunted them both down for the whole of humanity, for you wanted everyone to be safe. I know you did it for Robert Zachary and for what those evil men did to him, but you also did it for the whole world! I say thank you from all of lost children and their parents. Your grandfather smiles down from the heavens at you because you have his wit and intelligence. I've talked enough at you for this morning. You go to bed."

I kissed Della's forehead, whispered, "Thank you!" and walked to the bedroom.

Later that morning, the smell of warm bagels and hot steamy cream cheese enveloped my nose and hit my brain like drumsticks on a drum set! I did not want to open my eyes, but I did. I looked at my grandfather's watch… It said eleven o'clock in the morning, and my stomach was grumbling. I eventually did get up and put my clothes on. I walked out of my bedroom toward the warm bagels and the cream cheese, and Della looked at me. I answered her, "I know." I walked to her guest bathroom and washed my hands and face, then walked back to the table where all kinds of newspapers from around the world were displayed.

Della said, "I went over to the news stand across the street. I do it every morning, but this morning I looked at the headlines of all of the newspapers. They all said, 'The infinite molester was in our British Parliament.' Another one said, 'Forty years he molested and murdered boys in destitute countries while working in parliament.' I picked up another newspaper, and their headlines said, 'Two killers of children captured in the United Kingdom: The ambassador for Poland and a member of British Parliament.' The article went on to say that Fitzgerald hung himself before the assistant commissioner and his bobbies broke into his office to arrest him. I picked up another newspaper from Austria, and their headlines said that the British police have the serial killers of many children, plus one killer's diary."

Della continued, "I saw your father on BBC this morning, earlier in the coffee shop. I buy my coffee there every morning. I watched him, and he said that he wrote the bill C-145. It was the bill to allow Great Britain's judicial system to be able to prosecute any ambassador to the maximum that the law would allow for criminal acts against our citizens. This bill did not pass, as a consequence of a nasty rumour that was traveling through parliament at the same time his bill went to the Third Reading in the House of Commons. They wouldn't vote on it in the House of Lords. The interviewer said to your father, 'That rumor… What did it mean when you heard it?' He told the man he felt that his bill C-145 was not going to pass on to the House of Lords because everyone in the House of Commons was concerned about their children and families. If the bill passed, they believed that someone would capture their children and murder them. He confessed to lying about you and how you died. He had told the British people that his son Alban ran away deep in the forest and pack of wolves tore into his body and ate him. That is prevarication; he explained why he reported that, and it was on the grounds that he needed to hide his act of putting his only son in the Eastman Hospital. He said yes, that is right, he put him into that mental institution. He did it to protect his son from this molester, and he told them he was working entirely for the British citizens. He would not back down from anyone, and surely not the criminals. However, that killer got his innocent boy and he perished in that mental institution. Now he must deal with it for the rest of his life. Then the interview was over."

Della looked at me as a mother looks at their child. Her gaze could burn a hole through any untruth! She asked me, "Do you know why your father put you in the Eastman Hospital? I think you do because you read your father's journal. I know your father wrote about his feelings surrounding putting you in the Eastman Hospital, and you read it." Her brown eyes wouldn't let me go.

I waited couple of moments before speaking. "You are correct. I knew why my father put me in that hospital. I love my father, but I do not want other people to know that I apprehended Mr. Fitzgerald and Mr. Ezajasz and his gang. That is just the way I am. If I go back to live there, my father will realize I was involved in capturing the serial killers… and Mr. Rockdom, he knows about me too. They would tell the rest of the world. Anyway, my father would not like telling the British people that he lied again. I think my future is better off if I leave here."

"If your decision comes from not liking your family, just know that your grandfather ran away from his home at about your age. He had a great life while helping humanity the same way you did. So have you arrived at your decision?" Della waited for my answer.

"Well, I love my parents. And you are right about my grandfather. I want to go now, but I am worried about Robert. Who would look after Robert? You told me Mr. Rockdom would, and it would be amazing if life would work out, but only if the people let it, huh, Della?"

She swallowed hard and told me, "That's accurate, but it's a cruel world out there. You saw it in Mr. Fitzgerald and Wehczeslaw Ezajasz and their deeds! What happens if my ticker stops working in Berkeley? That would be a big problem for you because you don't have friends over there. Across the pond they have different laws for minors. You know that already. I know you could handle it, even as the young person you are. But you would be all alone there! Do you think you could manage it?"

I smiled a little bit, and I told Della, "You are Plymouth Rock and your ticker is like the minerals that formed it: they will not give up without a good fight!" Della smiled. I said, "Yes, I could manage it, but it will not happen."

"Okay then," she said, "your identification card and passport will be ready tomorrow morning. You get ready to leave here on early Wednesday morning. I'll call Mr. Rockdom and tell him I'm going to leave here on Wednesday and ask if he can watch over Robert Zachary for me. I'll tell him I promised that if anything happened to you, I would take care of Robert, and I'll confirm that unfortunately you had died and I need to go to the U.S. I'll ask if he'll look in on him frequently because he's been unconscious for a long time, thanks to Mr. Fitzgerald and his gangs, and I'll tell him they also killed you. I know he'll want to do that for me." Then she saw the look on my face, and said, "Alex what is wrong?"

"Nothing at all." I walked over to the kitchen sink and filled a glass of water and drank it down. I told Della, "There are two things I have to do before I leave here. One is I have to figure out how to tell those families! I have to tell them that Mr. Fitzgerald killed their children, but that they could never have prevented it! I promised all of the spirits that I would do that, and I need to do that for them."

Della smiled at me and said, "Look on this table. What do you see? I see many newspapers from around the world…53 of them…but do you not realize how many copies each one of these cities printed? I speculate 150,000 copies each. Do you know what the grand total is?"

"Of course, I do. It is seven million, nine hundred fifty thousand."

"I told you, you are smarter than the average bear! Then, normally, two readers per newspaper…that is fifteen million, nine hundred thousand people, and that's only for these particular cities represented here on my table. Those spirits, they told you about their parents, but I think they didn't mean that you needed to go to each family to tell them they could not prevent their child from being murdered. I think those spirits meant for you to solve the mystery and for the media around the world to do the rest! I love your heart. You are young, brave and sharp-witted, but you are wrong this time. All of the wars in history were caused by one thing, and do you know what that one thing is?"

"Yes, but I do not mistrust the media," I said. "They will tell all the people in the world, but they will only listen if they want to hear about it. I am concerned about whether there is a family living somewhere remote where they do not get any outside information."

"That could happen, but you are Alex, not God. You wouldn't have any way to find them. I'm trying to say that you solved a large problem in the world, and you must let other people do the rest."

"Maybe so."

"What date is today?" she said as she grinned at me. "I want to write on my calendar that I was right one time when it came to you."

We were both smiling, and Della said, "Okay then, I'll call up Mr. Rockdom."

I walked over to the sofa and watched the Thames from her picture window, vigorously flowing down its embankments. It flowed down this channel eons ago before the Cro-Magnon and the Neanderthals lived on Europe's soils. Then as time passed, the Neanderthals went extinct. Reason for that is they did not adapt to the dreadful climate change that the Cro-Magnons did. The Cro-Magnons evolved into modern Homo sapiens, and today's humans have Cro-Magnon genes in their gene pool. The Cro-Magnon and the Neanderthals could see the Thames River rushing down its embankments forty-five thousand years before me. Part of my genes are the Cro-Magnons' genes... I felt goosebumps on my arm. I watched the Thames rushing down its channel just like the Cro-Magnon did, and they can see it now through my eyes. Suddenly, Della scared me and I jumped.

"Are you all right? I'm sorry I scared you. What were you thinking about?"

"Well... nothing really."

"Come on, I don't believe that!"

I walked over to her picture window and told her, "I watched the river go by, and I was thinking about the Cro-Magnon and the Neanderthals living during the same period, but one died off completely and the Cro-Magnon are living through the European people even now. They are living all around the world.

"And with today's technology, it only takes the push of one button to exterminate a lot of cultures in one moment and to change the world's environment for at least a thousand years or more."

Della sat down on the sofa and whispered to herself, "I had to ask!" She said, "Sit down by me. It's very true that the nuclear bombs are a threat to be the end of the human race."

"I said that because I think it will never happen that way," Della continued. "Actually, the people who want to use the nuclear bombs already know their level of destruction. In 1941, Franklin D. Roosevelt was president of the United States of America. He had a mess on his hands at that time. He was concerned about Germany's attack on Poland in 1939 and that Adolf Hitler wanted the rest of the European countries, as he considered them to be his. Meantime, in the Pacific, the Japanese looked across the ocean to the Hawaiian Islands. The Japanese thought that the USA would be too busy with the situation with Germany, so they could easily attack the Hawaiian Islands. On December 7, 1941, they bombed Pearl Harbor. The next day, Franklin D. Roosevelt gave the famous speech to the American Congress that he declared war on the Japanese empire. He also announced war on Germany."

"Hey, a side note about the two world wars," I said. "Good technologies came out of them too. The technology that came from the First World War was the aircraft. I know that the Wright brothers brought the airplane into existence in 1903, but within ten years other countries in the world took notice—surely they knew this invention would be good for war. They knew ahead of the First World War. In World War II, most countries used aircraft in fighting. The technologies at that time were radar, increased speed, and aircraft carriers that allowed takeoff in the middle of an ocean. The military needed to know where their airplanes were at all times, so they used radar to put out radio signals to determine the range, altitude, direction, or speed of both moving and fixed objects, such as the aircraft or their ships. The radar dish would broadcast pulses of radio waves which would bounce off any object in their path, and those objects would return a tiny part of the wave's energy. However, one of the most dramatic single medical advances was probably the widespread use of penicillin. Many other great technologies came out the wars, too!"

"Okay, back to the nuclear bombs," Della said. "I forget where I left off.... Franklin D. Roosevelt had two wars to deal with on opposite ends of the country. He then had a larger problem, since the scientists in Germany discovered the nuclear reaction caused by either fission or a combination of fission and fusion. They needed two kinds of isotopes: uranium and plutonium. Uranium, which is fissionable by fast neutrons and is 'fertile'—meaning that it can be transmuted to fissile plutonium in a nuclear chain reaction. This generates the heat in a nuclear reaction.

"Here's my example," Della continued. What if you could put a couple of the sun's atoms, which have a conjugal bond, in one half of a bottle and two atoms of something else in the other half of a bottle? The other side of this bottle has two of darkness's atoms—I know darkness does not have any atoms, but my example does. The darkness atoms do not like having a conjugal bond to other atoms, and so between them is a barrier. It would take a powerful force in that bottle to take the barrier away, and let's say that happened. It would be so forceful that each sun atom achieved a conjugal bond together with a darkness atom due to the forcefulness. The sun's atom would not mind it all, but the darkness atom certainly would! They would then travel faster and faster around the sun atom's nucleus, while the darkness atom would just want to get away. It would go around the sun atom's nucleus a million miles per minute, and every minute that went by, that atom would double its speed and generate so much heat, it would cause an atomic explosion.

"As luck would have it," she said, "these scientists brought into existence the fission and fusion of uranium and plutonium. They were German scientists, and I thank God Adolf Hitler didn't get his hands on this technology. We can thank Franklin D. Roosevelt, who heard about these scientists and their discovery and ordered that they be captured. They apprehended only one scientist, and the Soviet Union also captured one or more of those scientists... that was another problem the American government had to deal with later. Roosevelt had brought back a head scientist from that group, and I wonder how he did that. I wonder how Adolf Hitler felt when he heard that two other countries had apprehended his 'ace in the hole' and his chance to rule the world had gone to waste. I think he probably could have taken over a large part of the world, and I know that thought is frightening, but it didn't happen because smart men did intelligent things! I know they did some illegal things, but they saved the world. Also, you did some illegal things too. You broke into the UK's Parliament building, but you needed to do that to protect the innocent from evil. You and those who helped you really did save the people.

"It can be difficult to make decisions to help your people," she continued. "America kept fighting in the Pacific for five years or longer, as FDR contemplated how to end World War II in that region. He knew he must give the command to drop an atomic bomb over Japan, but he still sat on that decision for twenty-two days. He made the tactical choice to drop an atomic bomb on Hiroshima, Japan at 8:15 a.m. on August 6, 1945, and another atomic bomb three days later on Nagasaki. This resulted in the deaths of approximately 200,000 Japanese people... mostly civilians. Their blood is stained on the flag of the United States of America forever, regrettably. I know FDR made the right choice at that time, though. He knew the power of the technology. In the wrong hands, the atomic bombs could have mostly wiped out human existence from the Earth for a thousand years or more.

"I see it like this," I said. "Franklin D. Roosevelt knew Joseph Stalin of the Communist Party of the Soviet Union. Stalin had this dangerous new technology in his evil hands, and Roosevelt knew Stalin would use it when the

Soviet scientists discovered the powerful potential of uranium and plutonium. FDR agreed to drop atomic bombs on Japan because everyone knew what this technology looked like. I think one component of FDR's decision to be the first to drop the atomic bombs was that he wanted everyone to know that their leaders had started to develop powerful technology like fission and fusion. It was a message for all people needed to stop their curiosity about nuclear weapons with the understanding that if any leader of any country dropped a nuclear weapon somewhere, it would affect the entire planet. It would look like hell on Earth."

"After America dropped the atomic bombs," Della said, "a new era began. People wanted political diplomacy and there was a new push toward war against totalitarian political regimes. The Cold War is going on even now, and it's 1973. Twenty-eight years after fateful day on August 6, 1945, we can still see that most wars in the world have American involvement. Even now, the USA is fighting in the Vietnam conflict. But no leader would drop the atomic bombs after that because they knew that the technology would eventually be advanced. The fission and fusion was no exception, and today an atomic bomb could be a hundred times more powerful than in 1945."

"But," I said, "if some leader launched an atomic missile to anywhere, what would that leader gain from that? He would not gain that land for over a thousand years because of the radiation. Air that is full of radiation would move out across the rest of the planet, and the rest of the people then would have to live underground. That leader would have to live underground, too, in order to survive, and in doing so, lose his own freedom."

Della said, "Yes, but the President of United States of America does have a bunker underground somewhere in the middle of Nebraska. Some leaders know far in advance of a launch of their atomic missile. He dug out his home underground before that happened. The Soviet Union's Nikita Khrushchev, I think, dug out his home before he put atomic missiles on Cuba aimed toward America. And John F. Kennedy's administration was exceptionally diplomatic. They learned quickly, thanks to 1960–1963 when they had four crises right after another."

Della and I talked about John F. Kennedy and his presidency. We talked about that for hours.

I looked up to the clock, and I saw that the time was 7 p.m. I told Della, and she was shocked at how late in the day it was.

"Are you hungry? I am sorry, I lost track of time. I don't like living in Britain because I can't see the sun. Most of the time it's dark and raining... I met my soulmate right here. He and I got married at the St. Mary Woolnoth Church in London. I want to be buried beside the man I loved. I hate this place, but I do not want to leave, either. Well, that's life. But this time I talked too much... I need to call up room service for some dinner for us."

I went to the bathroom to change the gauze on my left hand, and I saw that my wound had swollen up a little bit around the stitches, but only a little bit, so I cleaned that area and bandaged it up with new gauze. I walked back out into the hallway and saw Della get off the phone with room service. She said, "In a few minutes they will come with cottage cheese pie and a hot biscuit."

Suddenly, her phone rang again, and it was Aaron. Della handed me the receiver and I said, "Hello! It is the coffee beans special house! I will take your order!"

He said, "Very funny! I'm working a double shift over here. Do you want to come by and see Robert tonight?"

"Yes, I would like to. I will come by about nine o'clock."

"Okay, then I will unlock that door for you. I have to go now. I will see you later."

I hung up the phone, and about twenty minutes later a hotel server was ringing Della's doorbell. She pulled open the door, and as it moved, the air filled the entryway with the lovely smell of food. It stirred my appetite, and I quickly set the table up the correct way. Della and I sat down and started to eat. She asked me about my hand, and I reported a slight soreness and swelling.

"Aaron told me my hand was going to be this way for a few days. I only need to clean it every time I change the gauze. Oh, by the way, I need to buy some gauze for you because I used your last roll."

"You do not have to buy it. I want to buy the gauze for you in the morning."

I said okay. The clock said 8:36 p.m. I quickly drank a glass of water, picked up my plates and the glass and washed them at the sink. I turned around and said, "I was supposed to meet Aaron around nine o'clock so I can see Robert one last time. I know you want to see him."

Della stood up and hugged me. She said, "You feel like while your best friend is in his persistent vegetative state, you cannot help him. I know you're thinking about going on with your life while Robert remains in PVS. You feel guilty about enjoying yours to the fullest! I felt the same way when my husband died suddenly. That is life and history, and we have to live with it. You read lots of history books... Did you think about those people as being real and living and dying, being mourned by their loved ones, just as we do?"

"Although Robert is a little bit different—he is alive, and Robert's body is trying to revive his brain cells right now—in time Robert will do it!"

"True, but Robert won't ever be same as before. You know that already. Robert wants you to have a bright life... do you remember that?"

"Yes, I remember that, okay Mother?"

Della's eyes sparkled when I called her mother, and in an instant, it was gone. I immediately said to her, "I meant Della." I looked at the clock and said, "I have to go right now." I got my rain coat and put it on, then walked to her door. Della called me back as she walked toward me.

"You won't get far without any money." She handed me 12 pounds, which I put in my pocket. I smiled at her and closed the door behind me.

Chapter Twenty-Eight

I hurried down the hall to the elevator, but I saw the stairwell and rushed down the stairs instead. I failed to remember, though, that Della's apartment was on the 25th floor. After a long time listening to my heart beating and the *tap-tap-tap* of my feet hitting the steps, I opened the door to the lobby, out of breath. I walked through the large and elegant lobby and exited through the front doors, ran toward a taxi cab, and got inside. I told the driver where I wanted to go, and we drove off. London, England, is so full of bright lights that I felt safe and sound. I remember when my grandfather sent me letters using symbols from Sumerians, Assyrians and Babylonians to tell me what he was doing, and he was so happy sometimes. Reason for that is he felt like the world was safer after he finished an assignment. That is exactly how I felt, too.

My father's voice was talking on the cab radio. "Turn up the volume, please!" I could hear my father clearly, and it seemed to me he was giving an interview.

"This tragedy at the British Parliament looms over Great Britain... My co-worker has done atrocious, unthinkable things around the world and in our own country to families' children while he worked in parliament. Last night, Mr. Rockdom and his informant discovered evidence that the evil men are Mr. Fitzgerald and Mr. Wehczeslaw Ezajasz, including others comprising a small gang of thugs. This informant is intelligent enough to have found them, even as our police and Scotland Yard didn't know who the murderers were or where our children's bodies went. This informant knew who and where, and he is intelligent enough to have figured out how to capture these two men and their gang. If that brilliant informant watches me or listens to me on the radio, then I tip my hat to that informant, as do all of the citizens of our country. I tip my hat to you Sir.

"I do not give interviews... you know that already. But I asked the spokesman from the British Parliament to give me one interview, and this is it... because I know how those families feel. The British people heard the rumor about my son... that he ran away into the deep forest and was killed by a pack

of wolves. I started that rumor because I wanted to protect my son. I must end it right here and now! A few months ago, I worked on a bill to revise the criminal code with a conditional sentence that would have convicted any ambassador in our country for criminal acts against our citizens. The British judicial system would then have the right to prosecute any ambassador for the maximum term of imprisonment allowed for the crime. My bill was going to the House of Commons, and two of my co-workers asked me to drop my bill from the third reading in the House of Commons. There was a rumor in parliament that if the bill ever passed the House of Commons, if it went to the House of Lords, somebody would kill all the children of those in the House of Commons. I did not drop my bill! I was afraid my son was going to be murdered! So I made a plan. I was going put my son in the Eastman Hospital, a mental institution. I thought my Sir Alban III would be safe in there. But I was so wrong. Those S.O.B.'s still got him."

The radio went out, and the driver whacked it, but it wasn't successful. The driver said, "I'm sorry about that. My radio's so old."

I nodded my head, but my insides didn't feel right. My eyes shed tears, I wiped my eyes, and I remembered my grandfather's voice. "My little smart pants, whatever you do in your life, never let your emotions get involved in your decisions to help the world. On the other hand, you need to show compassion to all living things. It's a fine line, and you need to balance on that line. But if you can do that, you know you are becoming a man."

The cab stopped, and the driver said, "We're here at Eastman Hospital." I got out of the cab and paid the driver his fare. He said, "Thank you! Today I'm proud to be an Englishman because of that informant who captured those monsters in our government, and my hat's off to him."

I said thank you, and I walked away. I heard the taxicab drive off, and it started to rain on me again as I walked over the hospital's back field. I walked toward that door, and although my steps collected mud and mire, England's a lot cleaner. Reason for that is England is not dirty with two molester monsters living freely in our British countryside. I reached the door and turned the knob. I opened it quickly, quietly went inside, and softly closed it behind me. I locked it back up, took my shoes off, and quickly and quietly walked down the dark, empty hall toward the staircase. I opened a door to the stairs and heard a voice shouting for help. It filled up the stairway, but I tried to ignore it. With every few steps I took, it got a little bit louder. I went down another floor, thankfully away from that voice, and I was now almost at the hospital's basement door.

But I could not ignore it. I ran back up the stairs quietly and listened for any noises, but they had stopped. I opened the door and slowly walked out onto the third floor of the mental institution. I heard that voice again. "Could you help me out!? I need to pee, please!"

I looked around this long, white hall, and there was nobody around. I walked back to the staircase door and reached for the doorknob, but as I did, the patient said, "Please don't go away! If you were lying here instead of me, and you had to pee but couldn't walk, I bet you'd scream bloody murder just like me! If I were you, most likely I would want to leave me here too, but it isn't right!"

I let go of the doorknob, thought for a few seconds, and looked down the hall. It was dark and silent, and the long, white walls went on forever, it seemed. The voice came from the third door on my right. I silently walked toward that door and went inside that room to find a young man lying on a bed. He said, "Hello. Finally, you came to let me empty my bladder."

My voice hesitated, but I said, "Sure. Where is your urinal?"

"Over there in the small closet. I know you haven't been working here long because all of the urinals in here are kept in the patients' closets. Your muddy shoes are hanging on your neck, and you look like you're under fifteen years old."

"You are good observer," I said as I got the urinal from his closet.

"Yes, my observational skill is my downfall, my mother said. I am intelligent enough that I can think outside the box. She was right, God bless her soul wherever it is."

"I have your urinal. Now what do I do with it?"

He was laughing hard, and I smiled little bit, and I said, "No, I meant could you put your penis in the urinal, and I will hold the urinal for you. I know where the urinal has to go when someone needs to pee. Any ignorant person would know that."

He nodded while he kept on laughing. He pushed the sheet off the front of his body and asked me to "put it right here." He put his thing in the urinal and relieved himself. He asked me, "Did you hear the news today?"

I saw a newspaper on top of his nightstand. I said, "Yes. I heard those evil men got what they deserved."

"Yes, but our police didn't find them! That man or woman did. That person definitely thought outside the box."

I said, "Are you finished going to bathroom now?"

"Yes."

I went to the bathroom, dumped the urinal, washed my hands, and went back into the room. I walked up to him and asked him, "Can I ask you a question?"

"Yes, please do."

"When I look at you, I see an intelligent person. I am curious about why you are living in this place. It is the Eastman Mental Institution."

"I know where I'm living. I didn't choose to live here surrounded by deranged people. My mother didn't envision me this way, she said. She sent me off to great schools and I graduated with high marks in all my classes. After high school, I went to the University of California at Berkeley, majoring in applied science and technology. I got my PhD in A.S.T., and I wrote one hundred pages about alternative fuel. It was my PhD thesis. My professor at that time directed me in a small company that was researching alternative fuel. I worked there two years, and I discovered the gene to make oil in the lab. This oil made it easy to create gasoline that's carbon free! But my brother works for OPEC, and they were concerned with my research into this alternative fuel. My mother wrote in her will that my brother will become my guardian. She was a trusting soul, and I was that way once, but I'm suspicious of people now. My brother talked me into taking a trip with him through Britain. He tricked me... Just an hour after we landed here, he put me in this hospital."

"I can believe it because some people do evil deeds. I know because my father wrote British law in the House of Parliament."

"I watched your father on television this morning. Wait... He said on the telly that his only boy was killed by that molester and serial killer. That boy is you?"

"This newspaper on your nightstand told you about a person who apprehended those killers. Frankly, that newspaper wrote about me, and I am the son of Sir Albin Christopher."

I took almost two hours to tell him about how my father put me in this mental institution to protect me, although I did not know my father wanted to keep me safe, and I told him the rest of my story. I included every specific detail. I told him how Robert Zachary was almost apprehended by that molester's gangsters, and how he ended up in Eastman Hospital, too. I informed him that Robert's brain had irrevocable damage, that he remained in a bed in Eastman, and that his body was in a persistent vegetative state. I told him that I promised Robert that I would hunt down the people who did that to him, in every corner of the Earth, and that was hard, but I found them and the police had now apprehended them.

"My, my, my word... Three months was all it took for you to do all that? The police took years and didn't solve anything. You are ingenious! You are real live young James Bond! If I could walk, I still couldn't do that. I guess God gave you the skills for tracking evil people around the world!"

"Thank you, but I had to find those people who incapacitated my friend. Anybody could do that and find the monsters who put their friend out of action.

I am lucky I am intelligent and my grandfather taught me the knowledge of how to investigate and be aware of my surroundings." I caught sight of his clock, and I said, "I have to go!"

"Why?"

"I need to check on Robert for the last time. I am leaving this morning for Berkeley, California."

"Ah, I see. U.C. Berkeley is my *alma mater*. I wish I could go with you, but this place wouldn't allow it." His face changed suddenly with emotion.

It was hard to leave him, but I turned around and walked toward his dresser. I pulled the first drawer out and reached for his binder. I walked toward his bed and read the title on the binder. "Hi, Benjamin King."

"I'm sorry, I am bad at communicating with people. What is your name?"

"Alex T. Ottoman." I shook his hand.

"That name suits you. Ottomans built the authoritative empire in the Middle East, with their long-established government in Turkey. The Ottoman armies took over half of the Middle East at one time or another. Their empire lasted about six hundred years, and historians have written about them in the history books. It was a great empire, or it seemed to be through my high school teacher."

"It was a long-lasting empire."

He opened his binder up, and he said, "I know you want to go, but would you wait few moments? I'd like you to look through my binder at my formula for alternative fuel."

"Okay, I guess I have a few." I reached for it, and as I read, my finger was scanning his mathematical formulas. I couldn't believe his formulas... They were ingenious. I was wondering if it could be real. My eyes looked up at him, and I said, "Wow! I am not experienced at reading formulas for alternative fuel, but my understanding of these are good enough to see they are *profound*, and your alternative fuel would work if it were in the right hands." I closed his binder and handed it to him. He took it with shaking hands, and I smiled at him. "Well, I have to go now." I walked back to his door.

He said, "Wait..." He looked at his binder, then he looked up at me and asked, "Would you take my binder with you to Berkeley? It's sitting here collecting dust. I cannot put it in the right hands because I am lying right here, but you can!"

I walked back to him and reached for his binder. He handed it to me, saying with pleading eyes, "You need to be careful with it. It's my contribution to society."

I said, "I will," and I took it from him. I smiled and told him I would come back for him. "This is a promise. My grandfather told me to always keep my promises."

He smiled at me and said, "I know it." I shook his hand and reluctantly walked out of his room with his binder.

I shut his door quietly behind me and walked fast down the cold, dark hallway. I reached for the door to the stairwell and opened it just enough to squeeze through it. Walking up silently again, I went directly to Robert's floor. I did not hear a sound in his gloomy hallway. I got to his door and went inside his room.

There was my friend, lifeless on a hospital bed. I held his hand and my eyes wept as I relived our memories. "Remember that time you and I went to fight with swords in the forest in the Dover area, and you were a Frenchman and I was an Englishman? We were fighting just like our lives counted on our country's survival, swinging our swords ferociously at each other... The leaves were flying underneath our feet, we heard the waves of wet wind hit the leaves of the trees, and we felt it too... We felt like time travelers in the Hundred Years War with France and England. We were bashing our swords together and we positioned our feet and bodies in the right stance as we looked for that sweet spot... Just a few minutes of nimbleness with our feet on the leaves, and all of sudden, you fell down a hole!

"Do you remember that? Of course you do... You were nervous, and the ground was collapsing around your body into the hole... It seemed like in just a few minutes, the earth was going to swallow up your life! I knew I had to act quickly and precisely. I looked at our surroundings, at the humongous trees encompassing us with large limbs hanging over us, and with leaves blanketing the ground, and I saw a vine, which gave me an idea.

"I ran to get that vine, and I heard you scream, 'Come back for me!' It pierced my soul. I screamed back to you. 'You remember when we saved a dog from a deep hole?' You said, 'Yes, you tied up a long rope with a slip knot and you looped it around that dog. We lifted that dog out from that hole.'

"I said, 'Right! I am going get you out that way!' I looked at you and told you I got a big vine. I had to tie a slip knot on it, and few moments later, I threw the rope to you to put around your chest under your arms, and I told you to hold onto that vine. I threw the other end of it over a large limb above you, and then I tied that vine to my waist. I started moving away from the hole in the slippery mud the best I could, and that vine moved slowly across the top of the limb. I heard you in that hole saying it was working, slowly and surely. I took a long time, but you climbed out of that death trap! I ran toward you, and I said I wouldn't ever leave you. And we needed to go home because you needed a shower badly. There were earthworms in your hair just like Medusa! I said, 'Do not look at me because I do not want you to turn me to stone!' I smiled at you, you smiled back at me and pushed me away, laughing.

"You remember that? Of course you do… We were laughing all the way to your house. That was then, but this is now, Robby. I made a promise to you, but I have to leave you. I do not want to leave you. I have good news, though… I captured the men who tried to abduct you. I cannot stand to see you this way… I would change places with you in a heartbeat. I wish I could, but I cannot do that."

Robert's hand slightly squeezed mine. Just then, his door opened and Aaron walked in.

"Did you SEE THAT?"

Aaron said, "What?"

"Robert squeezed my hand very lightly!"

Aaron closed the door. He said, "Good, but the muscles in his hand could have spasmed involuntarily." Aaron patted my back and said, "It's time to go."

A small teardrop fell from my eye, and I turned around toward Robert again. I said to him, "My friend, I am leaving you with my body, but my spirit will keep watch over you, and Aaron here will keep watch over you, too."

I picked up Benjamin King's binder from the desk, and I turned away from Robert with my heart splitting in two. Aaron encouraged me to walk away, but I stalled for a few moments. Aaron encouraged me again, and he opened Robert's door and pushed me outside into the hall. "Robert will be okay. You have to go now because the nurses and doctors will have a shift change five minutes from now."

I turned my head toward Aaron and hesitated a moment. My thoughts in that fleeting moment were that Robert was going be all right in there.

I had to go right then because I did not want anybody to know I was alive. Robert was going be okay because Aaron would look after him. My blood surged in my veins, and I forced myself to turn and run toward the stairwell door. Aaron shouted after me, "I called the taxi for you! It will meet you behind the hospital!"

And then, the stairwell door shut behind me. I made my way very carefully to the back door of the hospital and calmly let myself out. I closed the door behind me quietly, stopped to put on my shoes, and ran through the mud and mire of the back field toward the street. I ran with Benjamin King's binder in my hand. My body was aching because I left my best friend helpless, but he would want me to live and not think about tomorrow. I saw a taxi and ran toward it. I got in, breathing heavily, and the taxi driver asked me, "Where you heading to, kid?"

"I am going to the Berkeley Hotel."

***

I remember Robert and I played all over London, and while we played, we learned about each other. I learned that when people looked at Robert, they felt and acted uncomfortable. I do not know the reason for that, but I have a theory that from the beginning of time, people formed small tribes. The men hunted, and the women cooked and cared for their babies. Tribes were segregated from other tribes because men needed to hunt and kill the nearby game for food. Those tribes would multiply, and other tribes would be in competition for those animals.

They tried to join with other tribes that had plentiful foods, but the men of the prosperous tribes got angry with having to fight for available food. It started racism. As time went on, tribes became kingdoms, and kings wanted more land. They started armies to fight other kingdoms, and they killed people for their lands, so their king could become more powerful. Mankind has always looked down at the weak and powerless because man wants to be powerful. Look at the Roman Empire. They had slaves to work their agricultural lands and industries. Slaves formed a very large part of their economy, and the Roman Empire built a large part of its wealth through slaves acquired by conquest. Unfortunately, the United States of America did it too, when the thirteen colonies went to war against the parliament of Great Britain to gain their independence. After this war, the United States arranged for boatloads of slaves from the continent of Africa to work the land in America's agricultural states. My own thought about that is, if in the early years of the United States there were no slaves, America wouldn't be as powerful today and the American people wouldn't be so racist regarding different cultures. People are naturally racist around the world, and I don't know how stop it. All of the wars that have been started and the future wars that will occur will be due to the countries' leaders' racism for other cultures and religions.

The taxi stopped, and the driver said, "Hey kid, we're at your stop." I opened the cab door and paid the man.

As I walked into this rich hotel, I saw Della in the coffee shop and walked over to her. I sat down across from her, and something told me she needed an ambulance. I said, "Della are you okay?"

Her voice was feeble as she said, "Time to go." She was struggling to stand up, so I helped her onto her feet. She reached for her purse and we tried to walk.

Della's legs buckled and she fell to the floor. I quickly dropped down and cushioned her body. I straightened Della out onto on her back, and I gingerly put her head on my lap. I screamed, "Call an ambulance! Please!"

Della's finger touched my lips and my voice went quiet. Della whispered, "I want to go home to see my stunning husband. My young man, your history is in front of you, and your dreams and aspirations are ahead of you, too. This world needs you because evil lurks around this place, and the people need your intelligence and quick decisiveness. You and only you choose what you will do, as your grandfather taught you. I know you will do positive work in this world. I want you to walk through those doors after this, and I want you to go to Berkeley and attend Berkeley High School. See Ms. Wilson. I have your ticket in my purse and a white envelope for you. Don't open it until your eighteenth birthday. I have your grandfather's gold watch in my purse, too." Her hand was resting on top of my arm as I pulled out my ticket, the white envelope and my grandfather's gold Rolex. I had them all in my hand as I looked at Della's face and into her eyes. I knew at that exact moment; she saw her husband… She was smiling. Suddenly, her body was spiritless and her freed spirit kissed me goodbye.

My hand closed her eyes gently. I dropped a tear onto her face as I moved her head from my lap to the floor. I was kneeling over her lifeless body, and I said to her, "I promise you, I will do great things in this world because you taught me everything I need to figure out my problems in the future. You were an awesome teacher. I love you for that. I wish you were my mom."

I heard an ambulance siren in the distance. "Bye Mom. I have to go. You are always with me." I stood up and picked up Benjamin King's binder from the table. I walked to the hotel doors, looked back at Della's lifeless body one last time as hotel staff rushed to her. I saw her and my teardrops fell. I wiped my eyes and walked through the lobby doors to get a taxi.

I said to the cab driver, "I am going to the airport."

The driver said, "Okay," and drove off. Just as we pulled away from the hotel, an ambulance drove up, and I saw it through the back window of the cab.

My body was quiet during the cab ride. I recalled everything Della had taught me about London's buildings. She did not like a few of the buildings because their architecture was not right for this city. She liked Baroque and English Gothic for England's architecture.

The taxi stopped, and the driver said, "We're here at the Great West Aerodrome."

"You mean the Heathrow Aerodrome."

"Whatever."

I got out of the taxi, walked to the driver's window, and I said, "I am really sorry but I have no money."

"I see, you waste my time and my gas! This taxi company, they'll take your cab fare out of my paycheck, do you understand? Do you?"

"Yes but…"

I heard someone say, "Hey cab driver, is this taxi free?" I was reluctant to run for it, but I did.

***

I was in Heathrow Airport. It was 7:30. I checked my ticket for the gate for American Airlines to San Francisco… I needed to be at gate 5, and I was at gate 35. I had a long walk, and as I went toward my future, I saw many people of different cultures walking to their destinations. Heathrow Airport is a gateway to every point of the world. I reached gate 5, my own destination, and many people were standing in line at the glass door waiting for a flight attendant to open the door and collect their tickets. I walked to the back of this line and felt a nudge on my left shoulder. Someone said to me, "Excuse me, what time is this plane leaving?"

I got my ticket out of my pocket and looked at the time on the ticket. "Take-off is thirty minutes away," I said, smiling at her. "What time did you arrive here?"

Her voice was unrefined. She told me, "I got here about five o'clock this morning."

"Why didn't you stay first in line?"

She told me, "I hate to have people in back of me because people are crazy. You have to know that."

I smiled. A person got in line behind her, and she walked away. Immediately after that, a flight attendant opened the glass door to the runway. I saw the stairs going up to door of the aircraft, and the flight attendant started to let people board. I shuffled forward in this line of people until a few minutes later I was handing my ticket to the flight attendant.

I looked back to see if I could find that lady I was talking to, but I couldn't see her. I asked the flight attendant if any lady with a rough voice had boarded the plane. She told me, "I am sorry for that woman troubling you. That woman is homeless. The airport police try to get her out of here, but this airport is too big sometimes."

"She was not a problem to me because I lost my mentor today. Like that homeless lady, my mentor and her mother were poor, but her mother taught her that knowledge is powerful."

"Okay then, do you have your ticket?" I handed her my ticket, and she said, "You have a nice flight to San Francisco."

I smiled at her and walked through the glass doorway. England's sunshine was hitting me, and for the last time its glorious rain hit me, too. Just like this rain, my brain was flowing with memories of Della's life. She told me about it uniquely, as only she could. I knew then she was holding her husband's hand, walking and talking with him and reminiscing of old times they had.

My foot stepped on the first rung of *the* airplane's stairs, and with my other foot still on my homeland, I waited few moments… My face looked up to the rainy English sky, I smiled to her, and I walked briskly up the stairs and into the plane. A flight attendant said, "Welcome, sir. Your seat is in the first row in first class."

I said, "Thank you," and I walked to my seat.

The End